FIRE-BREATHING?
NO, LASER-BEAMING!

There was no telling where the chest ended and the neck began, but the head was supported by a long, snakelike trunk that arched upward in a slow curve. Two red, beady eyes glared out above tiny, birdlike nostrils. The mouth was a grisly, horizontal slit filled with gleaming white teeth honed to sharp points. The creature was covered with a patchwork quilt of brown and tan scales.

A flash of light spouted from a gold-colored packet clutched in the right paw. A hot beam sizzled through the air between Scott and Rusty and hit the ground with enough energy to fuse sand into glass . . .

GARY GENTILE

◇ A TIME FOR ◇
DRAGONS

ACE BOOKS, NEW YORK

This book is an Ace original edition,
and has never been previously published.

A TIME FOR DRAGONS

An Ace Book / published by arrangement with
the author

PRINTING HISTORY
Ace edition / September 1989

ISBN: 0-441-81032-2

Ace Books are published by The Berkley Publishing Group,
200 Madison Avenue, New York, New York 10016.
The name "ACE" and the "A" logo
are trademarks belonging to Charter Communications, Inc.

PRINTED IN THE UNITED STATES OF AMERICA

10 9 8 7 6 5 4 3 2 1

◇ A TIME FOR ◇
DRAGONS

CHAPTER 1

"Rusty, I'm going to need a hand pulling this motor." Scott raised a greasy hand to his broad forehead and, with the back of his wrist, rubbed an itch below his blond crewcut. He laid down the worn socket wrench and spun free the last nut holding the motor mount in place. When he finished scratching he used both brawny hands to crank the motor out from under the cowling. An overhead vent pushed air gently across his face and evaporated tiny beads of perspiration. He picked up a rag and wiped his sticky palms on it, then unscrewed the shiny metal end cap.

Rusty sat at a computer console, typing with frenzied concentration. "Okay, I'm almost done with the exercise. I'm having a little trouble with the velocity-matching equations. The computer keeps throwing in variables." Scott could see that his mousy features were piqued. Pale skin reflected the cool fluorescent light.

"I got a little bit of that last week." Scott used a screwdriver to pry the shims apart and slide them along the steel shaft. "But I only had to worry about fuel consumption on the attitude controls—not vector analysis. It was enough to make me glad I'm taking missile maintenance rather than flight programming. Hey, while you're there, key in the work order and find out whether we're supposed to change the armature or just clean it."

"Will do. I'm tired of this anyway. I'll pick it up later down in my room. Maybe I can get Dad to help me." His fingers flicked over the keyboard with unerring speed.

Scott knew his job and did it efficiently. The four big air compressors and attendant ventilator and filter systems were rigidly maintained. They were the mechanical hearts that pumped the lifeblood into Maccam City and kept its two thousand underground inhabitants alive. With each compressor in a separate quadrant the city could function without difficulty on any three, and squeeze by on two for a while: there were

1

always bottled reserves. But it paid to never let them go too long without a complete checkup.

Rusty read the video screen. "It says here it should be inspected, and replaced or repaired at technician's discretion."

"Good. That means me, and I don't think it looks too bad. We'll just sand the commutator, file the grooves, and shove it back in place. And I'll be home in time for Mom's apple pie—while it's still hot. I can smell it now." He raised his nostrils into the air flow.

Scott was glad to take the easy way out. The ten-horsepower motor weighed easily a ton, so that temporary replacement required setting up a block and tackle, as well as maneuvering hoisting dollies. But the carbon traces could be filed off with a sanding block while one of them rotated the armature manually. He could change the brushes by himself in a few minutes.

"Nice try, Scott. But I happen to know you have a date with Becky tonight. Faron told me."

Scott blushed. "Sometimes I don't think that kid sister of yours has enough to keep her occupied. She spends too much time snooping." Under such confined living conditions, where everyone was physically close, Scott sometimes found it galling that everyone knew his business, his habits, his likes and dislikes. He was reminded of the differences of opinion between his father and Rusty's: between expansionism and continued incest, as his father stated it in his blacker moods. It just was not right for people to live in one another's laps.

"She doesn't snoop—she just listens."

"I wouldn't mind her plastering her ear to everyone's cubicle so much if she didn't blab everything she hears."

Rusty smiled. "Oh, she doesn't tell *all* she hears—not to everyone, that is."

"Just tell me what else is on the maintenance agenda."

Rusty stared at the monitor. "Oil the louvers and check the linkage, recalibrate the dampers, clean all the relay contacts—wow, what a bore—and vacuum the breaker panels. Then, we have to—"

Rusty stopped reading. For a moment the only sound Scott could hear was the whirring of auxiliary machinery and the clacking of contactors and relay switches. He looked up from his work. "What's the matter?"

Red eyebrows pinched over Rusty's freckled face. "I don't

know. The computer just went off line." Long, delicate fingers ran over control buttons lining the side of the console.

"What?" Scott put down his screwdriver, wiped his hands on the rag, and walked to the user terminal. Over Rusty's shoulder he stared at the blank screen.

"I've reset the power switch and tested the input channels, but they're all dead. And I'm getting no response from any of the mode switches. It doesn't make sense."

Scott stuffed the rag into a baggy patch pocket, next to the flashlight. "That's strange. I've never seen that happen before. What do you think it is?"

Rusty pushed the chair back on its slider. "I don't know, but I'm going to check the terminal blocks."

Sitting on his knees in front of the console, he turned the thumb screws that held the front access panel in place. Just as he pulled off the metal cover, the lights in the room dimmed.

"Nice going, Rusty. I don't know what you did, but you'd better undo it fast."

"I haven't touched anything yet." Rusty leaned the panel against the console pedestal. "What the heck is going on?"

Scott looked up at the flickering fluorescent lights, caught in the voltage drop. "Whatever it is, it's weird."

No sooner had he spoken than the lights went off altogether. Scott felt a tingling sensation run the length of his spine. For a moment the darkness was absolute. Then battery power took over and the emergency lights kindled on. The room was a contrast of black shadows and narrow white beams of light. Rusty was silhouetted with one hand in the act of reaching into the control panel.

"Listen!" Scott tried to shout, but it came out a whisper. He heard no machinery whirring, no contactors clacking, not even the minute buzz of arcing switches. And the whooshing of forced air that was subliminal to him was still. He dashed across the room to the workbench near the partly disconnected main drive motor. He thrust his hand below the vent. "It's stopped. Rusty, the air has stopped."

A three-dimensional picture of the city's ventilation system flashed through Scott's mind with tortured ease. Air drawn in from the surface by means of great compressors was pumped down hundreds of feet to the maze of underground passageways and the warren of cramped cubicles. It had to pump continuously or the inhabitants would soon suffocate.

"Let's check the power leads!" Rusty let the access panel slip to the floor, and vaulted past Scott. "There must be something wrong with this sector."

Squeezing through the crowded mechanical room, winding around auxiliary motors, exposed belts, and miscellaneous machinery, all of which was now still, Scott followed Rusty to the darkened corner where the main power distribution panels were crammed. A bank of tall metal cabinets housed circuit breakers, contactors, relays, control switches, and manual bypasses. The annunciator panel, which should have been lit up like a Christmas tree with red and green indicating lights, was blank.

Scott pulled the flashlight out of his pocket and bent over the instrument board. "The ammeter's dead. The voltmeter's dead. Nothing's coming through."

"There's got to be *something*." Rusty touched the gauges as if that would actuate them. "What'll we do?"

Scott took two steps to a nearby intercom station. He flipped a toggle and spoke into an acoustic diaphragm. "Compressor room three to central processing, come in please." After five seconds that seemed like an eternity, he repeated the command. "Compressor room three to central processing, come in please."

Rusty's eyes were as big as saucers. "The whole sector must be blocked off!"

"Yes, but they must know it by now. They'd have to. It would register on their monitors right away."

"But they might not know how bad it is until they run a check. Let's get down below and make a verbal report."

Scott could see the sense in that. "We'll probably bump into the contingency crew on their way up. And they'll need every hand they can get."

"Then we'll turn around and come back up with them. But if the problem is down there that's where they'll need us."

"You're right." From early childhood Scott had been drilled against every possible emergency, had been trained to think clearly and act decisively. "Let's go."

Scott led the way through a nearby doorway, ducking under the low lintel. He ran along a corridor that was only slightly wider than his broad shoulders. Fifty feet away he slammed into the door at the end of the passageway and practically flung it off its hinges.

Beyond was a closet-sized room packed with exposed conduits and electrical panels, one dim emergency light, and two steel doors that sealed off the elevator shaft and the stairwell. Scott's stocky finger gouged the recessed button. When nothing happened, he punched the button again.

Rusty opened the door of a small distribution panel. He reset the breakers by flipping them off, then on again. "The power's out here, too. The elevator's out of commission."

Scott wrenched open the adjacent door and charged into the stairwell. He barely reached the first step when he coughed and stopped abruptly. A vile, stinging vapor rose up the shaft, glowing green in the weak beam of the lone emergency light, and curled around his soft-soled slippers.

He inhaled only a whiff of it, but that was enough to send him staggering backward through the door, blinded and gagging. He tripped and fell headlong on the concrete floor. As he rolled out of the way, Rusty shoved the steel door shut: a momentary respite against the noxious fumes.

· Rusty knelt by his friend and grasped his shoulders with both hands. "Scott, are you all right?" Rusty had breathed only from the periphery of the acidic gas, but it had felt like swallowing nettles. "Wha—what is that stuff?"

Scott sucked in great lungfuls of fresh air. Slowly, the prickly pain subsided. "I don't know, but we've got to warn them. It's coming up the—"

Rusty finished it for him. "If it's coming up the shaft, the whole city must be inundated with it."

"But what could cause—" Scott had no time to finish his thought. The strange green vapor started seeping around the edges of both doors, eating through the rubber gaskets that kept the city hermetically sealed. As Scott watched, gray paint flecked off the sills and iron turned orange with rust. The doors became pockmarked with pinholes where the gaseous acid was eating through metal and dissolving steel.

An instant later the green gas flowed out the pipe shafts. Electrical panels foamed, plastic breakers melted. With a crash the elevator door fell in as its hinges were consumed. It hit Scott a terrible blow on the head and shoulder, and scraped Rusty's cheek. The virulent vapor boiled into the tiny room.

A blast of pungent gas hit him in the face. Rusty howled with pain and fell back, rubbing his eyes. Scott, still under the hissing metal, felt tears rolling down his cheeks. He threw

aside the heavy door. "Come on, let's get out of here." He
grabbed Rusty by the arm, pulled him out of the room, and
dragged him along the paneled corridor.

The gas curled wraithlike along the floor, green fingers that
destroyed everything that lingered in its path. Terminal blocks
and copper wires were eaten away. The emergency light
winked out.

Stumbling with his burden, Scott pushed Rusty into the
mechanical room. The redhead slipped to the floor, retching
violently. Scott slammed the door and leaned hard against it, as
if that would hold back the noxious gas. For the moment he
gathered his strength, thankful for the air that gave him life.
But the reprieve was short-lived.

At his back, the door started making crackling sounds. Rusty
looked up from the floor with tear-filled eyes. Scott moved
away from the noisy barrier, staring in the dim, gray light as
the green vapor seeped through the metal trim. The steel door
groaned and warped. BB-sized holes burst through the metal.
Gas hissed out like steam through a broken radiator.

"Let's go." Scott grabbed Rusty's arm as he raced by and
jerked him to his feet. In the middle of the machine-filled
room, Scott stopped. He stared at the still blank computer
screen. The dead console represented the city, the people. *His*
people.

He turned and looked up at Rusty. Rusty's words echoed his
own thoughts. "There's nowhere to go—but outside."

CHAPTER 2

To Rusty's knowledge, the emergency exit to the outside had never been opened. It had been practically forgotten for over a century—ever since the great plague, the result of human folly and biological warfare, had wiped out mankind. The barrier that had protected them all these years was now working against them.

Rusty jiggled the massive handle to no avail. "There must be a key here somewhere."

At the other end of the room the corridor door fell off dissolving hinges and crashed in smoldering ruins. White smoke boiled off the linoleum, the floor buckled as the underpinnings crumbled.

Scott bent to inspect the time-worn lock. "If there is, I never heard of it. Grab some tools." Then, amid the sizzling sounds of disintegrating electrical parts, collapsing stanchions, and the sagging of heavy machinery, he ran and got them himself.

At Rusty's feet he flung down a metal box full of sockets and wrenches. "Try these." There were no exposed nuts or bolts; the latch itself folded back and covered them. Rusty scrounged a plastic-handled screwdriver and tried ineffectually to bend the latch out far enough to get at the screws underneath.

The deadly, green vapor crept across the floor, enveloping everything like a hungry demon. The hissing and breaking-up noises sounded like the gnashing of giant teeth.

Rusty shook his head. "Socket tools are useless. We need something heavy. A chisel, or something."

Scott stared at him for a moment, then darted back to the workbench. He returned with a box full of hammers, chisels, and prybars, and dumped them on the floor. "Let's try the bruiser tools."

Rusty jammed a three-foot crowbar behind the latch, but the thick metal would not bend. "It's no use. It's tempered steel. Try the hinges."

He glanced over his shoulder at the advancing green menace. Sheet metal disappeared as if it were paper going up in flames, massive pipe racks broke away as their supports melted. The gas reached the computer console and attacked its delicate electronic components. Plastic parts softened, contacts fused, resistors and diodes broke down, chips became unstable. Insulation dripped off to leave copper wires gleaming, then the copper itself began to pit and corrode.

Scott picked up a long chisel and a heavy mallet. There were no screws on the hinges; the large pistons were welded to the framework the same as a vault door. He banged away along the tempered bead.

Rusty coughed. The first tendrils of pungent vapor reached him. He ignored the irritation in his eyes, continuing to look for another way out. He picked up the crowbar. "Scott, the intake shaft. It's our only chance."

The room was practically eclipsed as the green, poisonous gas rose to the ceiling and hovered thickly around the self-contained battery packs. One by one the emergency lights fizzled and went out.

Sneaking around the main compressor, Rusty led the way to where only a sheet-metal plenum separated them from the great air shaft that fed the city. Huge removable filters were taken out periodically and cleaned. The slit opening that was left when they were withdrawn doubled as an access trunk to the air ducts; accumulated dust was vacuumed out on a regular basis.

Rusty slipped the crowbar through the handle. The retaining clip that kept the filters from vibrating out was held in place by six hefty sheet-metal screws. Already the screwdriver was rusting away as the green gas billowed past the emergency exit.

Icy hands pushed him out of the way. Scott placed the point of the chisel against the first screw head. One mighty whack of the sledgehammer sheared it right off. In a few seconds he broke all six of them. Together they pulled the hundred-pound filter out on its track and sent it crashing to the floor.

With corrosive gas literally nipping at his heels, Rusty plunged into the darkness of the air duct. He started coughing right away, but this time it was because of the fine dust he had stirred up. Now he wished he had done a better job of vacuuming the month before.

Scott stepped in beside him and thumbed on the flashlight. "This way." He used the beam as a pointer. A green mist was slowly dispersing through the compressor vanes where the vertical shaft plunged into the depths of the city.

The horizontal connector extended fifty feet to the outside riser. An oily residue offered unsure footing. Static dust clung to the walls. At the far end of the plenum a series of rungs bolted to the wall led upward. Rusty heard loud crashes from the crumbling machine room, and saw a trace of deadly gas explore the filter opening.

With only the weak light to see by, Scott started climbing. The wrought-iron rungs were dust laden with an underpinning of aerated grease, making them slippery. He went only a few feet when the yellow glow disclosed a screen mesh blocking the shaft. The hinged gate was barely visible under a century of accumulated dirt and rust. Looping his arm through a metal rung for support, he wiped the barrier clean with his rag. "Oh, no. It's locked."

Rusty saw the glint of the brass mechanism, and handed up the crowbar. "Use this."

Scott took the tool, slipped it through the arched shackle, and pried against the antique casing. But the years had not affected the brass workings—it was still as solid as the day it was manufactured.

The acrid odor of gas stung Rusty's nostrils. He climbed up behind Scott, shaking. His raillike arms were not built for strength and he was weakening fast. "Hurry it up."

Scott strained against the lock. "I'm working as fast as I can." He leaned hard against the crowbar and pulled not only with his free arm but with his whole body weight. The lock snapped with an abruptness that caused him to topple backward. He caught himself with one hand, tucked the crowbar under the arm that was hanging onto the ladder rung, and worked the shackle out of the hasp. He pushed hard. The gate moved an inch on rusted hinges, and stopped.

Using the crowbar again, he pounded it open by degrees. When it swung partway out from the wall he slipped through the gap. Then, with both feet planted on the grid, he lifted his friend through the opening.

Rusty rolled onto the grillwork and lay gasping. Gobs of dust stuck to his mop of red hair. "I need to rest. My lungs are stinging, and my arms can't take it."

"Don't give up now." Scott shone the flashlight down

through the grating. The thin sheet-metal walls were melting away like butter, revealing rough hewn rock.

Rusty rolled over, and nursed his aching arms. His shallow cheeks were twisted in pain. "You'd better get going."

Scott shone the light up the riser. Fifty feet above a dim light filtered through another grating. "All right." With the crowbar in one hand and the flashlight in the other, he jumped onto the ladder and started climbing by hooking his wrists over the rungs. He stopped after ten feet. "Come on."

Rusty rose weakly to his feet and started up. "I'm right behind you."

Scott ascended rapidly. From the bottom of the shaft the metal grating hissed as it dissolved in the acidic gas. "Are you all right?"

Rusty saw nothing below in the darkness. Above, Scott was a smudge clinging to the wall. "Just keep going."

Scott surged ahead. Rusty rested, and watched him stop just below the next landing. There was another gate, and another lock. He inserted the crowbar under the slider, and wrenched hard. The brass lock did not give, but the hasp ripped completely off and fell away, crashing on the disintegrating grillwork fifty feet below.

"The gate's still stuck." The metal was twisted as if some minor earth movement had jammed it in place. With great upward swings of the crowbar Scott smashed at the barrier. Loud clangs reverberated off the metal walls of the riser. The hinges remained stuck, but the screen mesh sprung out of its holding bracket. He pushed through to the landing, heedless of the sharp points that tore his clothing. "Hurry," he shouted. His voice echoed tinnily.

In the light that shone down Rusty saw the green gas surging after him. He clung to the rungs with aching arms. Scott was only ten feet above him, yet he seemed so far away. Rusty scaled the ladder slowly, laboriously, reaching out for a rung, pulling himself up, and reaching out again. He thought he would never make it when suddenly Scott pulled him through the twisted grill.

He leaned back against the wall, and felt the metallic coolness through his thin suit. "I need a rest."

"There's no time." Scott shone the flashlight through the grating at his feet. There was no bottom anymore, only a green, swirling mist that beckoned menacingly. "We have to go on."

"On to what?" They had nothing to go on *to*. They were merely running away. Except for what he had seen on disk, Rusty knew no world other than the narrow confines of corridors, closets, nooks, and pigeonholes. All available living space was filled with essential computers, machinery, and life-support equipment. Walls were lined with shelving for hydroponics. All his life had been spent in a subterranean dwelling surrounded by people and imbued with constant clamor. He felt secure in cramped quarters.

Outside was space on a different scale. It was a cold, quiet, inhospitable world. Through history disks he had seen the endless expanse of desert, the limitless sky, the unimaginable emptiness. Outside there was nothing but barren land, torturous rocks, rugged mountains and wild rivers, burning heat and unfathomable cold. Outside was so—*uncontrolled*.

"I don't know. The unknown, I guess." Rusty could see the uncertainty on his face, his bland features. Fifty more rungs led to another landing. And beyond that—what? More grates? More ladders? Rusty did not fear just the unknown; what he feared was the sheer *openness*. Scott put a helping hand under his arm. "But I'm not giving up. And I won't let you give up, either."

Rusty groaned, and stretched his sore muscles. "Yes, you're right. But you'd better let me go first, in case I—slip."

Scott grinned and punched him lightly on the shoulder. "You're doing fine." He helped Rusty to his feet and pushed him toward the ladder.

With the first faint tendrils of green gas rising through the grating, Rusty grabbed the lowest rung and pulled himself up. He had already climbed more than fifty feet, and there was no telling how much farther the riser went beyond the next grate. After ten rungs he stopped and rested. Then, through sheer will of mind, he climbed ten more.

Scott bumped his feet. "You're doing great." He had put away the flashlight, for now there was sufficient light filtering down from above to show the way. "But don't stop now. I can smell gas."

Rusty, too, could smell it: a few wayward molecules wafted ahead of the main body. He could also hear the dissolving metal, and pieces of the lower grate giving way and crashing down to the bottom of the riser. He climbed ten more rungs, counting each one to himself so that he could rest on the tenth. He looked up; there were only twenty more to go.

"My arms—" Something pungent entered his lungs. Sweat beaded on his forehead, and ran in rivulets under his arms. His eyes began to sting. But it had to be worse for Scott.

"Don't stop now."

Rusty climbed five more rungs. "I can't—" But when he heard Scott cough, he did. He was only ten rungs from the top before his strength waned to almost nothing. "I'll never get the gate open."

Scott coughed again, uncontrollably. "Let—me—get—past—you."

"How?" Now Rusty went into a spasm of coughing. Oh, how his arms arched.

"Pull in close—and I'll—climb over you."

Rusty had no choice but to comply. His arms were so weak he was afraid he might fall any moment. Was a quick, merciful death preferable to a choking, lingering one? Scott scrambled over him like a spider, stepping on the sides of the rungs. He climbed right up to the gate and started beating on the lock with the crowbar.

Instead of corrosion-resistant brass this lock was case-hardened steel—and rusted solid. He inserted the crowbar under the shackle and pried. The lock remained immobile, the hasp secure. He applied a twisting motion, with more leverage, and pulled down with his whole body weight. Then he used the crowbar like a maul and beat against the lock, the hasp, and finally the gate.

A few feet below the green gas thickened. Rusty's meager strength paled. Breathing in starts, he watched Scott's mighty efforts. The grating that covered the rest of the shaft was oddly bent, the reinforced seams separated in places. Peering through the mesh he saw in the half light that great sheets of rock had dropped off the natural cave roof onto the protective grating, stressing the metal to the breaking point.

"Scott, the frame—" Scott looked around, and noticed the crumbling condition of the entire gate assembly. He jammed the crowbar into a tear in the mesh, and pulled. Although the gate, independently fastened, remained unmovable, the entire framework around it shook.

"I can't—hold on—much longer." Rusty's voice was a

harsh whisper. With his eyes tightly shut, he breathed through the upper fabric of his jumper, and watched helplessly as Scott worked.

"Hang in there, Rusty. I'll get through this thing yet." Holding the rung with one hand, he leaned out and pulled down on the snagged crowbar with the other. A ribbon of green gas curled up the riser. Fresh air was only a few feet away, but it might as well have been a mile. He took a deep breath and held it. Pulling hard, the gap opened an inch, then another. Metal screeched on metal as the welded framework slipped farther apart.

Rusty was beginning to tremble from the strain of clinging to the cast-iron supports. And he was weakening from the lack of oxygen in the air. He stood close to the wall, so most of his weight was on his legs. "Scott." His voice was a feeble gasp.

The shriek of tearing metal made Rusty's spine quiver. He jerked to attention and saw the crowbar ripped out of Scott's hand, saw one foot slip off the rung, saw him dangling by one sweat-covered hand. He gasped involuntarily, and took in a great lungful of fiery air. Then the entire grating, along with several tons of rock, thundered down the shaft, passing by him because of the notch left by the still standing gate. The plummeting mass took the partially dissolved remains of the next grating with it, then piled up on the floor of the riser in a great cloud of dust.

Scott regained his grip on the ladder. The green gas had been sucked down with the debris, offering a temporary respite as fresh air from outside poured in. Partially revitalized, Rusty coughed the dregs of poison from his lungs.

The only thing in the way now was the gate that had just saved them from being torn off the ladder. Reaching out, Scott grabbed hold of the torn edge and swung out into the air. He dangled freely for a moment, then pulled himself up onto the narrow lip to which the grating had been attached. He took only a moment to catch his breath. "Come on."

Rusty clung to his perch, ten feet below. His eyes were glazed, and his grip was loosening. He could breathe, but his strength was gone. "I—can't—make—it."

"Sure you can." The green gas was already streaming back up the shaft. "It's only a few feet. You can do it."

Rusty closed his eyes, reached up, grabbed another rung. He hesitated, then pulled himself up. Scott yelled encouragement.

Rusty coughed. His knees were shaking like reeds in the wind. But he reached out for another rung, pulled himself up, then reached out for another.

Rusty was no longer looking up. His head hung limply, resting on his clenched fist. His other hand groped blindly for the next rung.

"I can almost reach you." Scott leaned out over the edge and dangled his right arm. "Just a couple more steps to go."

Rusty climbed up another rung, and rested. Then he climbed another, and rested longer. The gas was getting thicker. His coughing sapped his strength. When he was within reach of the grate, he stopped.

"I'll never—get around."

"Reach for my hand," Scott ordered. Slowly, Rusty let one hand go and reached out. Scott caught it and guided it to the ledge where he could get a grip. "Now the other."

"I—can't—" Rusty's muscles were beyond aching—they were going numb. He was afraid to let go.

"You have to. It's the only way."

Now Rusty went into spasms, caught with one hand on the ledge and one on the ladder. His jerking weight proved too much for the ancient bolts. With a sudden wrench the rung tore out of the wall and went spinning down the deep shaft.

Rusty screamed as sweaty palms slipped off the ledge, and his body swung outward into the void. Scott's face and shoulder were slammed against the metal, but he did not let go. Instead, he clamped down harder on Rusty's wrist until the pendulum effect brought him swinging back into the wall.

Rusty grappled instinctively with his free hand and found the ledge. Fear gave him uncommon strength, and he hauled himself halfway up while Scott rolled back and added leverage to his contortions. With legs flailing against empty air, Rusty kicked hard and hooked his heel on the metal shelf. Scott grabbed the back of his collar, and Rusty squirmed right over on top of him.

As soon as they stopped flopping, two more bolts gave way and the metal ledge sagged dangerously in the middle. Rusty kept scrambling, felt solid rock under his hand, and rolled into a cold, granite floor. Scott landed beside him, breathing hard.

They were inside a low, rock-strewn cave flooded with a bright, yellow light.

Rusty breathed deeply. He started to take stock of his

surroundings when he felt a stinging sensation on his feet. The corrosive gas was still rising up the air shaft. With a gasp that gave Scott warning, he crawled away on all fours.

His body was bruised and bleeding, his stamina was at an end. Yet somehow he inched over the sharp rocks until he reached the base of the scree below the entrance. His fingers were scraped, his nails torn. He lay there quivering like a fish out of water. Scott, he noticed, lying next to him, looked the worse for wear.

Scott glowed triumphantly. "Well, we made it."

Sucking in the hot air, Rusty was not sure what they had made. Behind him was his home, his family, his friends, the only life he had ever known. Tears welled up in his eyes, this time not from the pungent gas. The awful dread of loneliness swept over him. In a matter of minutes his life had become without meaning.

Still, he was urged on toward survival. The back of the cave was filling with acrid fumes. Like an insect pursued by a relentless spider, he did not have the time to grieve. Scott got up silently and moved on. Painfully, Rusty followed him. On hands and knees he climbed up the rubble of loose rock. From the top of the pile he had his first real view of the outside.

He saw waste and desolation, craggy rocks and dry ravines, hot sand, and a frightening, infinite blue sky. And somewhere in that great beyond was the rubble of once great cities, the ruin and destruction of a once mighty civilization. It was a vast unknown. Yet, behind was certain death. Forward there was a chance of life. Rusty steeled himself to take that chance.

"Our folks—"

Scott stood tall, and faced the outer reaches. "I know." Without looking back he took a step forward, and became the first of his people in over four generations to feel the burning rays of the sun upon his tender skin.

CHAPTER 3

Scott sat on a smooth boulder whose cool surface lay close by the shadowed cliff face. "How about a short rest? I feel like a wet noodle." He pulled his arms out of the sleeves of his jumper, pushed the material down to his waist, and let the air dry his chest.

The ravines cut deeply into the rocky terrain, with sheer walls that sometimes blocked out the sun. Even though he knew nothing of shade, it did not take long to discover that it was cooler there. Aimless wandering soon pushed Rusty into despair. He would long since have given up hope for survival had it not been for Scott's dogged persistence.

"I thought you'd never ask." Rusty squatted on the uneven ground and pressed his back against the rock. The bright sun beat down unmercifully. Thirty minutes in its withering heat and he was thirsty, an hour and he was parched. Walking was easy exercise for him, but dehydration was sapping his energy. Where was there water in this barren desert?

Scott flexed muscles cramped by years of tight city living. The thin material of his one-piece uniform was pockmarked with holes where the acidic gas had eaten through. His back was covered with red, round pustules. Yet, he gave no sign of discomfort.

The sun distorted into an orange ball as it neared the horizon. Rusty was thankful that it would soon be night and the inexorable heat would be gone. The short exposure to the sun's radiation enhanced the freckles on his face, and changed his color to a glowing red. Silent and brooding, he was drifting into a shell of loneliness when he was snapped from his reverie by a sharp, loud clap.

From history disks he remembered the sound of thunder. He also remembered that it was associated with atmospheric electrical discharge. But there were no clouds in the sky, or signs of a storm approaching. Then there was another thunderclap, followed by a piercing scream.

17

Rusty's hackles rose and he became instantly alert. "That sounded like a man."

Scott jumped off his perch and shoved arms into sleeves in one easy motion. "Let's go."

They ran toward the south, urged on by some deep-seated instinct. The narrow ravine curved slightly, and the high walls sloped downward until they merged with the ground. The gully emptied into a flat, boulder-strewn arena hundreds of feet across.

Again there was a loud retort, and a cry of pain. Several other ravines terminated in this natural amphitheater, and from one of them someone stumbled out, with hands thrust forward, and collapsed onto the ground. When Scott and Rusty reached him they found a small, wizened man with a blackened face and singed hair. He was wearing a tattered uniform like their own. The soles of his slippers were worn through, and the side walls hung ludicrously around his ankles.

The man gasped, one arm clutching spasmodically at his side. His jumper was partially burned off. His thinning hair was covered with dust, his lips dry and cracked. Scott knelt down and cradled the man's head in his lap. Rusty pulled the protective hand away from his rib cage; he gasped when he saw the horrible wound under the charred cloth. The skin was still smoldering, and the putrid scent of burnt flesh permeated the air. Rusty gagged.

The man's mouth worked futilely, but no words came out. He coughed, and a clod of blood hit the ground and soaked into the sand. With his last remaining strength he gestured behind him. Then he slumped over and went limp. As he did so, Rusty saw another, smaller, hole in his back, as if an electrical arc had gone right through his body.

Rocks crunched up the ravine from which the man had come. A searing beam of intense light, pencil thin, burned through the air with the smell of ozone, and exploded against the rock wall above Rusty's head. Molten droplets splattered outward like tiny brands of fire, spraying his clothing and leaving black scorch marks on material and skin.

A long shadow appeared; above it was a creature that was something out of a nightmare. Eight feet tall it stood, on two stout, slightly bent legs that thinned below the knees to raised heels with dewclaws and three-toed, splayed feet. A fat tail dragged on the ground, balancing the forward-leaning body.

The bulging abdomen tapered upward to a narrow chest from which sprouted two scrawny arms which ended in taloned paws.

There was no telling where the chest ended and the neck began, but the head was supported by a long, snakelike trunk that arched upward in a slow curve. Two red, beady eyes glared out above tiny, birdlike nostrils. The mouth was a grisly, horizontal slit filled with gleaming white teeth honed to sharp points. The creature was covered with a patchwork quilt of brown and tan scales.

A flash of light sprouted from a gold-colored packet clutched in the right paw. A hot beam sizzled through the air between Scott and Rusty and hit the ground with enough energy to fuse sand into glass.

Scott lurched out from under the dead man and rolled to his feet. Rusty jumped the other way with catlike agility. Together they ran across the open arena as light beams crackled from behind and licked fire at their heels.

Rusty reached the head of the ravine first, running with a fleetness that Scott could not match. Another blast of energy singed a rounded boulder and ricocheted into the cliff face to Scott's right. He darted to the opposite wall and charged after Rusty.

The ravine twined through the desolate wasteland. The lizardlike creature dogged them relentlessly with the long reach of its flaming weapon. Rusty ran like a deer, but Scott was soon gasping for air. Before long the twists and turns took them out of the line of fire.

"I can't catch my breath." Scott sprawled across a large boulder, dripping sweat.

Rusty stopped and ran back. "We can't stop now."

"How much—of a lead—do you think—we have?"

Rusty looked down the ravine. "Not enough for me."

"Well, I can't run—forever. Let's find a place—to hide."

Rusty nodded silently. While Scott trotted along as best he could, Rusty flitted from side to side checking out rock outcrops and boulder groups. Finally, he stopped in front of an overhanging ledge barely a foot high. He dropped to his belly and scurried into what appeared to be a small cave.

He poked his head out. "Scott. In here."

Scott lay flat and worked his body into the crevice. His chest scraped dirt off the top. "I think we're in the clear."

Rusty sat against the back wall where the ceiling was high enough for him to crouch. He felt much more comfortable in the cave, surrounded by close, solid walls. The agoraphobia was telling on him. He drew his knees up to his chin, and listened. Several minutes passed in silence. Just as the tension was beginning to wear off he heard a scraping sound outside. He got down low so he could see out the opening.

The reptilian creature slithered past on its two bulky legs, the long tail making a track in the dirt. The periscopelike head veered from side to side, but the bumpy lidded eyes did not see their hideaway.

The gold packet in its paw was attached by a shiny metallic cord that passed under the right arm to a square, contoured box worn on the humped back. Stout straps came over the narrow shoulders, crisscrossed the chest, and went around the bulbous waist, holding the box firmly in place. A moment later the beast passed out of view.

Scott rolled up on his side, facing Rusty. "What was that thing?"

Rusty slid to the back of the cave and curled into a fetal position. "I don't know. I've never seen anything like it."

"Let's hope we don't see it again." Scott pulled out the flashlight and sat up. He thumbed the switch, and slashed the beam through the dank air. The shelter was twenty feet long and ten deep, but the way the ceiling sloped near the back some of it was inaccessible.

"Where there's one there's bound to be more." Rusty felt secure in the cave, as if he were back in his cubicle and the lights had been dimmed for sleep. In fact, it was getting dark now that the sun was almost below the distant ridges. And the coolness of the cave was a welcome relief. He kept a wary eye on the low entrance.

Scott explored a far crevice. "That was Roger, you know."

"Who was Roger?"

Scott worked his way back until he was right next to Rusty. He picked up some withered strings that looked like dried stems, or perhaps roots. "That man back there."

Very quickly, coolness was giving way to chill. "You mean, Roger the motor mechanic?"

Scott continued to study the curled strings. "He must have been working in one of the other ventilator rooms."

"Then—others might have escaped?"

Scott picked up more of the curious strings, some still green. "Maybe."

"We've got to look. We've got to find them. Alone out here—"

"Ah—*ha*." Leaning on his haunches, Scott shone the light at the low ceiling. Between him and Rusty a patch of moss clung tenaciously to the gritty sandstone, a colony of tiny tendrils with white spore caps growing down. "Well look at this." As he flashed the beam around, it became evident that there was not just one cluster, but many.

Rusty ignored the discovery. He was close to hysteria. "Scott, we've got to go look for the others."

"We've got to survive first."

"But we need them." Rusty's skin was like ice under the remnants of his jumper. The unbearable heat of the day was escaping rapidly in the dry, nighttime air. "We need them."

"Snap out of it, Rusty. We're no good to anyone dead." He pulled Rusty close and pointed the flashlight beam at the ceiling. Glistening drops of water, condensed in the cool air of the cave, collected on the stems and ran down to the enlarged tips. Each clump of moss was a miniature sponge. "We need water, and food. We need to stay out of the way of—whatever that thing out there is. And we're not going to do anything until morning. So take it easy. Let's just wait and see what happens."

Rusty wanted to wake up from this terrible dream. "Sure, Scott. I'm—I'm sorry. I'm just not—well, I'm just frightened."

Scott put a reassuring hand on Rusty's shoulder. "Don't worry about it. We're both a little spooked. I'm just as scared as you are. But we've got to face up to it. We have no choice. Maybe tomorrow—"

Rusty felt momentary solace. "Thanks, Scott. Thanks. I'm just glad I'm not alone."

"Don't worry about it. Now, what do you say we take a drink and get some sleep?" He pressed his lips to a patch of moss and sucked loudly.

Rusty followed his example. The water was bitter, tainted with iron, but it was wet. He slurped greedily. The pangs of hunger still gnawed at his stomach, but at least his thirst was quenched.

When the moss had been sucked dry, Rusty said, "You know, I'm actually freezing?"

"And I thought it was only me." Scott wrapped his arms about his chest. He turned off the flashlight and lay down.

In the darkness Rusty could imagine that he was back in his cubicle—that none of this was happening. But when he lay down on the cold, hard floor the illusion fled. Sore muscles ached, cuts and bruises throbbed, his skin was on fire. And outside, as stones cooled and contracted, they snapped in the stillness in a way that reminded him of those terrible lightning bolts. He slid down next to Scott and, side by side, they lay on the dirt-covered stone, touching for warmth.

He had no idea of where they would go, what they would eat, or how they would find water. Throughout his youth the simple amenities of life had always been provided. Like everyone else he had had to tend the hydroponic gardens, maintain well pumps and air compressors, help manufacture goods, make repairs, and learn a multitude of occupations. Each individual was a functioning unit of the whole, with a basic understanding of the complex and delicate balance of life in Maccam City.

Never had Rusty had to fend for himself. There had always been those more knowledgeable to be questioned, or more experienced to look up to. There had been father and mother to comfort him, brothers and sisters to confide in, aunts and uncles and nephews and nieces and cousins to provide different degrees of love and a sense of belonging. Now he was on his own, full of fears and self-doubts. He was glad he had Scott's strength to rely on.

Rusty did not fall asleep for many hours. For the first time in his life he felt heat, cold, hunger, and thirst. For the first time he experienced fear and loneliness. And for the first time, he did not know what tomorrow might bring.

CHAPTER 4

"Ooooh. Rusty, I sure hope you feel better than I do."

Rusty stirred, but emitted only a groan.

Scott sat up, shivering and racked with pain. His back felt like ice from lying on the cold ground. He reached for the light switch, but jerked back his hand when it smashed against the jagged rock wall. For a moment he sat still in the darkness: staring, feeling, remembering. Gradually, he rolled onto hands and knees and crawled out of the cave. The sun already flooded the ravine with a delicious warmth.

"Rusty, come on out." He chafed his stiffened limbs and managed to work out some of the chill. A couple minutes of calisthenics left him breathing hard, but feeling good. Then he crawled back into the cave and shone his light into Rusty's face.

Rusty's eyes were half closed and his hair was twisted into knots shooting out at odd angles. "I feel awful."

"You look awful. But a little exercise will make you feel better."

"I'm too sore to exercise. And my face stings like the devil."

Scott sat cross-legged on the ground. "Sunburn. I had a taste of it once when I fell asleep under an infrared lamp."

"So what do we do about it?" Rusty curled tighter into a ball.

"I plucked some moss off the ceiling during the night, and held it against my face. Here. It's soft and cool."

Rusty took the patch of moss and dabbed it on his reddened skin. "Any sign of that thing?"

"I forgot all about it, but I'll check." He squeezed back out and scanned the length and breadth of the ravine. He studied the ground, but was not able to discern any tracks the beast might have left. "I don't see anything. Come on, it's nice and warm out here."

23

Rusty peeked out warily, squinting in the bright sunlight. "Where do you think it went?"

"I don't know. I don't even know where it came from."

Rusty slowly eased out of the opening. He got to his feet and walked in a slow circle, hunched over like a gnome. "I want to go back."

"Back where?"

"Back to where we found—Roger. There may be others wandering around."

"But that's suicide. I don't want to bump into that thing again. I think we should keep going."

Rusty stood straighter now, but still grimaced. "Keep going where? This way, the way that lizard went? What makes you think it isn't still up there, waiting for us?"

"Well—"

"Maybe it was on its way home. We don't know that. We don't know anything about it. And we can't assume anything. It's just as likely to be behind us as in front of us. Or maybe they're all around us. No, I say we go back and look around. We have to be careful, and keep our eyes open. But we have to see if there are any others."

Scott ran his hand through his short hair. "I guess it doesn't make any difference which way we go. All right—but I'm going to carry a couple of rocks just in case."

Just what he would do with them, if they came across another creature, he was not sure. He had never attacked anyone—or anything—in his life. Yet, in a different sense, he had spent his whole life preparing to attack.

They stayed long enough to drink whatever water had accumulated in the moss overnight. Then they cautiously picked their way along the ravine. After thirty minutes, with the converging of ravines nowhere in sight, they sat down to reason it out.

"This doesn't seem familiar to me," Rusty said.

Scott looked around, shaking his head slowly. "These ravines have so many twists and turns and offshoots—and they all look alike. We might be walking in circles."

"I don't suppose there's a food dispenser anywhere around?"

Scott placed a hand on his own grumbling stomach. The mention of food reminded him of apple pie; apple pie reminded him of his mother; his mother reminded him of . . . Those kinds of thoughts would lead to madness, he thought. "I'd settle for a raw leaf and a drink of water." He wiped sweat off his brow. "Or just a drink of water."

Rusty indicated the rock wall to his left. "Why don't we climb to the top of this hill and see where we are?"

"Good idea." Scott led the way, climbing slowly so as not to get too far ahead of Rusty, and so he could point out handholds and footholds. Despite the aches and pains, thirst and hunger pangs, he felt strong. He had a strange sense of going somewhere.

The view from the top revealed in one direction an almost infinite plateau, and in the other a land broken by draws and gullies. The sky was a deep blue studded with white clouds that hugged the flat horizon. The land was a light brown with rock outcrops that were a dark shade of gray.

"Doesn't it look green over that way?" Scott pointed across the plateau.

"I can't tell. My eyes are a little blurry."

Scott surveyed the sparse flora: tiny shoots only inches high, and patches of wire grass. "Well, where there's vegetation there's wa—" Suddenly the air vibrated with a curious, deep thrumming. Scott looked around, shading his eyes with his hand.

"Look! Over there!" Rusty pointed over the canyonland from which they had just come. "What's that?"

In the sky a golden dot reflected the sun. It panned above the craggy desert on a shimmering heat wave, coming closer and looming larger, but still too far away to be distinct.

"I'm not sure, but I'll bet it's—alien." For a moment Scott thought that this was what Maccam City had existed for all these years, and he longed to be arming a missile to shoot the invader down. But the word foreign did not seem to fit this particular menace, not since they had run into that monster yesterday. The world was not the way he had been taught—it was much, much worse. "Let's take cover!"

Scott found a crevice in which they could both fit. It provided shade as well as protection while they watched the flying perambulations of the alien machine.

"Do you think it's looking for us?" Rusty said.

Scott shrugged. "Or other survivors—if there were any." He lapsed into silence. He did not want to say too much for fear of getting Rusty's hopes up. They had escaped by the sheerest coincidence of being on maintenance duty at the time of the attack. Roger must have been repairing a motor in one of the other compressor rooms. The lizards had tracked him down with little effort, and Scott did not intend to fall into the same trap.

The golden dot flitted back and forth across the sky for an hour before the thrumming muted with distance and the object receded from view. When they came out of concealment Scott turned away from where the machine had flown off, and headed toward the plateau where he thought he could see a touch of green.

"Well, I guess we know where we're going."

"No we don't. We just know where we're going away from."

"Have it your own way."

"But what if there are others? How are we going to find them if we don't stay and look for them?"

"Rusty, we don't even know where we are. We can't find anything in this wilderness. We can't live without food and water, and that's what we have to look for. We have to keep going. I don't know where, I just know that we won't find anything by sitting still."

By midafternoon, Scott did not think that walking would solve their problems, either. There was no shade at all in the rough, rocky terrain, and the sun shone with unrelenting heat. His tongue felt like a ball of cotton in his mouth. His sores stung as sweat deposited salt into the wounds. His sunburned face and hands were a bright cherry red, and the skin was blistered. His feet were constantly tormented by pebbles and sharp rocks; the soft soles of his slippers were almost worn through. And the knees and elbows of his jumper were torn from rock scrambling: the material was delicate and not designed for rough outdoor life.

Still, because there was nothing else to do, they kept on. Then Scott spotted something on the ground besides the dry, twisted sprigs. "Look. A flower." He stooped low and inspected the yellow blossom. As did everyone in Maccam City, Scott had a good knowledge of botany and horticulture.

"It doesn't look like anything I've ever seen before." Rusty fingered a pointed leaf. "Ouch!" He drew his hand back sharply. "It bit me."

"Plants don't bite." Scott got down on hands and knees and

looked closely. "It's covered with little hairs, probably razor sharp."

Rusty plucked the tiny filaments from his fingertip. "I don't think it's edible."

"I agree. But maybe that is." Scott pointed to a twelve-inch bulbous tube that grew next to a boulder. As he approached it, he reached through his memory for identification. "It must be a baby cactus."

"Yeah, don't these things grow twenty feet tall?"

"Hey, there's another one. Rusty, let's get up this hill where we can see."

A moment later they were surrounded by sparse, crinkly vegetation and gnarled, stunted trees. More of the cactuses were here, as well as some larger ones. Several were in bloom, their yellow petals unfolded to catch the rays of the sun. And the ground was covered all over with a variety of grass.

"It's a forest," Rusty said.

"Yes, and if we only had a processor we could grind it into extract." Scott plucked some flowers and shoved them into his mouth. He chewed thoughtfully for a moment. "Well, it's not great, but—"

"Forget the flowers. Let's see if we can find some water."

"Good idea." Scott plucked another flower anyway. He plodded over the soft sand after Rusty. "There must be a stream around somewhere."

They walked quickly, going deeper into the woods where the trees grew thicker and the vegetation taller. Forgotten now were the aches and pains, the cuts and bruises. They jogged along through the stunted forest until they bounded into a cliffside clearing—

—and ran right into an eight-foot-tall, scaled lizard!

The monster was walking parallel to the rock face, looking upward, when it swung its snakelike head in their direction. It made a creepy, sibilant sound, reached behind its back, and brought its huge paw around clutching a gold firing capsule.

Scott and Rusty jumped away from each other at the same time there came a crackle of thunder and a blast of fire. Where they had been standing was now a molten puddle, slowly solidifying, while droplets of searing sand were spewed up into the air.

Rusty, in his eagerness to get out of the way, struck his foot against a protruding root. He went down hard, air whooshing out of his lungs. The reptile swerved the gun in his direction.

Scott was momentarily paralyzed, the rocks hanging limply in his hands. Then he leaped into action and hurled one straight at the scaled creature. The granite projectile bounced off the tough hide and, while it did no discernible damage, it unsettled the reptile enough so that Rusty had time to clamber out of the way of the lightning bolt.

Now the creature swung back to Scott. A beam of light shot out of the gold-colored gun. Scott rolled to the side and avoided the blast, but was showered with molten debris as the heat ray plowed into the ground.

The sound of the lightning bolt no sooner died out than something else clove the air with a whoosh. The creature struck forward, its head jerking as if pulled by an unseen string at its feet. It tried to hiss, but a thin, wooden shaft had pierced its throat.

The gun fired another blast, but it was harmlessly spent into the ground. The monster wavered on its powerful hind legs for a moment, then crashed sideways where it lay with its left hind foot clawing futilely at the blue sky.

A loud whoop-whoop-whoop rent the air from the rock ledge. Scott looked up and saw a nearly naked savage, wearing only a loincloth and moccasins, standing with legs spread wide, and holding a carved wooden bow in one hand. Even as he watched, the savage reached over his head, past black, shoulder-length hair, and tugged another arrow out of a quiver on his back. He notched it to the string, drew it back, and let it fly past Scott and into the trees.

A bolt of lightning crackled out of the woods and singed the rock at the savage's feet. This was followed by a loud hissing sound, and the crash of a body as another lizard fell into the clearing eyeball to eyeball with Scott. A fat tongue licked sharpened teeth, and the jaw worked reflexively. Thick, viscous blood drained out of the wound in the throat. The dying gasp of air that exhaled in Scott's face was fetid and nauseating. Yet, the legs and paws continued to move mechanically, as if animated by an unseen puppeteer.

Revulsion made Scott sick. He rolled over just as the savage leaped off his perch and landed with a thud on tautly muscled legs. "Come quick. Follow me." He gestured with his free hand, then turned and fled without looking back.

No more invitation was necessary. Scott scrambled to his

feet and, picking up Rusty on the way, pursued the scantily clad man across the clearing. Another reptile plodded out of the woods next to a fallen comrade and chased them with a beam of light. There were two more behind it. But by the time they drew a bead, their targets had vanished into the trees.

Once out of sight of the conflict area, the savage wove a circuitous course around the trees and brush. He was so fleet of foot that twice he had to stop and wait. Even so, they soon outdistanced the slow, bipedal lizards.

They entered the shadow of a line of hundred-foot-high cliffs. Dragging Rusty by the hand, Scott did his best to keep the savage in sight. He watched in awe as the man danced over a field of loose boulders as if they were pebbles on the beach. He and Rusty had to negotiate each rock at a snail's pace, either by walking around or climbing over. Day-old wounds were aggravated by the acrobatics.

The savage waited patiently whenever he got too far ahead, and stared back with dark, watchful eyes. It was not until they reached an area where great sheets of rock sheared off the cliff face offered concealment that he waited for Scott and Rusty to catch up.

Scott eased his worn and weary body to the ground. "Thanks. . . . Thanks—a—lot."

Rusty pressed one hand to his side. "Yeah. You—really saved—our necks."

The bronzed savage studied them without expression. His chest was deep and muscular, his abdomen flat and strongly delineated. Blue veins coursed over the muscles of arms and legs, and protruded from the sides of his thick neck.

"Men stick together. It is code."

There was an odd enunciation to his words, as if each syllable was supremely important. He stood stoically, with hands hanging by his sides. Then he untied a smooth, bulging pouch from his waistband, removed the corded line that snugged the top, and offered it to Scott. Still catching his breath, Scott only stared at it and wondered what it was. He was at the point of asking when the savage took it back, put the tip near his lips, and squeezed the soft, rounded base. A stream of clear liquid shot into his mouth.

When the pouch was handed to him the second time Scott took it eagerly. He wrapped his cracked lips around the opening and sucked out the life-giving water—and would have drunk it all had not the savage pulled it away from him with the ease one would use in taking a toy from a child. He handed the pouch to Rusty, who greedily drained the rest of it. When the empty flask was handed back, the savage meticulously wound the cord around the top and retied it to his waistband.

Rusty lay back on a slab of rock. "Thanks again."

"Yes, I'm sure glad you happened along. They would have gotten us for sure."

The savage looked at them blankly.

"You really know how to shoot that thing." Rusty indicated the bow which was still clasped tightly in one brawny hand.

Suddenly the impossibility of the situation exploded in Scott's brain like a rampant warhead. There were not supposed to be any people living on the surface of the Earth. "Hey, who are you anyway? And where did you come from?"

The savage, still standing tall, stabbed a thumb at his chest. "I am called—Death Wind." Then he extended his arm and pointed. "I live south." His pronouncement stated, he folded his arms across his chest.

"Uh, yes, well, it's nice to meet you, uh, Death Wind. My name's Scott."

"And I'm Rusty."

"Where from?"

"Maccam City," Scott replied.

"City?"

"Yes, an underground city. Back there." Rusty made a sweeping gesture with his arm. "Somewhere."

"Underground?"

"Yes, we've always lived underground. Ever since the plague."

Scott got up from the ground, and approached Death Wind. "In fact, we didn't know there were people living on the surface anymore. I always thought nothing could live out here—not even animals."

"Nomads live here. My people are Nomads."

"You mean, there are others?" Rusty stepped forward and stood by Scott's side.

"Many people. Many tribes. All Nomads."

"And you live around here?"

"Live here in summer. We hunt. In winter, we go south. Plant crops. Soon, we go south."

"You hunt? You mean, like—animals?" Scott licked his lips. "Do you have—food?"

"And more water?" Rusty added.

Death Wind nodded imperceptibly. "You need." It was not a question, but a statement of fact. "You friend." He thrust out his hand, fingers outstretched. Scott stared at it, wondering what it meant. When he did not react, the savage grabbed the inside of his arm, just below the elbow, and held it firmly. With the other hand, still holding the bow, he took Scott's fingers and wrapped them around his own dark arm in the same manner. His touch had a gentleness that seemed odd for one who appeared so coarse.

"Men stick together. It is code." This time it sounded like a chant.

At last, Scott understood that this was a bond of friendship. He clamped down on Death Wind's arm, and repeated the formula. Then Death Wind and Rusty exchanged the same greeting.

"You come with me." Death Wind turned and continued the march. Scott and Rusty traipsed along behind.

"Say, where did you get the bow and arrows?" Scott asked. He handed the bow to Scott. "I make."

Scott ran his hands over the carved wood, and marveled at the balance. He plucked the taut string. "How about the arrows? Do you make them on a lathe, too?"

Death Wind plucked an arrow from the quiver and let Scott have it. "Lathe?"

"Yes, lathe." He nocked the arrow and pulled the string. It hardly moved at all, and he wondered how the savage had bent the bow almost in half as he had. "I've never worked with wood but this is obviously machine made."

"Machine?"

"Yes, don't you make this on a machine?" Scott released the arrow and inspected the tip. It was triangular shaped, and appeared to be some kind of stone.

The savage touched a sheathed knife at his waist. "I make with this."

Rusty took the arrow when Scott was through with it. "What are these purple things sticking out the end?"

"Feathers."

"*Feathers!* You mean, like from birds?"

Death Wind remained silent.

"You mean there are birds still alive?"

"You never see?"

"I've seen them on disk. But I thought they had all died out—along with everything else."

"Disk?"

"Yes. You know, a computer disk."

"Computer?"

Rusty shoved the arrow back into the quiver. "Don't you know what a computer is?"

"Animal?"

Rusty stared at Scott, and burst out laughing. "No, it's a—well, a—kind of machine." Rusty launched into an explanation of what a computer was, and all the things it could do. Death Wind listened, but made no comment. His face remained impassive, so Scott could not tell whether he understood or not.

By that time Death Wind had led them up a nearly vertical climb to the base of an immense overhang. It was high above the surrounding plateau, offering an overview of the desert and the faraway ravines from which Scott and Rusty had recently escaped. The cave was large enough to fit a fair-sized house. It was Death Wind's solitary campsite, consisting of a fire pit, a collection of pine needles, a pile of wood, and a pack with carrying straps.

"Sit." Death Wind pointed to the pine needles. Rusty collapsed on the makeshift bed, obviously worn out. Scott took off his slippers—or, what was left of them. The soft sole had worn right through, and his feet were cut and scraped. He kneaded them tenderly.

From the pack Death Wind produced what appeared to be a loaf of bread, except that it was too solid. When he took out his steel-bladed knife, Scott saw that the blade was almost as long as his forearm. He sliced off a chunk of spongy matter, cut it in two, and handed it out. "Eat."

Scott had no idea what the stuff was, but he was too hungry to ask. He tore off a bite and knew right away that he had never tasted anything like it before. It was chewy, and required quite a bit of effort to swallow, but it was not unpleasant.

Between mouthfuls, Scott said, "This is good. What is it?"

"Meat."

"Meat? You eat meat?" Death Wind did not answer. By this time Scott figured out that he never answered questions that were either rhetorical or self-evident. "Yes, I guess if you hunt animals you must eat them."

"Stands to reason," Rusty said.

"What do you eat?"

Scott talked and chewed at the same time. "Vegetables. Plant food. Anything that grows, really. All our food is cultivated in hydroponic gardens."

"Hydro—ponic?"

Without stopping his intake, Scott explained. "Yes, you see, it's like farming, but more scientific. We live—lived—in a closed environment. Everything has to be recycled. Human organic waste material is used for fertilizer for plants grown in trays, in nutrient solutions, under artificial sunlamps. We grow—grew—mostly things like roots, tubers, and nuts; things that could be plucked from underneath. Any part of a plant we couldn't eat raw was converted into meal in processors. We made bread out of it. Nothing went to waste."

"You have rain?"

Scott laughed. "No, it never rains underground. We recycle our water, too. Or, at least, most of it. When water was thought to be unusable it was sprayed outside to be carried away by the wind—atmospheric dispersion, we call it. But we had wells drilled below the water table, and pumps that ran constantly."

Scott found it impossible to tell from Death Wind's expression how much he understood—or believed. His dark eyes carried no emotion. He sat unmoving, like a rock. He breathed slowly and deeply; even his chest did not move. Scott had the impression that the savage's body was a well-trained machine; trained, perhaps, for survival. And Scott found himself admiring that trait.

Death Wind rummaged through his pack and pulled out another smooth-skinned pouch. He took a small drink, then handed it to Scott. This time he was careful to leave some for Rusty. Death Wind stood up when Rusty returned the empty pouch. "I get more water."

Scott watched the graceful motion of the savage's body as he climbed down the rocks. He flexed his own muscles. He thought of himself as strong, and in good physical condition. But compared to Death Wind he was badly out of shape, and incredibly weak.

When he turned to address a question to Rusty, he found him dozing peacefully on the bed of needles. It made Scott realize how sleepy he was himself, how sore he was, how woefully exhausted he was. He wanted to wait up for Death Wind, to talk some more, to find out about this strange and wonderful, and awful, world into which he had been thrust. But he was gone so long that Scott found himself drowsing off. He lay back for just a moment to rest his eyes, and fell instantly asleep.

When Scott woke up the lighting was somehow different. He could not place it because his mind was fogged, as if in a drugged stupor. He lay for a long time staring at the roof of the cave, seeing nothing more, hearing nothing stir. When he finally rolled up to a sitting position, he saw Death Wind hunched over a sheet of brown material, working quietly.

"What are you doing?"

The savage looked up expressionlessly, then pointed to his feet. "Moccasin."

Scott inspected his own, practically nonexistent, footgear. "I guess I could use a new pair of shoes. And some more food, if you don't mind my asking." Death Wind stopped his work long enough to slice off two portions of meat. Scott chomped into the food ravenously. He poked Rusty in the ribs. "Hey, wake up before I eat your breakfast, too."

Rusty groaned and rolled over. "Is it time to get up?"

"It's morning already." He handed the other slice of meat to Rusty, then cocked an eye toward the low-lying clouds. "And judging by the light, it's not early either."

"I don't need food. What I need is a cool shower and something for this headache."

"We're lucky to have enough water to drink, much less bathe in." When Scott got up to claim the water container, he found a new ecstasy in pain. He sat back down with a moan.

Death Wind quit his project, and brought water to the two invalids. "You sick. You need rest. I take care until you are better."

"Thanks." Scott accepted the water with a grimace. "But why are you doing this for us? You don't have any idea who we are."

"No matter. You are men."

"Sure, but you almost got yourself killed by taking on those big lizards."

Death Wind seemed neither proud, nor embarrassed. Scott took this as a measure of his confidence. The savage had not made any decision on the matter; he had acted only as gravity acts when something was let go and it fell to the ground.

Rusty cleared his sore throat. "Uh, **Death Wind**, I know this is asking a lot, especially after you've done so much for us already, but—could you help us look for our—for other survivors?"

The savage poured gray powder from a small sack into a hollowed-out log, then added water from his smooth-skinned canteen. He stirred the concoction with a stick. "No others."

Rusty stopped chewing. "But, there must have been. We couldn't have been the only ones to get out of there alive. Yesterday we found another man who had escaped, so there should be others."

Death Wind kneaded the mixture until it had the consistency of a thick glue. "He wore clothes like you. Your tribe?"

Rusty nodded eagerly. "You saw him?"

"Dead. I follow trail. See track of many dragons. No others."

"But, there must have been—"

"Rusty!" Scott found himself irritated by his friend's insistence. "Face the facts, will you? We were the only ones to get away. The rest are all dead. I know it isn't nice, but that's the way it is. And the sooner we accept it the better off we'll be."

Rusty lapsed into silence, glaring at Scott. Death Wind looked from one to the other. He took a handful of paste and rubbed it first on Scott's hands, then his feet.

"That feels cool. What is it?"

"Medicine from plant. Help heal. Soon you be better." He applied it to Rusty's wounds next, smearing generous portions wherever he found cuts, scrapes, or blisters. He also laid a thin layer on his face, where the sun had burned his skin to a painful cherry red. When he was done he went back to his task of making moccasins.

Scott realized that the material from which he had cut the triangular pattern was animal hide. He watched in fascination as Death Wind, using his own broad foot as a last, converted the flat, tanned skin into footgear. With his foot in the middle of each sheet he wrapped the hide in such a way that one pointed end became the tongue and the flat end became the heel. With the point of his knife he punched holes along the other two sides of the triangle, folded them over the top of his foot, and laced them with thin strips of previously prepared

hide. When he was done he had a moccasin that wrapped
tightly around the foot as high as the ankle bone.

Scott was trying his on for size when the air started to
vibrate. There was an all-too-familiar thrumming sound in the
near distance. Immediately Death Wind dragged them to the
back of the cave. Soon a gold-colored disk floated into view.
It hovered at a thousand feet and was close enough so he could
make out details.

The aircraft was shaped like two curved bowls, one inverted
over the other. Square cutouts along the rim appeared to be
ports. Underneath, in the middle, was a tubular protrusion
about a quarter the diameter of the disk. Surrounding this,
hundreds of needlelike projections spouted purple beams
downward which, after a while, merged into one shimmering
heat wave.

As it cruised out of sight, and the thrumming sound was
swallowed up by the intervening cliff face, Death Wind said,
"You bring."

Scott said, "What do you mean by that?"

"You bring dragon. You bring airboat. They never come
here before. Three days ago I see boat in air, dragon in woods,
in desert. They search. I hide. Then I follow, watch. Strange
smoke fill air in desert. I find dead man, killed by dragon. I
follow your trail, bring you here. I think dragon seek you."

"But, who are they? And how did they find our city?"

Tears rolled down Rusty's cheeks. "And why did they kill
our people? What did we ever do to them?"

"Dragon bad. They kill men." That seemed to sum it up as
far as Death Wind was concerned. "Tomorrow I go to my
people. You come and live. We take care. Men stick together.
It is code."

Scott realized that for him and Rusty there was no other
choice. Thrust into a hostile world about which they knew
nothing, they could never survive alone. Their future was
irrevocably tied to this man of the wilderness.

Death Wind offered them more than security: he offered
them life.

CHAPTER 5

For Rusty it was another miserable night. Asleep long before sunset, and wakening long after dawn, he still felt exhausted even though he did nothing but lie around eating, talking, and healing. His sunburned skin was peeling in layers which he picked at constantly. And the bed of pine needles was not exactly like the linen-covered foam rubber he was used to.

Death Wind twice again refilled the canteens. He gathered leaves for bedding. He kept a constant vigil for dragons. And he collected a supply of plant sap for medicinal purposes, to help soothe Rusty's painful skin and to prevent Scott's acid-burned pustules from getting infected. The savage worked constantly for their benefit.

With his huge knife Death Wind cut off another portion of meat. "You eat much."

Scott licked his lips before taking a bite. "After a lifetime diet of vegetables and ground greens, this is quite a change."

Rusty lay snug at the back of the cave, nibbling. "Meat doesn't have the concentration of protein or vitamins that our processed food has, nor is it as easy to eat. All this chewing is a waste of energy. And besides, the high fat content is unhealthy in the long run."

"Where did you hear all that?"

"Oh, I've read a lot of disks on nutrition. Our diet is a lot better than what it used to be."

"You read much. You smart." Somewhere in this world of scrub brush and twisted pinon pine, Death Wind had found two long, slender tree trunks. He shaved the bark off them with his knife, then indicated Scott with his chin. "You strong."

Scott blushed. "He's spent as much time at computer terminals as you have in the woods. There's nothing he doesn't know about them, or can't figure out. Just like you know all this stuff you've been telling us about plants and animals."

"What I don't understand is why you move around so much.

37

Instead of migrating back and forth, wouldn't you be better off staying in one place?"

With the bark off, Death Wind started whittling one of the trunks into a pole. "Stay still, dragon find us. We move, they not know where we are."

Rusty wrestled with the tough meat. "But you're out in the open all the time. Do you really like it?"

"You like living in cave, like groundhog?"

"He's got you there, Rusty."

"Yes, well, it was the only kind of life I ever knew."

"You should have watched more movies instead of text disks. You always thought I was wasting my time, but I was looking for something like this. The only way I could get it was on a computer screen."

"But *this*"—Rusty swept his arm toward the arid desert—"is not what I saw on disk. Life was different in the old days, before the plague. I don't think I can get used to this kind of life."

"Well, as Death Wind says, you don't have much choice."

Death Wind worked on the end of the pole, shaping it into a nasty-looking point. "I teach. You learn. Work hard, you become warrior."

Rusty pouted. "I don't think I like the sound of that."

Scott leaned forward, eyebrows knitted. "What's involved in becoming a—warrior?"

"Child stay with family: cook, sew, mend. Learn to fight: bow, arrow, spear. When ready, go on trial. Alone. Many days. When he kills, he becomes warrior. Two day ago, I was child. Today, warrior."

"You mean, you have to kill one of those dragons to become a warrior?"

"No, kill beast of field."

"What kind of beast?"

"Sometimes small." Death Wind held the palm of his hand two feet above the rocky floor. "Sometimes big." He made a great circle with both arms. "But he who kill dragon be chief someday. My time come. I go on trial, look for beast. Many day, travel far. See airboat. See dragon. I hide. I stalk. I kill. Now I am warrior, someday chief."

"Well, you're a warrior in my disk." Scott finished eating, and wiped his mouth on his tattered sleeve. "And you certainly lived up to your name."

"I choose name. All children named by mother, father. But when kill, become warrior, choose own name. I kill dragon. From now on I am called Death Wind."

Rusty decided it was less dangerous to take an examination in guidance control or trajectory computations. "And how do we go about becoming warriors? We don't know anything about killing."

Death Wind passed the sharpened pole to Rusty. "You take spear. I teach. Soon you kill, become warriors."

Rusty viewed the spear askance. It was carved so the pointed end was thicker, and heavier, and the tip needle sharp. He passed the device to Scott. "Suppose I don't want—to kill." For some reason he found the act of shoving this wood into flesh appalling.

"Must kill to survive."

Rusty swallowed hard. If he disliked the outside world before, he was beginning to detest it now.

Scott's eyes were aglow. He hefted the spear over his head, and made short, thrusting motions. "You show me how to use it, Death Wind. I don't care about becoming a warrior—I just want to get even."

They did not leave that day—or the next. Scott and Rusty were simply not well enough to travel.

"Skin like baby." Death Wind applied more paste to Rusty's sunburn, to Scott's back. He also made them sit in the sun an hour at a time, in order to accustom them to the searing effects of solar radiation. At the same time, by converting a hide blanket into clothing, he taught them to sew. With a large cactus spine for a needle he fashioned tunics that were loose enough to allow circulation, but which kept the hot sun from bearing down on tender skin.

Rusty did not like the exposure of the breechcloth. The purpose of the unconnected front and rear panels was one of sanitation—it never had to be removed. "If you don't mind, I'll sew the flaps together and make a pair of shorts."

"Civilization dies hard." Scott laughed. He seemed to soak up everything Death Wind had to say. Already he could throw the eight-foot spear with a fair amount of accuracy. And Death Wind allowed him to carve the second pole. It was less than perfect, but good for a first try.

At the end of a week they were dressed, armed, and ready to leave.

"We not wait any longer. Need food."

In all that time there had been no more sightings of the dragon flying machines. But Death Wind led them through the pinon pine forest with his usual stealth, instructing them on the importance of always being alert, of being at one with the environment. He also interpreted the plant life they encountered along the way, naming flowers and edible herbs. By afternoon they passed out of the arid desert terrain and entered a forest of spruce and fir, and juniper with its dull blue berries. The world was transformed into a land of green, from the soft grass to the low-lying bushes and the tall treetops.

"Legend say dragon bring plague, clear the land for their seed."

Rusty dragged the tail end of his spear, for his spindly arms were not used to such weights. When Death Wind indicated a halt in a shallow ravine he was more than relieved. "What did they seed?"

"Eggs." The savage dropped his pack on the sandy soil, and started to scrape a hole with his bare hands. "Not like mammal kind, so bring egg of lizard. After mammal dead, lizard grow and take over land."

Scott leaned against his spear, using it as a third leg. "But where did the dragons come from? How did they get here?"

In a purely human fashion, Death Wind shrugged. "Not know."

"But your legends must say something."

Death Wind gathered leaves from the ground and stuffed them in the hole. "Legends speak only of fact, not make-believe. Anyway, it not matter. They are here, they are in control, and we must live in their world."

"Isn't there some way of fighting them?"

"Too many. Too strong. Mighty weapons." The leaves soaked up moisture like a sponge. Death Wind held them over the opening of a canteen and squeezed the water out.

"Ouch!" Rusty jumped, and slapped at his foot. A small creature, about the size of his thumb, fell to the ground and scrambled away. "What's that?"

The savage pounced on it. When he held it up Rusty could see the six madly moving legs, the brown, chitinous body. "Bug." Death Wind plopped the still living insect into his mouth, chomped down once, and swallowed. Rusty promptly threw up.

"We certainly seem to have different eating habits," Scott said. "And I'm not sure I care for all the things on your menu."

"When hungry, you eat."

"Not me." Rusty wiped his mouth on a large green leaf. "I'll never be that hungry." When Death Wind scavenged under a rotting log and found half a dozen slimy, mucus-covered white grubs that he promptly threw down his throat, Rusty got sick all over again.

"Take it easy, Rusty. You're losing all that valuable breakfast."

"Go ahead and laugh, Scott. I don't see you sticking your hand out for any grubs."

Death Wind continued to wring out the wet leaves. It took two hours of tedious work to fill both water pouches. Rusty was astonished at his perseverance. And the water he collected the three of them drank in minutes.

"Is that how you got the water you gave us in the cave?"

"Desert dry. Water scarce. Later, we find stream."

But before they found water again, they found food. Death Wind froze in the thick of the dense forest. He held up his hand for silence. Rusty heard movement. At first it sounded like something crashing through the underbrush; then it was tearing bushes out of the ground, ripping them asunder. Whatever it was, sounded big.

"Stay. Keep spear ready. I circle."

Death Wind slipped soundlessly away, like a ghost fading into mist. Rusty clutched his spear with nervous fingers, half hidden behind a fir tree. Ten minutes passed, then twenty. Still, he heard only the rutting of a wild animal.

Then there was a squeal like a fire alarm that went on and on, punctuated now and then by louder war whoops. Scott took off at the first sound, spear at the ready. Rusty chased after him. By the time he got to the action, it was all but over.

The animal that Death Wind was calmly watching in its death throes was a giant chameleon. Its strangely frilled head was fully a third of its five-foot-long body. An equally long tail writhed wildly. The arrow in its breast was snapped off close to the smooth, bright green skin, and blood was pouring out as if from an open faucet. It sucked air in labored gasps, like a fish out of water.

Scott got close, held his spear over his head with both hands, and stabbed down with all his might. The thrust carried the spear through the neck and pinned it to the ground. There was a momentary resurgence of activity as the creature leaped about with newfound energy, but it quickly faded. Scott held the spear in place until all movement ceased, and blood stopped flowing.

He pressed his foot to the ugly head, and worked the spear back out. "I thought you were going after food."

Death Wind nodded imperceptibly. "Food."

Rusty pointed a trembling finger. "But that thing's a lizard. You can't eat it."

The savage picked up the broken, feathered end of the arrow, and stuck it in his pack. "Lizard is beast. Beast is meat. You ate. You liked."

"You mean we've been eating lizard meat all this time?" Rusty's question went unanswered. "But, I thought we were looking for pigs, or cows. Livestock animals. That's what the computer disks say."

"No pig. No cow. No big mammal since plague. Only man and small mammal hide—live."

Scott wiped the blood off the end of his spear by rotating it on the ground. "Is this what the dragons brought? Are these the kind of creatures that hatch out of their eggs?"

"Are—are there many—beasts like this?"

"Many." Death Wind drew out his knife and started dissecting the chameleon. One thrust from chin to crotch disemboweled the animal. As the still warm viscera poured onto the ground, he cut one out of the bloody mess and tossed it aside. "This one small."

Scott touched the organ with the tip of his spear. "What's that for?"

Death Wind tapped the water pouch on his belt. "Bladder."

Rusty put a hand to his mouth. "You mean, we've been drinking out of some lizard's urine sac?"

As was his way, Death Wind did not answer. He peeled back the skin and cut away great chunks of meat.

Scott followed the savage's example. With his hands he waded into the mass of flesh and blood and took the steaks as they were cut. "Are we going to eat it raw?"

"Raw meat go bad quick. We cook tonight. Last many days."

The skin made good carrying sacks and before long all three marched off under a new load. Rusty's scrawny arms had all they could bear. He switched his load from one shoulder to the other, each time taking a new grip on the folded skin. The smell of blood was nauseatingly close.

The sky was turning from a pale blue to a light purple by the time they reached Death Wind's objective. The stream was barely two feet wide, and only several inches deep, but in seconds it carried more water past than they had seen in a week. Weapons and supplies were dropped unceremoniously. All three lay flat on their bellies, placed their lips on the surface of the cool liquid, and sucked in great quantities of water.

"I never thought I'd have enough to drink again." Rusty cupped the water in his hands and washed the grime from his face and neck. "It feels so good to be clean."

"Your hair could use a shampoo, too. And a comb wouldn't hurt." Scott sat by the stream, splashing water in Rusty's direction.

While Scott and Rusty played and got cleaned up, Death Wind cleaned out the chameleon bladder. He opened it wide at each end, put a rock inside, and sank it in the creek.

Scott started unpacking the meat. "Death Wind, when do we eat? I'm starved."

"Make camp first. Then gather wood for fire." The savage cleared a circular area of brush and grass until only bare earth remained. He lined it with large stones from the creek, and filled it with leaves, dry needles, and wood shavings. He took a flint from his pack and struck it against the back of his knife. Sparks flew into the tinder and, after several tries, ignited it. Then he blew on it until he had a small blaze going. Gradually he added more needles and shavings, then small sticks, and eventually round logs with peeling bark.

Rusty laid chunks of meat by the fire. "Death Wind, don't we have to worry about the dragons seeing all this smoke?"

"Dragon not travel at night." He lashed together two sets of sticks into "A" frames, skewered several pieces of meat, and laid it over the hottest part of the flame. "They cold."

Rusty was cold, too. He moved closer to the fire, exhilarated not only by its physical warmth but by the quieting effect it had on his mood. "Don't they have clothes?"

"Blood cold." He tapped himself on the chest with his fist,

and said, "Blood warm." Then he pointed to the meat on the stick. "Blood warm."

"You mean, the dragons are cold-blooded animals, but the lizards are warm-blooded?"

Scott shoved a small piece of meat on a spit and held it over the fire. "That isn't the way I remember my biology."

Death Wind cut off a thin slice of meat, and tasted it. "Good." He cut more and passed it around. "Eat while hot."

Rusty passed the meat from hand to hand because it was burning his fingers. The freshly cooked meat had a fragrance that whetted his appetite; he suddenly found himself famished. "I take back all I said about meat before. This is delicious."

It tasted so good that Rusty ate more than he thought possible for his stomach to hold. With darkness all about them, he stared into the red blazing logs, hypnotized by the flickering flames and coruscating embers. In his mind he was catapulted back to a time when men gathered around fires for protection from the elements and wild animals. And for a moment this horrible world was not so bad after all.

When all the meat was cooked, the fire was allowed to die out. Finally, with eyelids drooping, Rusty could stay awake no more. He lay back on the bed of leaves, staring up at the nighttime sky. What he saw made his eyes spring open, and sent a chill down his spine. "Look!"

Death Wind bolted for his bow and arrow. Scott stared upward, blinking sleep from his eyes. "I don't believe it."

The savage had his first arrow notched. He looked up and all around, half crouched and waiting for the attack. "What you see?"

"Why, they're all over. It's beautiful," Rusty said.

"I never thought it would be like this."

In the disks they had always been cold and uninspiring, but when seen through atmospheric heat waves they danced about like living entities. Rusty glanced at Death Wind. In the partial darkness he could see a sign of expression in the savage's face. Confusion? Disbelief? Disorientation? It was nice to know that he *had* emotions. Rusty laughed right out loud. "The stars!"

CHAPTER 6

"Up! Up! Up!"

Before Rusty could do more than open his eyes, the savage picked him up and pushed him into the cover of a nearby bush. A moment later Scott landed on top of him. After the rustling of the leaves stopped he heard the thrumming that meant that a dragon flying machine was in the area.

Scott pushed branches out of his face. "What's he doing out there?"

Death Wind stood right out in the open, and stared up at the sky. The sun sat on the horizon like a dull, orange globe, pinking the heavens. The hum grew louder for a moment, and the savage's dark eyes locked in intense concentration. When the sound of motors reversed pitch, and the machine started receding, he motioned them to come out.

"It is safe."

Scott brushed himself off. "Why did you stay out in the open like that?"

"See airboat, avoid danger. Take weapon, come with me. I show you."

Rusty squinted his eyes. The dragon machine was only a golden speck, moving directly away. With his spear over his shoulder like a rifle, he followed Scott and Death Wind through the woods. The tall trees offered faint comfort, but they dispelled the feeling of openness. The air was filled with the same odor of burnt wood he had smelled the night before while they cooked the meat, except that this was thick and sickening.

They stopped at the edge of a blackened swath of destruction, a hundred feet wide, as if a giant blowtorch had been played across the ground incinerating everything in its path.

"Airboat pass high, safe. Pass low, death. Sound is different. Be ready to run."

While there was the sign of a great conflagration, there was no flame or smoke. Trees were scattered everywhere like a field of fallen monarchs, denuded of leaves or needles. Patches

45

of cinder were all that showed where bushes had stood. There was dry, blackened earth where once had been fields of verdant, green grass.

Rusty remembered the shimmering that emanated from underneath the machine. "Scott, can rocket propellant do this?"

"No, the ground isn't scorched. This is no chemical reaction." He scraped a fingernail full of soot off a charred trunk. "This is some kind of molecular vibration."

"Whatever force they use to power their aircraft must discharge an awful lot of energy."

"They've got a kind of science that we know nothing about." Scott turned to the savage. "Death Wind, how long does it take to learn all the dangers of this world?"

"Whole life of child is learning. Once learned, go on trial." Death Wind led the way back to camp.

"But you just became a warrior the other day. How long did it take you? How old are you?"

"Two hundred fifteen."

"What?" Rusty tripped over a lichen-covered log and hit the mossy forest floor with a thud. Scott helped him up. "Two hundred and fifteen *years*."

"Moons," the savage said.

Scott pushed vines out of the way. "How old does that make him?"

Rusty calculated quickly. "Why, he's younger than we are. He's only seventeen."

"Believe it or not, Death Wind, we're adults in our world. We've learned most of the necessary material and passed our tests."

"Sure, we're just taking postgraduate courses now."

"That not make you warrior."

Rusty rubbed a sore elbow. "I'm not saying it does. I'm only saying that we're equal in our knowledge with respect to our own societies."

"All men equal."

They reached the campsite, and Scott immediately unwrapped a helping of meat and cut portions with Death Wind's knife.

"All Rusty's saying is that you'd have as much trouble adjusting to our way of life as we are adjusting to yours. The difference is that here a simple mistake can mean death. You don't have makeup tests."

Instead of eating right away, Death Wind took the bladder out of the creek. The overnight immersion had purged it of residue. He looped and knotted one end, filled it with water, and tied off the other end. Then he presented it to Scott.

While Scott and Rusty ate, he went about the task of making packs out of the giant chameleon skin, stitching with cactus spine and strips of skin. "You say you always live underground. How you know about stars and constellations? How you know about the moon? How you know about the North Star?"

Rusty laughed. "We have science courses along with everything else. It's like I told you before, everything is on computer disk."

"I do not understand this—computer disk."

"And Rusty's too smart to be able to explain it to you. Let me just put it simply. The computer is a device full of knowledge, and the disk is a way of retrieving that knowledge. A disk is like a book."

Death Wind's face brightened. "Book?" He stopped working for a moment and rummaged through his pack. He brought out a musty, moldy object and held it out. "Book."

Scott reached out for the slender volume. "That's it. That's it. Disks are like this, only the print is so small you can't read it. The computer enlarges it so you can."

Death Wind nodded. "I like books. Read pictures all the time."

"Do you understand the words?" When Death Wind did not answer, Scott opened the picture book to the middle and pointed to the large typeface. "Do you know what these mean?" The savage shook his head. "Then maybe we can bring you some knowledge from our world by teaching you how to read."

Rusty took the book from Scott, and opened it to the faded title page. It read, *The Song of Hiawatha*, by Henry Wadsworth Longfellow. "Death Wind, where did you get this book?"

"City. South. Much broken."

"By broken, do you mean it's in ruins?" Death Wind nodded. "Will we be passing this city on our way to your village?"

"Way south. Maybe pass later."

"Can we stop there, do you think? I'd like you to take us to where you found this book. If we can find a library, we may be able to learn what happened after the plague. Our history disks stop when the input terminals went blank."

Scott said, "You see, we're still waiting for a counter-attack."

Death Wind looked from one to the other.

Rusty handed the book back to Death Wind. "Our city was originally built as a missile coordination center with intercontinental capability. We integrated high orbital command modules and military telecommunications—"

Scott put a hand on Rusty's shoulder. "Rusty, you're talking way over his head. Let me try it." Facing Death Wind, he continued, "In the old days people fought with missiles, not bows and arrows. These missiles are like, well, like giant spears, only much more deadly. They could be launched at targets thousands of miles away. But the missiles aren't kept all in one—quiver. They were scattered all over the country. Maccam City is a control center—we directed the throwing of these spears, so to speak."

"I have heard of these weapons that kill at a distance. Called—guns?"

"Not exactly. Guns are small weapons, hand held."

"Like dragon lightning thrower?"

"Exactly, except that the guns we had threw pieces of steel. But missiles are much bigger, as big as—" Scott looked around for a moment, then pointed upward. "As big as those trees." Death Wind looked up at the fifty-foot ponderosa pine. "And one of them could level an entire city."

"What you mean? Weapon for animal or dragon, not city."

"Not in the old days. There were no dragons then. But there were great wars, nations fighting other nations, in which millions of people were killed."

Death Wind's expression contorted into a mixture of horror and disbelief. "You lie. Men not fight men. Men need men—for food, for protection, for family. Why you make up this story?"

"It's not a story. That's the way it was."

"Men need men. To live."

Rusty said, "Maybe now, but not a hundred years ago. Then, man's worst enemy was man. There were always other nations—"

"Tribes," Scott interrupted.

"—trying to take over weaker na—tribes."

"You come from these men who kill men?"

"Yes. And all these years we've been waiting. We never knew which side started the plague, but in case they started throwing missiles at us we wanted to be ready for them."

"I not like this. You speak maybe truth, maybe lie." Death Wind's eyes narrowed. "You still—kill men?"

Rusty saw they were treading on dangerous water. "No, you don't understand. Our ancestors were trying to prevent this from happening. These aggressors had missiles, too, to throw at us. We never intended to use ours except in self-defense."

"And besides, the world is different now. There may not even be any others. The plague may have backfired and gotten them, too. I don't know. But what Rusty is saying is that we would like to find out."

"And if you could take us to this city we may be able to determine who won the war."

Death Wind had not moved in many minutes. "My heart is troubled over your words. When we get to tribe, we talk with chief. He is warrior for many moons. He will understand. Let him decide."

CHAPTER 7

By the time the sun reached its zenith, the trio was on the trail.

Each was now carrying a well-stocked pack, and had his own canteen. Death Wind carried his bow over his shoulder. Scott and Rusty practiced spear throwing as they walked through the green, fertile forest. Rock outcrops and rolling hills provided relief in the terrain.

Death Wind picked up a rock chip. "Flint. You save. Start fire, make arrow tip." Later, when he found mushrooms growing on a log, he broke one off, sniffed it, snapped it in half and inspected for infestation, then ate it. "Never take from ground, get sick. From log, okay."

Scott plopped a mushroom into his mouth. "Tastes kind of musky." He handed a piece to Rusty.

"No thanks. I'll pass."

"Come on, Rusty. You've been eating mushrooms all your life."

"But they were grown under sterile conditions, then purified and processed."

"And we don't live like that anymore. From now on we're men of the forest, and we have to start thinking that way. We can't cling to our old values. Instead of striving for good grades we have to find food and water, make clothing and shelter, live each day at a time."

"But I don't like it. I don't like being outside, I don't like all this moving around, and I don't like killing animals and eating food off the ground."

"Well, whether you like it or not, you'd better get used to it. Because we're going to live this way for a long time."

Death Wind picked up a long stick. "Nomad have no village, have no home. He wander forever, escape dragon. No choice. We do what we must."

A tear hung on Rusty's cheek. "That's easy for you to say. You were brought up that way."

Death Wind held his stick out sideways, halting Scott and

51

Rusty in their tracks. He put a finger to his lips. Soundlessly he tiptoed toward a hollowed tree stump. Scott detected movement, as if something were flashing in and out of sight, at the upper end of the rotten wood.

Suddenly the stump exploded with living creatures. They leaped out in all directions and hit the ground with all four legs clawing for traction. Death Wind swung his stick with unerring accuracy, catching several of the lizards in the air and batting them left and right, and clubbing others on the ground.

Scott leaped after one, but when he tried to grab the creature it stood up on its hind legs and was gone in an instant. The rest that made it to the ground and got out of Death Wind's reach scattered through the underbrush. Rusty stood rooted to the spot as several raced right past him.

"Those things sure are fast." Scott got up and brushed himself off. He picked up one that Death Wind had killed, and noticed that the skin was smooth, that the animal felt warm in his hand. "Are these things warm-blooded, too?"

"All warm, except dragon." He dismembered the lizards with his knife and discarded the bodies. "Legs good. We eat."

That night, Scott took a turn at starting the fire. He scratched his flint across the steel blade and tried to aim the tiny sparks into the tinder. Time and again they either missed, or were swallowed up without igniting the leaves and dried moss.

"It looks so easy when you do it." Eventually, by blowing gently into the tinder, he coaxed the fire to life.

Death Wind pushed a sharpened stick through the fat legs and roasted them over the hot flames. After they had been cooked, the skin peeled off readily and the meat underneath was soft and tender.

Rusty grudgingly nibbled on a leg, held delicately with a leaf so he would not get his fingers greasy. "It's not bad, but it could use a little salt."

Scott smiled. "Do you have to complain about everything?"

"I can't help it, I'm tired. Trying to keep up with Death Wind is like running a race."

Scott turned to the savage. "How far is it to where your people are camped?"

"Me, two days. You, four days. All, three days."

"There, you see. He's going slow for our benefit."

Rusty put a small piece of mushroom cap on his tongue. "Great."

Scott scooped some water out of the stream. It was cool in his throat. "And how long does it take your people to move to their winter location?"

"One moon. Maybe two." He chewed heartily on his sixth lizard leg. "No hurry."

By late next morning the dense pine forest gave way to fields of open grass dotted with rock piles and hillocks, and populated by deciduous trees such as quaking aspen, cottonwood, and birch. The land was much brighter, and the ground was covered with flowers of delightful colors.

Scott continued to practice with his spear. He had carved a comfortable grip that was just the right size for his hand. The balance point was one-third of the way back from the tip. He liked the feel of it, for it gave him a sense of power.

"Hey, what's that?" Rusty pointed to something that fluttered by with random, jerky movements. It pierced the air on saffron wings, which folded delicately over its tiny body when it landed on sun-seeking blossoms.

"Butterfly."

Rusty chased after it in the open field, dragging his spear. He tried to catch it with his hand, but could not anticipate its quick, darting motions. "They're all over the place."

Scott turned cheerfully to Death Wind, but saw the Nomad standing stock still, staring off in the distance. His nostrils flared as he twisted his head, catching a scent. "What is it? What do you smell?"

"Lizard." Death Wind cocked his head, listening. "Big lizard."

Scott tightened his grip on the spear. He looked across the idyllic glade, full of colorful flowers and flitting insects. Then he heard a crash, followed by something that was a cross between a snort and a bark. "Can we eat—"

Before he could finish, he saw an animal step out of the cover of tall brush from beyond a hillock. It was a dark gray mass the size of a tank. The massive head was at least five feet long. Two spearlike horns reached out from above the eyes, while another, shorter and stubbier, pointed upward from the nose. A flared shell stretched backward, protecting the beast's thick neck. It moved on four trunklike legs.

Rusty froze in the middle of a living bouquet of flowers. A gasp escaped his throat. "That's a triceratops."

The ten-ton beast grazed noisily, uplifting roots and bushes and small trees. It crunched limbs and leaves in its powerful jaws and swallowed indiscriminately whatever passed its smooth-skinned lips.

Death Wind motioned for caution. Loud enough for Rusty to hear, he said, "Beast have dim eyes. Maybe not see."

Even as he said it, Scott felt the wind shift. The triceratops stopped in midstride. It raised its mighty head and craned its neck. Large, round eyes peered myopically from under bony brow ridges. The three sharp prongs triangulated on Rusty.

"Run!"

Scott chased after Death Wind as he ran a zigzag course through the woods, dodging trees and leaping over bushes and broken logs. Rusty was on his heels one moment, then soaring past the next. Scott cast a glance over his shoulder and saw the ungainly looking creature catching up with him. Thundering hooves propelled the triceratops closer every second.

He broke out into another clearing and saw Death Wind waving him on toward a large rock mass several hundred feet away. The moss-covered rock, topped with shrubs and saplings, stuck sharply up out of the ground to a height of twenty feet. The sides were broken with jagged edges draped with vines.

As Death Wind neared the outcrop he made a tremendous leap that carried him halfway to the top. He grabbed onto a narrow ledge and with the strength of his arms he pulled himself onto it.

Following the savage's example, Rusty dropped his spear and vaulted as high as he could, but fell a foot short of the ledge and fell back down to the soft earth.

"Spear!"

Rusty picked up his weapon and thrust the blunt end up the rock face. Death Wind took the spear and pulled it up hand over hand, with Rusty hanging on. Sinew strained and veins protruded until Rusty's hand found the ledge. A dark brown hand clamped down on his wrist and hoisted him up.

Without letting go of his spear, Scott hit the rock at full speed and tried to run right up the side. His momentum carried him just to the level of the ledge where Death Wind's hand reached out for him. They missed by inches, and Scott slipped back down the rock face scraping skin off knees and knuckles.

The spear imbedded in the ground and could not be dislodged. Without wasting an instant he climbed the eight-foot pole like a monkey and was almost at the top again when the triceratops crashed into the base of the rock pile. With a single thrust of its powerful head the spear snapped in half like a toothpick.

Scott fell right onto the head of the triceratops, between the bony plate and the base of the two long upper horns. The beast thrust its great head up in a stabbing reflex and flung him over its tanklike body as one would fling off a fly. He landed on his side and back, the pack taking the brunt of the fall, and rolled over dazed. He saw the short, pointed tail flicking across a broad rump, and expected to be trampled any moment. But the triceratops, despite its great size and its massive head, was too stupid to turn around to see what happened to its quarry. It continued to make spear thrusts with its horned snout, gouging deep furrows in the rock face.

Death Wind shouted war whoops to distract the beast. This kept the triceratops so enraged that it continued its senseless attack on the wall.

Scott crawled out of the way of the swishing, whiplike tail. He stood behind the creature, wondering what to do next. Death Wind sidled along the ledge, drawing the animal to the side. As the triceratops changed its angle of attack, Scott slipped around behind it until he reached the rocks and found a place where he could, with some difficulty, climb up to safety.

As soon as Scott was out of danger Death Wind lapsed into silence. Now the beast snorted aimlessly, its imaginary enemy gone. Its head was showered with dirt and debris, its large eyes blinked away dust. Within moments it forgot why it was pounding its head into rocks. It ambled on its way, snorting and gouging bushes out of the ground with its stubby central horn.

When he recovered his breath, Scott said, "I'm beginning to think this outdoor life's not all it's cracked up to be."

CHAPTER 8

"Where did that—dinosaur—come from?" Scott blew on his knuckles where the skin had been torn off.

Death Wind mixed a salve from his meager supply. "Dragon bring."

From the top of the outcrop Rusty watched the dull-witted beast trundle off into the woods. "But you don't understand. Dinosaurs lived on the Earth a hundred million years ago. I've seen them on disk, and that horned monstrosity is a dead ringer for a triceratops. It's inconceivable they could have evolved on another planet in exactly the same form. It just doesn't make sense."

Death Wind concentrated on applying the healing goo to Scott's wounds.

"How about the smaller ones, Rusty—the ones we've been eating? Did you recognize any of them?"

"No, there were thousands of different dinosaurs—tens of thousands, I guess. In their heyday they were as plentiful as mammals were before the plague. The paleontology disks I've seen were just overviews. A lot of the dinosaurs we know about were reconstructed from a few bone fragments, sometimes only one, so there are bound to be differences in their real appearance. But something like a triceratops is well known, from many intact specimens."

Scott grimaced as Death Wind smeared his concoction on his skinned knees. "And you have no idea where they came from, other than they appeared on Earth the same time the dragons did?"

"Many moons ago, men plentiful. Cover earth like grass in field. Live everywhere, without fear. Together. Then disease come, kill all: mammal on ground, bird in air, fish in river. Some hide, live. Then dragon come, hunt down men. More than that I do not know. Must move always, stay away from dragon, find food, take care of little ones."

With the danger past, they climbed down to the grassy field.

Scott picked up the broken pieces of his spear, picked at the splinters, then discarded the tail end. "Yes, I guess it doesn't leave much time for study."

Rusty combed leaves from his hair with a short-needled pine branch. "First dragons, now dinosaurs. This world gets crazier all the time."

The world got crazier the next day when another dragon flying machine passed by. Death Wind cupped his ear. "Listen to sound."

At first, Rusty heard nothing. But as the gold saucer got closer, riding on its shimmering beam of purple radiance, the high-pitched thrumming sent irrational chills of fear down his spine. He wanted to reach out with his spear and strike the hated enemy craft out of the sky.

As if the dragons were cooperating with Death Wind's lessons, the machine descended. Then Rusty could distinguish the lowering of pitch that meant its deadly beam was reflecting off the ground, and that molecular destruction was occurring.

Just before dark it passed by again. "Many airboat, not good."

Scott carried the stub of his spear over his shoulder. "Do you think your tribe will move away or take cover before we get there?"

Death Wind scanned the forest. "If so, we find. We camp here tonight. But be on watch for dragon. Be ready to run, or fight."

"I think I'd rather run," Rusty said.

"Run if possible. But if you fight, move quick. Dragon think slow, move slow. You get out of way easy, like butterfly."

Rusty slept restlessly. His dreams were full of dragon airboats that flew by and incinerated them in the propulsion blast. He tried sleeping close to a birch tree, using an exposed root for a pillow. But ants and other nocturnal insects crawled over his body without any regard for his terror, and after several rude awakenings he was forced to move out into the open where he had nothing but stars for a ceiling.

Death Wind roused him early in the morning. Groggily he accepted the piece of cold meat Scott handed him, and chewed it absently while he stumbled through the forest in the half light. The pace was telling, and it seemed to him that the Nomad was showing some anxiety about his tribe. Three times in the morning airboats were heard, but always too far away to be seen.

"What's that low rumbling noise?" Rusty said.

Now Death Wind broke into a trot. "River. We close."

Rusty, who found he could run fast in short spurts, was not so fast in the long haul, especially carrying a spear and a pack full of food. Periodically, Death Wind called out in his stylistic war whoop. But the only answer came from aspen leaves quaking in the gentle breeze. Still, he ran on toward his brethren. Rusty was exhausted when he caught up with Scott and Death Wind.

They stared at a blackened clearing, a smoldering circle of destruction, as if a dragon airboat had dropped close to the earth at this one spot and had taken off again. All around it was green and beautiful and untouched.

"Watch for dragon," Death Wind whispered. He led the way around the ugly scar, moving as gracefully and as silently as only one who was born and bred in the forest could move. His bow was held in front, an arrow notched. Despite its weight, Rusty cocked his throwing arm and prepared to launch his missile—or run.

Rusty could detect no discernible footprints around the burn zone, and if Death Wind saw any signs he made no mention of it. They veered close to the river, slinking through the thick vegetation that grew upon the banks. The roar of rushing water became thunderous, and Rusty caught a glimpse of the raging torrent as it cascaded down a large cataract, tossing spume high into the air. The spray landing on Rusty's shoulders brought with it a sharp coolness.

Suddenly the once thick vegetation ended. A blackened swath of fallen trunks and shriveled limbs lay rotting on the ground. The path of destruction went right into the river, where the tumbling water obliterated any further traces.

The forest continued on beyond the dead zone, and Death Wind wasted no time leading Scott and Rusty through the debris. Rusty's spear kept hanging up and he fell far behind the others. His moccasins filled with mud as he waded through the sooty swampland. When he reached the trees on the other side he saw that it extended only a few feet before opening up to another patch of charred destruction. And beyond that, there was more black death.

They came to a great clearing, crisscrossed by so many burnt tracts that hardly a tree stood within a mile. Huge boles, shorn of bark, were flung like giant matchsticks lying pellmell on the ground. The wood was blackened, the earth glazed, and the land pockmarked as if hundreds of explosions had torn it apart. Nothing was alive, nothing was intact. Nothing even remotely resembled any form in nature except the whitely gleaming remnants of human bones partially melted into a gray ash. Disembodied fragments like broken pipe stems attested to what they had once been. The dragon airboat, held aloft on its deadly, purple beams, must have traversed this area again and again with ruthless abandon.

Death Wind stood like a statue, uttering not a word. A wayward breeze tossed his long hair off his shoulders, revealing muscles that now sagged with despair.

Then the great statue that was Death Wind, killer of dragons, began to wilt. Great, gleaming tears streaked down his dusty cheeks, rolled off his quivering jaw, and dropped onto his outflung, heaving breast. The muscles in his neck bunched into knotted cords. And still the silent tears flowed.

After many minutes Death Wind strode out into the ruin and desolation that had once been his people's camp. He kicked violently at anything that got in his path. Scott kept at a respectable distance. Rusty lagged behind, struck with fascination and horror.

For an hour they roamed the former encampment, seeking signs that some of the Nomads had gotten away. But of the many footprints that Death Wind pointed out, none had been made in the act of escape. It appeared as if the dragon airboat had made increasingly smaller circles, herding the people to their deaths.

Rusty's spirits sagged. In the span of a week he had lost not only one family, but the promise of another.

Death Wind stooped down and picked up a clod of clay fired into brick by the sudden, intense field of force from the dragon machine. In his strong, brown hand he squeezed it until it crumbled into dust. He let the particles sift through his splayed fingers.

"I feel now—what you feel. Your grief is my grief. I share your sorrow." He paused for a moment and looked up at the sky. "From this day on, till death take my spirit, I vow vengeance against the dragon and their ilk. I, Death Wind, killer of dragon, have spoken."

Later that night, while the stars plastered the velvet sky like scintillating diamonds, and embers burned brightly in the fire, the three orphans ate in disconsolate silence. Scott carefully arranged three felled trees so their ends met in the flames. As they burned down he snapped off the cinders and pushed them in farther.

"What about the other tribes?"

Death Wind stood on the rocks above the falls, listening to the rumble of cascading water. He stared listlessly over the churning foam. "All south."

Rusty knapped a piece of flint, as Death Wind had shown him, and made his first arrowhead. "Well, can't we find them? Can't we join them?" When the savage did not answer, Rusty persisted. "After all, they're your people, too. You said all Nomads are the same."

The quiet that followed was ominous. After many minutes Death Wind spoke sibilantly. "I vow vengeance. No seek Nomad. Seek dragon."

"But what about us?" Rusty said.

"Tomorrow we part. I go my way, you go yours."

Scott jumped up, his eyes burning red like the fire. "Go? Go where?"

"You follow river. Find Nomad."

Rusty ran to Death Wind's side. "But, we can't do that. I mean, you can't just leave us. We don't know this world. We'll die out here."

"You smart, you strong. You live."

"No!" Scott screamed. "You're not leaving me here. If you're going after dragons, I'm going with you."

"Now, wait a minute, Scott. We don't have a chance against the dragons. There's no sense getting killed for nothing."

"Was your father nothing? Was your mother nothing? Your brothers and sisters? Are you going to just write them off? Well, I'm not. I'm going with Death Wind to get even with them—or die trying."

"No." Death Wind folded his arms across his chest. "I go alone. I take my sorrow. You take your sorrow. May our sorrows never meet again."

"What are you talking about? Why can't I go with you?"

Death Wind faced the crackling fire. His face was as impassive as ever. "Dragon seek underground city. They find.

They destroy. But you escape. They track, and find my tribe. Kill my people. Because of you, they are dead."

"Hey, don't think you can blame us for that." Scott stood between Death Wind and the fire. He forced the savage to look at him. "How do you know they weren't looking for your people and just happened to stumble across our city?"

Death Wind would not be prodded into an answer. "You know not the way of fighting. I must go alone. I go fast, you not catch. I have spoken." Death Wind calmly sat down and lay by the fire. He closed his eyes, but Scott would not leave him alone.

"You just try to get away. I'll follow you, I'll track you down. Maybe I can't keep up, but I'm sure going to try. I'll keep going till I drop. And if I lose you, I'll fight them alone. You hear me, Death Wind? You hear me. I'm going with you."

Rusty curled up on the scorched earth. There was a hollow pang in his chest, as if his heart were pounding to get out. And there was no solace in his dreams.

CHAPTER 9

Scott looked up at Death Wind in the first hint of dawn, when the brighter stars were still visible and the black sky was fading to purple. "Up. Eat. Soon we go."

Wary eyes pinched at the savage. "You mean, you're going to take us with you?" Death Wind nodded slowly. "How come the change of heart?"

The savage was silent for a long time, his face twitching. "Maybe you right. Maybe I right. I not know. All—confusion. But this I do know: according to code men help each other—always."

A smile broke out on Scott's face. "That's the way to go." He reached over and punched Rusty on the shoulder. "Wake up, sleepyhead. Death Wind says we're going with him." He gathered his legs under him and stood straight and tall. He grasped Death Wind's extended arm in the Nomad greeting, then he threw his arms around the savage's shoulders and hugged him like a long-lost brother. "Now you're talking. And you won't be sorry, either. We won't let you down, will we, Rusty?"

"Huhn?" Rusty jammed a fist into his eyes, and rubbed away cobwebs. "Uh, well, no. I guess not."

"We go east. Through abandoned city. Over tall mountain. Across Great Desert. Into Dark Swamp. Where dragon live. There we die—for our people."

"I'm not too crazy about dying, but I'll give it my best shot." Scott's voice was full of enthusiasm. "Won't we, Rusty?"

Now Rusty was awake, or almost. "Yes, sure we will." The uncertainty in his voice gave way to sincerity. "We'll launch a tirade against those dragons they won't forget for a long time."

They veered away from the river, heading east. On the trail Death Wind marched like a living machine: his legs pumped like pistons and his lungs moved air like a bellows. His long

63

hair streamed back in itinerant breezes, sometimes entangling in the quiver full of feather-studded arrows.

Scott soon found that his determination did not make up for his still soft muscles. He was in a constant state of fatigue. He worried about Rusty, but if his friend had any trouble keeping up the pace he did not complain about it. His long skinny legs stretched out two steps to Scott's three.

All that day, and the next, and half the third, they trudged inexorably on toward the abandoned city where Death Wind had found the chronicles of another, and earlier, wandering soul. When they reached the outskirts of the ancient, once-thriving town, Scott was sorely disappointed.

"It isn't exactly what I expected."

What he saw was a hundred years of decay and deterioration in which wooden houses had long since collapsed, brick facades had fallen in, and multiple-story buildings had toppled. Sand and dirt and dust had swept over the whole, leaving an amorphous mass that hardly resembled anything with pattern and meaning.

"Dragon airboat fly low over city, roads, houses. Always destroy. First kill man, then kill memory." After a wistful moment, Death Wind added, "Book this way."

He stalked off through crumbling walls and uncertain foundations. The one-time residential district was now nothing but rotted wood and disjointed cinder blocks, and a morass of broken-up blacktop that had once been a busy street. Weeds and small shrubs grew wherever they could find enough dirt to hold a root.

"But why? Why do they want to obliterate us?"

"It doesn't matter why," Scott said.

Closer to the heart of town, in the former commercial district, rusting steel frameworks, like twisted, garish skeletons, were all that was left of the sharp clean lines of skyscrapers. Mounds of detritus completely smothered the streets under many feet of brick, marble, and slivers of glass. The trio climbed and scrambled over the broken tumulus.

An eerie silence hung over the abandoned city. Since the time of man's defeat the only sounds made were by the wind, or by the gradual collapse of his construction.

Death Wind raised his hand and tilted his head with great concentration. He notched his bow.

"What is it?" Scott whispered. "What do you hear?" In the

pale quiet he heard the hissing of steam, and something heavy scratching across the stone debris. He fingered the splintered end of his spear where the shaft had been broken.

A leering lizard head rose above the mound of rubble in front, mottled gray and tan, swaying on the long stalk of a neck. As it stood up straight on thick hind legs the unwieldy paw swung around, gripping the firing apparatus of its lightninglike gun.

An arrow sliced the air and pierced the soft part of the upper neck. The beast let out a hiss of pain. It was hurt, but not to the point of death. An instant later the gun was brought to bear and a shaft of fire spat from the nozzle.

Where the beam struck, Death Wind was no more. Dodging to the right, he loosed another arrow. This one sunk into the broad breast between the short, gnarled arms. Lightning flashed unaimed, its energy spent uselessly in the air.

Rusty launched his spear. The finely honed point clove the broad abdomen with such force that the animal spun partly around from the momentum. Another arrow glanced off the forearm and into the chest. The creature hissed horribly and drew back its injured limb. The gun dangled by the cord from the power pack.

Scott rushed from the left. As he leaped over the rubble embankment he delivered the coup de grace by ramming his stubby spear into the unprotected underbelly. The creature twisted away, ripping the spear out of his hand. But the two-chambered heart had been pierced, and the dragon died on its clawed feet while its jaw still worked silently from side to side. After several seconds the autonomic reflexes stopped and, levered sideways by the thick tail, it crashed to the ground.

Death Wind ran up beside Scott. He cast furtive glances all around, then looked down at the drooling mouth. "Dead."

He placed one foot on the dragon's coarse scaled neck and pulled out his precious arrows. After wiping the blood off on the leathery skin, he returned them to his quiver. Then he pulled out the two spears, held them high over his head, one in each hand, and faced his companions.

In a voice that was triumphant without being loud, he proclaimed, "Hail, warriors, killers of dragon."

Rusty was too stunned for words. Scott threw his arms around him and lifted him off his feet, dancing with him in a small circle. He tried to make a war whoop like Death Wind's, but as soon as he made a sound the Nomad squeezed them both together with his muscular arms.

"Where one—more. Always quiet."

Scott curbed his tongue but could not stop grinning foolishly. Meanwhile, Death Wind lost no time in unsheathing his knife. He knelt by the fallen foe and started hacking away at a scaled leg.

"Hey, what are you doing?" Rusty asked.

Death Wind kept cutting. "Meat almost gone."

"But that's—that's a dragon. You can't eat it. It's—it's an intelligent—being."

"If you can call that intelligent." Scott tried to hide the revulsion in his voice, even though he felt the same sense of impropriety at eating one's enemy. But, after all, Death Wind was the teacher. . . .   "Hey—the gun."

He leaped forward and picked up the hand-held unit of the weapon. The gun was a molded plastic box with a power lead coming out of one end and an eight-inch nozzle out the other. It was too large to fit comfortably in his hand, but holding it awkwardly, he found he could reach the firing stud with his index finger. He aimed it away from him and pressed the trigger. A bolt of lightning shot out and incinerated a nearby stone wall.

"This—beamer—still works." He fumbled with the unfamiliar buckles and released the straps from the dead owner. The power pack and holster came free. The pack was contoured for the curved, humped back of the dragon, but with a little restructuring it could be worn by a man.

He started adjusting the straps when an ear-piercing shriek echoed off the ancient crumbling walls, and sent shivers down his spine. A loud, sharp bark was followed by the release of energy from a beamer. Three more barks rang out in rapid succession.

Scott swung around to see Death Wind off and running. He hefted the power pack by the straps and dragged it along with one hand. Rusty hesitated long enough to retrieve his spear and Scott's stub.

They dashed through the rubble between two buildings that still stood as high as three stories. Flashes of light could be seen through the city ruins some two hundred yards away. They came to a low stone wall, all that was left of a building front. Scott looked over it to see a squad of dragons moving ponderously past them only a few feet away.

Six of them marched in staggered formation. With beamers in their clawed hands they were firing rapidly after a lone retreating figure dressed in a smooth, light brown burnoose that billowed in the breeze.

Momentarily exposed, the lone human turned and spat fire from a tubular weapon cradled in one arm. Holes appeared in the chest of the leading dragon, and it fell to the ground hissing. The lone defender drew fire from five beamers, but ducked out of sight before the air was riddled with lightning bolts.

Scott aimed his newfound beamer at the nearest reptilian body and pressed the firing stud. Instantly a beam of light shot out and sizzled through flesh. It left a black, burning hole from which blood poured like water. As ponderous heads turned to see what was nipping at them from the side, Death Wind pierced one in the eye with his deadly, flint-tipped arrow.

Temporarily out of the line of fire, the cloaked figure jumped up and made more barking sounds with the rifle. *Crack, crack, crack,* and down went another dragon. Scott fired again, and there were only two pursuers left. A squad of reinforcements came into view, shooting their beamers as they approached.

In the heat of first battle Scott stayed too long in one spot. A bolt of lightning stabbed between his legs and hit a steel supporting beam behind him. The flash singed hair off both calves, and the backs of his legs were scorched by bits of molten metal. Then he leaped to the side, and remembered to keep in motion.

Rusty launched his good spear into the stomach of a dragon. It hissed and writhed and, while not dead, was at least out of action. With glacial speed the dragons of the second squad redirected their fire, but by the time the lightning bolts were let loose Rusty was long gone.

Ducking beamer blasts, Death Wind shot another arrow with less precision than usual—it missed completely. Fist-sized holes burned through the crumbling wall he hid behind.

While Scott scurried for protection an intense staccato of rifle fire sprayed the dragon platoon, taking the heat off him. In the confusion, Rusty jumped up and threw the half spear. It wobbled in its wild flight, and glanced off the hamstring of the nearest dragon. As it spun around, Death Wind took careful aim and pierced its cold-blooded heart with an arrow.

The air blazed with beamer charges. Scott flitted from brick pile to brick pile with the agility of a cat, and while the dragons concentrated their fire on him the stranger's weapon continued to take its toll. As Scott's protection melted down in front of him he ran back and dived over a wall, crashing right on top of Rusty.

Death Wind joined them a moment later, and led the way toward the lone defender. Scott stuck his head out long enough for several more shots, but most of the damage to the dragon squad was coming from the continuous barking of the automatic rifle.

Cupping his mouth, Scott shouted, "Run for cover." If the stranger heard him there was no time to answer, for the surviving dragons now drew a bead on the rifleman who stayed too long in one spot.

The broken wall offered some defense until the trio gained the safety of a doorway into a brick-strewn ruin that had once been the lobby of a building. The rifle barked out of the adjacent window.

The cloaked figure stepped back behind the safety of the pitted marble slabs, and threw aside the shawl. "Nice shooting, fellas, but this is no time to duck your tails. We got 'em on the run."

Under the cloak she was dressed in a coarse skin blouse and matching skirt. The loose-fitting clothes tied about her slender waist in a way that did nothing to hide her appearance. Bandoliers carrying ammunition pouches were draped over both shoulders, crisscrossing between two bulging breasts. Long hair hung loose down past her waist.

"Hey, you gonna give up now, or what? We got a battle to win."

Without waiting for an answer she discarded the empty clip from her rifle, snapped in a full one from her bandolier, and stepped back outside and started shooting. Scott and Death Wind exchanged shrugs, then went back out to help her fight.

Two more squads of dragons moved into position, firing with precision now that their quarry was pinned down in one place. So many beamer blasts hit around them that the air seemed to crackle with live electricity, and the dust from blasted stone walls was getting too thick to see through.

The trio spread out and formed a line behind a mound of rubble. The dragons kept coming. The girl mowed them down: she was deadly accurate with her automatic rifle.

Scott was quickly getting used to the awkward firing mechanism and returning fire at a prodigious rate with growing success. Death Wind stayed calm, shooting his arrows slowly and deliberately.

Suddenly Rusty clawed at Scott's back. "Look out behind."

Over the din of battle he heard the peculiar thrumming in the sky. Turning to where Rusty was pointing he saw the golden airboat, glinting sun off its smooth back, moving directly toward them. It flew low, purple beams thrusting down like neon stilts. The excess energy ate up the streets, the rubble, and the remaining parts of buildings, like a hungry demon. Wreaths of black smoke rose from the ground as stone and steel structures were pummeled into unrecognizable slag.

"Hide," Death Wind shouted. Scott wasted no time ducking into the doorway after Rusty. He stopped there to cover the others' retreat. Death Wind punched the girl hard on the shoulder and stabbed a finger at the approaching machine. "Hide."

But the girl kept firing. As soon as she sprayed the dragon soldiers with a clip of bullets she dropped the metal holder and replaced it with another. She kept up such a rapid rate of fire that her pouches were quickly being emptied.

"Run, you cowards," she taunted as Death Wind ducked into the doorway next to Scott. "I'll do the fighting."

Beamer bolts came so thick by now that the wall in front of her was quickly disintegrating, and the ambient temperature rose by many degrees. With sweat streaming down her stolid face the girl remained steadfast and continued to shoot into the advancing horde. She seemed determined to engage the enemy until her own life was forfeit. She swung around and, with a full clip, fired fiercely up at the bottom of the hovering aircraft.

"She's crazy," Scott uttered.

Steel-jacketed bullets laced into the glowing purple cones, dousing the pillars of light and sending out shrapnel that damaged others. The machine was only a hundred feet high, and a mere fifty feet away; the air smelled of heat and ozone. The thrumming sound rose in pitch as it soared upward to get out of range. But it was still coming forward.

"Down here," Rusty shouted from the bottom of a debris-filled stairway.

Scott stood riveted in place. Pride would not let him leave his post. Following the girl's example, he fired the beamer at the energy thrusters. The cones shattered like glass.

Death Wind slung his bow over his shoulder, grabbed the girl around the middle, and lifted her off her feet. She screamed obscenities and kicked futilely while the Nomad dragged her into the building. Then all sound was drowned out by the thrumming of the fantastic motors.

The savage carried her down the stairs to where Rusty waited. Scott leaped without a moment to spare, reaching the concrete floor without touching a single step. He barely got under cover when the building overhead burst apart, and a blast of heat rained down with all the fury of an active volcano. Scott tumbled forward on top of Death Wind and the girl as wooden beams and a cloud of plaster showered down from the floor above.

The heat was insufferable as the multistory building settled down. Bricks and stonework fell like raindrops, filling the cellar with tons of dust and debris and smoldering wood, threatening to bury them.

But the worst enemy was the heat. The air was as hot as boiling oil, and clung as tightly. It seared his lungs as Scott tried to breathe, turned his clothing into furnace lining. He pulled the loose skin of his shirt over his mouth and sucked air through it; he screamed when hot air flowed like molten lava into his lungs.

As suddenly as it came, it was over—except for the occasional dropping of loose bricks and splintered wood. Outside, all was silent as the machine swooped away to lick its wounds.

Brushing debris aside, bleeding from a dozen wounds, Scott found himself miraculously alive—but sealed inside a dark, dusty tomb. For long moments he coughed and gagged, and tried to find clean, fresh air.

The girl cleared her throat. "We really brought the house down, didn't we?"

Scott groaned as he disentangled himself from her and Death Wind. "Rusty, are you all right?"

From somewhere in the darkness came a weak voice. "I guess I'll live."

Scott heard the Nomad crawling over the rubble. Death Wind found him, and practiced hands ran over his body and limbs. "Hurt?"

Scott grimaced. "Nothing a few weeks convalescing wouldn't cure." He had no broken bones or severed arteries, just cuts and bruises. But he was beginning to view such wounds as an accepted norm.

Death Wind checked out Rusty, then moved to where he had left the girl. "Hey, keep your hands off me."

"Hurt?"

"Not as much as you'll be if you touch me again." There was a scuffle in the blackness, and Scott felt a board come loose and land in his lap. He pushed it aside. "Hey, anybody here got a name? I'm Sandra."

"I'm Scott, and that board you just threw landed on top of me."

"Sorry. Who's the stringbean with the red hair?"

"Rusty."

"How original. And Mr. Hands?"

There was a moment of silence before the Nomad pronounced his name. "Death Wind."

"You must be joking. Where'd you pick up a moniker like that?"

After another silence, Death Wind said, "You hurt?"

"Just a coupla scratches, if it's anything to ya."

Scott started moving around, to test the size of their prison. Fallen beams prevented most of the debris from hitting anyone with full force. In absolute darkness they worked together to clear out some of the boards and bricks until there was room to move around.

"Hey, anybody got any water? I sure would like to wet my whistle."

Scott dug around in his pack and brought out his water pouch. "Drink sparingly. We don't have much."

"It might be all we need unless we get some air in this coffin." Sandra slurped noisily from the bladder, then slapped it against Scott's chest, still half full. "Thanks. You know, you guys came along at the right time. Whatcha doing in this burg, anyhow?"

Scott seemed to be the only one willing to hold a conversation with her. He let some water clear the dust from his throat. "Looking for the library."

"Nothin' better to do, huhn?"

It had been a hard day. It looked like it was going to be a harder night. He handed the bladder to Rusty. Death Wind moved debris out of the way, passing bricks, stone, chunks of mortar, and broken beams to Scott, who passed them on to Rusty.

"We were looking for information—about the dragons."

Sandra moved out of her corner and helped in the digging. "The only thing you need to know about them is that they're vermin to be shot on sight." She huffed and puffed as she lifted large sections of masonry and pushed them behind her. "Listen, now that we all know who we are, how about if I start the biographies?"

After a moment of silence, she went on. "Okay, I can see the curiosity's killing you, so here goes. I come from a long line of administrators. They're the people who tell others what to do, 'cause they don't know how to do it themselves—or because they don't have the guts to do it. My folks have been running from the dragons ever since they were born, moving all over the country instead of staying in one place and fighting them. For a hundred years they've run us ragged, picking us off one by one. About fifteen or twenty years ago our big cheese decided the gang was getting too big, so they split up and spread out. They figured that small units could move faster and hide better. And that's what I've been doing all my life, running and hiding."

"Where's the rest of your, uh, gang, now?" Rusty said.

"They smoked us out about a month ago. There were about a hundred of us living in a subway in an old burg north of here. We—"

"Excuse me, but, what's a subway?"

"Don'tchu know nothin'? It's a bunch of tunnels—part of an underground railway. You know—trains? Anyway, we been living there about eight years. Ran into a small group that had built quite a complex down there, so we merged with 'em. Been there ever since."

Scott hoisted a heavy beam out of the way. "I thought you said your bands moved around all the time? Eight years in one spot isn't what I call traveling. We've lived in Maccam City all our lives—"

"Hey, who's telling this story, anyway?"

"Sorry." Scott concentrated on his work. They reached the

base of the stairs and started making a pathway up to the surface.

"Now, where was I? Oh, yeah. Well, it was all right, I guess, living there. The place had a lot of advantages, and we spent a lot of time out in the open, shooting dinosaurs for food. That's the part I liked best, even in the winter. I always liked the snow."

"You mean, there were dinosaurs living where it was cold?"

There was a long silence following Rusty's outburst. "You gonna let me tell this story, or not?" The work went on. "Okay. So we went out on hunting trips, we worked the fields for grain and vegetables, we picked wild fruits. And every once in a while we'd—lose a few people. We'd see a flyer in the air, then we'd scatter, run and hide like rabbits, crawl into a hole and pull it in after us. But they would never fight back, said it would give us away, and we didn't want to attract any attention."

Sandra stopped working and got quiet. "Anyway, about a year ago we started seeing a lot more activity: flyers, war parties, dragons, were turning up all over the place. Before that, it was always chance encounters. Then, they started going after us actively. They seemed to be—searching. That's when I lost—my father."

Scott felt a pang in his chest. He was glad no one could see his face in the dark cellar. His hands were suddenly clammy.

"He was out hunting with three other men. Flyer musta come down right on top of 'em. Never found more than a puddle of slag, an' some liquefied bones." Sandra sniffled faintly. "Anyway, that was a year ago. Then, last month, the dragons found our hideout. I was in the fields with my mother, so we were lucky—if you can call staying alive lucky. When we got back to the tunnel that night, after they'd gone, we couldn't even get in. The place was filled with some green, poisonous gas that ate through metal like acid—"

Scott found himself gasping. He managed to keep quiet until he heard the end of her story.

"Well, we ran into Tom and Ned that night. They'd been out hunting, an' we were the only ones left alive. We hightailed it out o' there, but as soon as the sun came up they were onto us again. We played hide-and-seek for a week before they caught us at the edge of town. Tom was gunned down before we knew what hit us. I blew two of 'em away before my gun jammed.

Then we started to run. When it looked like we were circled, Ned an' my mother shoved me into a dumpster—a stinkin' dumpster—an' took off. They didn't get far—"

Sandra's bravado faltered. She whimpered for a moment, managing only to utter, "They were picked up and taken away—" Then she burst into tears, sobbing hysterically.

Scott froze with a brick in his hands. The pathos of the story was too vibrant for him to hear without a strange feeling of deja vu.

Death Wind said, "What you mean, take away?"

Scott heard the scuffle as blows landed on the savage's body. "I told you to keep your hands off me." The rifle clattered in the confined space. "You touch me again an' I'll fill you full of holes."

In his deadpan voice Death Wind repeated his question. "Dragon take?"

"Something wrong with your English, fella?"

"What mean, take?"

"I mean what I said. They were carried off, up in the air, in one of those golden spaceships from over the rainbow."

Scott could hardly contain himself. "You mean, they were kidnapped?"

"Hey, am I talking funny, or what? I said they were taken away, captured. They didn't leave no ransom note, or nothin'."

"Death Wind, is this possible?"

A shaft of light shone through the hole, and the way to the surface was almost open. The Nomad stopped working for a moment. "Dragon always kill. Always."

"You guys must be thick-headed or dull-witted. I'm telling you I *saw* them. And if you're calling me a liar I'm gonna pull your tongues out by the roots."

Scott could see light glinting off beads of perspiration on Death Wind's face. Cheek muscles bulged as he clenched his jaw. But it was Rusty who broke the charged silence.

"Sandra, listen, we're just trying to understand something that is very—foreign—to previous dragon activity. So, please don't get angry. But, are you sure your mother was alive when they took her aboard the—flyer?"

"She walked."

"Ned, too?"

"Ned, too."

Scott watched dust particles glimmering in the light as they were siphoned upward in the exchange of air. "This is something new. What do we do now?"

Death Wind stared at Sandra with dark, fathomless eyes. "Wait till dark," was all he said, until dark.

CHAPTER 10

Under the cover of darkness Death Wind went out on his own. He was gone more than an hour, and when he returned he brought back full canteens and a section of meat. "Still warm."

Scott coaxed a small fire to life in the artificial cave. He took the water gratefully, drank a conservative amount, and passed the rest on. A warm glow suffused through the close confines, reflecting off four dirt-smeared faces.

"Gee, thanks." Sandra took a slice of meat and sank her teeth into it. She chewed and swallowed the first bite. "You may talk funny, but you're a pretty good scrounger."

Death Wind did not answer. Scott looked askance at the meat. It had an unfamiliar taste, and he was fairly sure where it came from—but he refrained from asking. It was something he would rather suspect strongly than know for sure.

"So you guys are gonna conquer the world, huhn?" Sandra garbled with her mouth full. "What makes you think I wanna go along?"

"You alone," Death Wind said.

"Yeah, an' what makes you think I'd be any better off hanging around with you guys?"

"Men stick together. It is code."

"Gee, where'd you pick up that corny line? An' look here, buster, I'm not a man, see."

"You man."

"Yeah? An' you been in the woods too long. I'm a girl, you know, like in woman, female, opposite sex. Or hadn't you noticed." She settled her arms in her lap and unnecessarily thrust out her chest.

Scott almost choked. "I noticed."

Sandra's eyes twinkled in the flickering light. She seemed to take pleasure in Scott's admiration. Scott smiled at her.

Death Wind gestured with his hands. "I man. You man. All man." He pointed dramatically at her upper chest. "You warrior. You very brave."

"I must be, to sit here next to you, wearin' nothing but a codpiece." Sandra pointed to the loincloths and tunics that Scott and Rusty were wearing. "And you two aren't exactly overdressed."

Rusty drew his legs up under him, as if to hide his nakedness. "This isn't my normal attire."

"What Death Wind means is you killed a dragon today," Scott explained. "In the Nomad culture that makes you an adult."

A smile touched her lips. "No kidding? Then that must make me an old woman 'cause I blew about ten o' them suckers away."

Scott sighed heavily. This girl just did not seem to have any respect for convention. "Look, all Death Wind's trying to say is that we can't just go off and leave you—alone. It's too dangerous."

"And you're gonna take care of me, is that it?"

Scott tried to be patient. "No, but there *is* safety in numbers."

Sandra finished eating, and wiped her mouth on her sleeve. "Well, I'll think about it. Ask me in the morning. Right now I wanna get some shut-eye."

Scott still wanted to talk more with this outspoken girl, but once she made up her mind to go to sleep, she did just that. He cradled his head in his arms, and watched the dancing phantoms in the fire until he drifted off into dreamland.

In the morning it was a cautious crew that climbed out of the hole and listened for dragons. A careful survey revealed none that were still alive. Scott looked at the dead bodies that were lying where they had fallen, burnt to a crisp by the escaping flyer. The dragons had little of what in human terms would be called reverence. The only thing they had done for their dead was to strip them of their weapons.

Death Wind collected water out of a puddle writhing with mosquito larvae. Sandra viewed it with disapproval, taking instead a drink from Scott's canteen. "If you think I'm drinking from that cesspool, you're crazy."

"You drink last night. No complain."

She spit out what she had not swallowed. "You idiot! What's the idea of giving me that rotten water?"

"You thirsty."

"Of course I was thirsty. That doesn't mean you have to poison me."

"You look very much alive to me," Scott said.

"A corpse would look alive to you. You know, I'm beginning to hate the bunch of you. You didn't look too eager to fight yesterday, an' yet you're talking about attacking the dragon capital. I think you'll all get killed before you even get there."

"At least we're going to try."

Rusty shuffled along behind. "Maybe if we could find this library we could find out something about our past, or discover a weakness in the dragons."

"They ain't got no weaknesses, an' the sooner you learn that the better. They got technology, transportation, and superiority in numbers."

Scott said, "So what are you going to do? Pick them off one by one?"

"Ever hear of guerrilla warfare?"

"Sure. I guess that's what this is."

"Oh, you're gorillas, all right. But that isn't what I meant. I'm thinking about heading back up north an' hanging around the subway till I can get captured. Maybe they'll take me to my mother."

"Assuming they don't kill you instead, what good will that do you?"

"I figure on carrying some concealed weapons and escaping after I find her."

"We go south," Death Wind said.

"Well, wait a minute. Why don't you stick with us until we find the library? We can talk about it then."

"Library gone. I check last night. Airboat smash."

Rusty slammed a rock on the ground. "Oh, that's just great!"

"Watch your temper there, skinny. You almost hit me."

"Sorry."

They paused at the top of a huge pile of rubble. They could see many miles in all directions, and everywhere there was ruin and desolation. There were no flyers in the sky.

"You come with us."

"Let's get one thing straight right now, buster. *You* don't give me orders. No one does."

"It is safer to be together."

"I'm not so sure I'd be safe with you." Sandra dimpled her blouse with her thumb. "Besides, I've got my own way of doing things."

"Mind made up?"

"That's right. My mind's made up."

Death Wind stared at her hard. Then he stuck out his hand and grasped her forearm. "Then, we part here. May your path be safe and healthy. May you find what you seek. Maybe we meet again." The Nomad turned and started to walk away.

"You're leaving? Just like that?" Sandra turned pleadingly to Scott. "What is this, a one-night stand?"

"Hey, Death Wind, you're not really going to leave her here on her own, are you?" Scott was aghast.

"Yes, what about the code?" Rusty added.

"Code of honor, not force." To Sandra he said, "You want, you come. You want, you go."

"Yeah, well, maybe I'll just go my own way. I got along fine without you before. An' you don't need me anyway, so go on an' get outa here."

Death Wind checked the straps on his pack, and realigned his bow and quiver. He raised his hand in the universal gesture. "Peace." Then he walked calmly away.

Scott was torn with indecision. Here was a girl, alone, and in need of company. And there went the savage, possibly his only salvation in this world. Something had to be done to bring the two opponents together. Rusty broke after Death Wind, pleading, and Scott soon followed.

"Hey, Death Wind, we just can't go off and leave her. It's not right."

"Maybe we can talk it over some more, come to an agreement."

"She'll get killed out here."

"How about if we just sit down for a powwow, or something."

By the time they were a hundred yards away Scott heard a yelp from behind. "Hey, wait up." Sandra ran after them, with long hair flying and bandoliers slapping. Her petite moccasins beat a dusty path over the loose debris.

Scott stopped, holding onto Death Wind's arm so he could go no farther. Sandra caught up with them and stood leaning on one leg, swinging her rifle casually.

With forced nonchalance, she said, "You know, two's

company and three's a crowd, but four's got the making of a pretty good little army. An' I think you can use a good gal with a gun. So maybe I'll tag along—for a while. But don't think you're gonna give me any orders, see?"

Scott smiled. "Glad to have you along."

"Yeah, well, your long-haired buddy don't seem too happy about it. But I like you guys. You got spunk."

Rusty slapped the savage on the back. "Aw, Death Wind just keeps things in. He'll get to like you, too. Won't you?"

Death Wind stared at Sandra with unspeaking eyes. He turned and led the war party out of the ruins.

By the campfire that night Sandra toasted meat on a spit. "Where'd you get the name Death Wind?"

The Nomad stirred the coals with the tip of a new spear he was fire hardening for Rusty. "As small boy I hear of legendary man known as Death Wind: traveler of great distances, chief among his people, killer of dragons. When growing up I think that I want to be great traveler, chief of my people, killer of dragons. I go on trial many time, always come home empty-handed. Always I wait—not kill lizard. I wait for the day when I kill dragon. When I killed, I chose name. Not because of what I am, but because of what I want to be."

"You know, my father used to talk about the Nomads. I don't think he ever met any, but he knew about them. He used to say my mother was just like them. Do you know what he meant by that?" When Death Wind did not answer, she went on. "My mother isn't like most women—she's a tough cookie. What kind of women are Nomad women?"

"All Nomads warriors. Men, women, all the same."

"An' what about this trial of manhood you're so proud of? Is there a trial of womanhood, too?" Death Wind inspected the spear tip. "Well, what do the women have to do to—prove themselves?"

Death Wind let the spear cool a bit, then handed it to Rusty. "Woman kill lizard."

"Oh, is that all? Well, I guess that does make me a woman by your standards. Maybe I should choose a new name for myself. Whaddaya think?"

Death Wind chewed a slice of warmed meat. With a flat sandstone Rusty honed the soot off the spear and sharpened the tip.

Scott eased his feet out of his slippers and scraped ground-in sand from the bottom of his feet. He wriggled his toes with newfound freedom. Then he fluffed up the leaves and branches he had collected for his bed. "I think Foot-In-Mouth would be fitting."

Fire leaped into Sandra's eyes. "You shut up, you, or I'll—I'll—"

"Talk me to death." Scott rolled over and stared up at the stars.

Sandra hit him with a stick. "You know what's the matter with you guys? You just ain't got any fun in your life."

"Is there something wrong with your English?" Scott said.

This time Sandra got up and kicked him—but not too hard. "You know, if I had a brother I'd want him to be just like you."

The solitude of the thick green forest was suddenly broken when a raucous scream bellowed down from the treetops. Death Wind yanked an arrow from his quiver, staring skyward. But when Scott pulled the blaster from its holster, the savage stayed his hand.

"I want to kill, not destroy."

Scott had no idea what he meant by that, but he put the gun away anyhow. He could see nothing in the air besides green flicking leaves and a blue sky. Slowly Death Wind stalked through the woods, gazing upward and listening for a repetition of the strange caw. Whenever he heard it he stopped and stared. Finally, his right arm drew back on the string, the arrow flew, and an animal fell out of the trees.

"What kind of lizard is that?" Scott stared at the still living beast. It weighed perhaps five pounds, and was as long as his forearm. Four taloned paws fluttered in the air; loose folds of flesh stretched from the forearms to the scrawny body. The pointed, toothless beak jabbed at the arrow protruding from its furred breast. The tail fanned out like a horizontal rudder.

"Bird."

"That ain't no bird, it's a flying lizard."

The animal expired as Scott scooped it up. What he at first thought was fur was really a network of horny shafts, from each of which sprouted a closely woven mesh of soft, silky barbs.

Death Wind took the animal and pushed the arrow through the flimsy body. "All same."

"Rusty, what do you make of this?"

Rusty did not touch the bird, but looked at it closely. "I've seen pictures of early birdlike reptiles. This—this is probably some progenitor in the beginning of the evolutionary scale."

"In plain English it's still a lizard, feathers or not. Besides, I've seen real feathers and they're a lot finer than these." Sandra plucked out one of the slender tubes. It proved to be hollow.

Death Wind held the bird carelessly by the neck, and looked forward to where a small brook sliced through the forest. "We camp here. Climb mountain tomorrow."

"Mountain? Where's the mountain?" Scott looked around and saw nothing but trees.

"Come here." Death Wind walked a few steps into an open glade and pointed up.

From under the cover of the forest the mountains were not visible, but in the open the tall peaks stood out in stark relief against the heavenly blue: dark mounds of craggy granite that were streaked with white near the top. The tall peaks stood so close that Scott felt as if a strong wind could topple them right on top of him.

"Wow," Scott said, his jaw dropping. "I never realized they were so—grand."

"You seen one you seen 'em all. Let's get a fire going."

That night Death Wind carefully plucked the precious feathers from the prehistoric bird, then cooked it along with the rest of the day's catch of small lizards. And early in the morning, long before dawn, he roused them all for the climb.

Scott flexed his arms and legs, eager to put them to use. But he soon found that climbing brought new muscles into play. As they got higher and higher his thighs and calves ached at every step. At times they went straight up, searching for handholds and footholds and resting occasionally on narrow ledges with a spectacular view of the forest. Even the ruins of the city could be seen as a brown smudge in the middle of the vast greenery.

"Can we rest a moment?" Scott sat down on an outcrop, but Death Wind kept on with his tireless, machinelike gait.

As Sandra walked by she said, "What's the matter, can't you take it?"

Scott grimaced, and forced his legs to respond. He trudged along last in line. The air became thin, causing headache and fatigue. The pack grew heavier, especially since he was further burdened with the dragon beamer. Finally, he was forced to pause every few steps to catch his breath and regain his strength.

Hours passed, and still they toiled upward. Scott at least had the satisfaction of knowing he was not alone in being out of breath, for hardly a word was spoken during the climb. For the hundredth time he stopped to gather in a few lungfuls of air before continuing, when something smashed him on the top of the head.

He had the beamer in his hand even before he looked up. But all he saw were three backs, and nothing else around. "Hey. Something hit me." Then Sandra turned around and threw a rock straight at him. It came so fast he could not dodge it, and it slammed into his chest and broke into a thousand pieces of cold crystal.

"What is this?" he said when he realized he was not hurt. He wiped a smear off his tunic; it was like ice.

"It's snow, silly. Don't you moles know anything?"

Scott climbed up to their level. Rusty scraped a handful of white fluff off a rock and molded it into a ball. "Scott, this is really snow. It's wet, and cold." He tossed it to Scott.

"So this is what snow is. But what's it doing out here, in the summer?"

"It's the altitude. It stays colder up here, especially at night. So there's snow all year long in the shade."

"So that's why we're trying to make this climb in one day. Death Wind, why don't you tell us these things?"

"Everyone know this. I forget that you live in ground."

"Well, it's nice to know you're not perfect."

"Come. Soon we be at top."

Soon turned out to be a way of reckoning that was not Scott's. By the time they reached a pass below one of the lower summits it was late afternoon. They stood on a vast field of snow.

"Isn't it gorgeous?" Sandra faced the wind coming from the east, her hair flying back in a wild torrent.

Scott chilled quickly as the sweat evaporated from his skin. "I'm not sure I'm in any condition to appreciate it."

Many thousands of feet below stretched a green and verdant pine forest fed by clear, cold mountain streams visible only by the jagged stands of cottonwoods that lined their banks. Unlike the western forest, this one ended a few miles away. From there, and for over a hundred miles, Scott could see nothing but a flat, endless desert.

"Look at that." Rusty pointed to darkened streaks that marked the sand at irregular intervals. They all pointed east.

Scott shivered now, and was anxious to get going. "Flyer tracks. It looks like we can follow them right to the dragon city."

"How long will it take to cross the desert?" Sandra asked.

"Half moon. Maybe more."

Rusty said, "Two weeks in the open? Without shelter?"

Scott did not balk at it for an instant. "Then let's get going. I'm freezing already, and I don't want to get caught up here after dark." He took the lead for a while, eager to keep moving in order to build up some warmth.

Scott soon discovered that climbing down, while easier physically, was more difficult technically. He often found himself searching with his feet for a ledge he could not see, or hanging onto a handhold afraid to let go. It was not until they got to a point where the slope was not so steep that he found a comfortable gait. Then he made up for lost time by running, and leaping from boulder to boulder, as he had seen Death Wind do the first time they met. Sore muscles were forgotten for the moment as he exhilarated in the unbounded freedom.

Nightfall found them camped beside a meandering brook, on soft grass, and totally exhausted by the day's strenuous activity. It was almost too much of an effort for Scott to even gather wood for the fire. But once it was done he collapsed by the burning coals, thankful that the mountain had been climbed, that one more barrier between him and revenge had been crossed.

"I don't know about you, but I'm taking a bath." Sandra showed no shame as she shed her dirty clothes and waded into the water where it pooled chest deep. She plunged completely out of sight and came up with her long hair plastered against her head. "Boy, is this water cold. But it sure feels good. Come on in."

Rusty was already on his way. "It sounds good to me." However, he doffed only his tunic, and splashed into the stream wearing his shorts.

Death Wind and Scott watched them gambol in the water, playing and swimming. When the Nomad handed the slender book to him, Scott said, "Sorry, but I'm too tired for tonight's reading lesson."

Scott sat comfortably by the fire. Even if he felt like taking a bath he would not have gotten in the water with a nude girl.

Rusty was out of the water within a couple minutes. He raced barefoot to the fire and stood there shivering, great goose bumps covering his freckled skin. He picked dirt out from under his nails. "I don't know how she can stand it in there. That water is freezing."

Sandra washed all her clothes before she came back to the fire with her shawl only loosely wrapped around her. Scott tried his best to look away. If she had strong inhibitions about having her body touched, she did not seem to mind it being seen—and admired.

"You know, I'm getting attached to you guys, even if you are a little stuck-up." After wringing out her tresses, Sandra tilted her head and rotated her neck so that her hair stroked the fine skin of her back. She sat cross-legged by the fire. Scott noticed that her tan spread over her entire body, without any lines of discretion.

"What is that?" Death Wind pointed to Sandra's earlobe.

"That? Oh, that's an earring. I have two, see?" She bared the other ear. The jewels caught the sparkle of the fire, each facet glittering.

"Why?"

"Why what?"

"Why do you wear it? What is the use?"

"Well, it doesn't really have a use. It's just ornamental—and sentimental."

"What this mean?" Death Wind looked at Scott, and repeated, "What does this mean?"

Sandra pouted. "Scott, you better stretch your English lessons to include vocabulary."

"He's doing fine, soaking everything up like a sponge."

"What is sentimental?"

Sandra sighed heavily, and covered her ears with her black tresses. "You see, my mother gave them to me. Besides making me look pretty, they remind me—that is, they make me feel—I mean, they give me a feeling of—oh, forget it. I'll explain it later."

"Maybe you can explain something to me." Scott laid his weary bones down before he fell down. With his head resting on a log, he went on. "Did you have computers where you lived? In the subway, that is."

"Whaddaya think, we were savages, or something? Of course we had computers. That's why we moved in with those people. And we had all kinds of gadgets, too. I'm quite a repairman, used to tinker with the machines all winter long, when it was too cold to go outside."

"And did you have movie disks?"

"Oh, yes. I used to watch them all the time."

"Hmmmn." Scott was thoughtful for a moment. "How old were you when you moved in there? You've picked up quite a bit of old colloquialisms, so I figured it must have made an early impression on you."

"Well, I guess I was about eight. My mother and father had already started tutoring me, and when we found the subway people they showed me how to use their computers."

"Oh, so you're sixteen years old." Sandra looked stunned for a moment. Then Scott started laughing, and could not stop.

"You tricked me," Sandra screamed. She looked from face to face, but found no sympathy anywhere. "Oh, you men are despicable. And just when I was beginning to like you." She got up and walked off in a huff.

Scott winked at Rusty. The latter smiled back. Then Death Wind leaned over and said in a secretive voice, "Strange woman."

CHAPTER 11

Scott studied the dragon gun with the intensity of a mechanic. "It's definitely a laser beam. I can hear the capacitor recycling after each shot." He took his ear off the power pack. It was one piece of molded plastic with no visible means of access.

Rusty looked at the funneling nozzle. "I don't know what kind of battery can store that much power, and there's no telling how long the charge will last. What does the nozzle do?"

"Focuses the beam, like the ones we used to use for cutting metal. Only this is a lot more powerful. I can burn a hole through one of these lizards at a hundred feet. At two hundred feet—"

"If you can hit anything at that distance," Sandra interrupted.

"At two hundred feet it will singe, but the beam is spread too wide to be deadly."

Sandra patted the rifle butt. "I can hit a bull's-eye at a thousand feet with this."

"Yes, but I'm afraid to practice too much because I don't know when this thing will die out on me."

"But you don't hafta allow for droppage—it shoots exactly where you aim it."

"Listen, do you have to show off all the time?" Scott's face clouded with anger. "If you want me to admit that you're better than I am, all right. You're better. Now get off my back."

"Well, sor-*ree*. I didn't think you were so sensitive about it. Come on, Death Wind, let's go for a walk and leave the two brains alone."

She dragged the Nomad off by the hand. Once they were out of hearing, she said, "Which do you think is better?"

Death Wind kicked over a rotten log and picked up a handful of grubs. One by one he popped them into his mouth. "Bow is best. Always make arrow."

"Yeeck, how can you do that? Those slimy things make me sick just to look at 'em."

"No taste. Throw past tongue. Swallow."

"But why do you do it? Don't we have enough meat?"

"Habit." Then, remembering Scott's schooling, he said, "It is habit. Always take opportunity. If stomach is always full, there is no hunger."

"Yeah? Well, let me show *you* something."

The forest was green and fertile and full of all that was wonderful in the world. Tall grasses wisped in gentle breezes, colorful flowers adorned the ground, and wildlife abounded. Insects added a melodic drone that was a lure into serenity. Feathered lizards flitted in the treetops, gliding from one branch to another rather than actually flapping their forearms and flying. This was the kind of life that Death Wind knew and appreciated.

Sandra bent down and picked a spiderwort. Its purple blossoms were taking in the sun. She stuck it in Death Wind's face. "Smells good, right?"

The Nomad wrinkled his nose. He shrugged.

"Don't give me that. If we're going to be friends you have to be honest with me. Now, does it smell good, or doesn't it it?"

Death Wind gave in reluctantly. "Smell goo—yes, it smells good."

"That's better." Under some bushes Sandra found a cluster of wallflowers, whose golden petals rivaled the warmth and color of the sun. She snapped off several of the foot-long stems and held them together like a bouquet. With a long, deep inhale she sniffed the freshness. "Well, they don't smell all that great—but they're beautiful. Right?"

"They—are pretty."

"Right. And if I take this purple one and place it over my ear, like so, it makes me look pretty, too. Don't you think so?"

For the first time Death Wind took a long, deep look at her. She was from a different culture, but she had many of the same qualities of the women of his tribe. And, in some ways he could not yet identify, she had more.

"Yes. You are pretty."

"Why, thank you." Sandra pirouetted daintily, hugging the wallflowers close to her breast. He did not even notice the incongruousness of the rifle slung over her shoulder. He saw only her gay eyes, her flowing hair, the shape of her body, the softness of her skin. "And I would like you to have these."

Sandra handed the bouquet to Death Wind. He took them, not quite knowing what to do with them.

"You see, these are like the earrings my mother gave me. I give you the flowers because I want you to have them, because I want you to think of me when you look at them. And because I hope you'll remember me in some special way. That's kind of what sentiment is all about. It's a way of feeling."

Death Wind was not sure he understood it any more than he understood the strange churnings going on inside his body. He only knew that this girl brought with her a new kind of friendship.

Death Wind and Sandra returned to camp bearing three dead lizards, as well as fruit and berries, for the larder. Rusty separated strands of lizard gut that could be used as threads, while Scott stitched a new pair of moccasins.

Scott held up his latest creation. "Hey, what do you think of these?"

Death Wind inspected the dried skin. "Good. You make more?"

"Will you make more," Scott corrected. "And we already have. Rusty and I have ours, and this pair's for you. Now, if the lady will supply her foot for measuring I'll see if she's really Cinderella."

"Don't you think I can make moccasins?"

"Oh, I have no doubt about your ability to do anything you set your mind to. But I had to do something while you were out, uh, bringing home the bacon."

"All right, wise guy. If you're trying to shame me into making my own, forget it." Sandra put her best foot forward. "I never look a gift horse in the mouth."

Scott removed her badly worn slipper and placed her foot flat on the dried sheet of lizard skin. He said "Hmmn" several times, marking places by making creases. "Any particular style you'd like? Left folding? Right folding? Double folding? Get them while they're cheap."

Sandra's face softened into a smile. "Come on, silly. Are you done?"

"Not quite. Would you like to see our line of shawls? Yours is lovely, but not very practical."

"Oh, yeah? Says who?"

Scott smiled broadly. "Says Death Wind. He says we're all going to need hats in case we're out during the day, so we don't go batty. I figure we can attach a hood to your shawl, like a burnoose."

Sandra thought about it. "Well, if you say so." She removed her outer layer and allowed Scott to affix a makeshift hood to it.

Death Wind ignored the banter and rechecked the packs to make sure they had everything they would need for the crossing: freshly cooked meat, sheets of skin for tarps, and plenty of bladders filled with fresh water.

As the strongest of the group he carried the largest pack, loaded down with meat and water. Rusty carried a smaller one, suitable to his weight and leanness, filled mostly with fruits and tubers the savage had collected. Scott, besides the heavy power pack for the beamer, had slung underneath a small pack with odds and ends. Sandra was weighted down with her two bandoliers and a small pack of essentials. All carried water, as much as they were able, as well as a tarp for shelter.

That night, in the cool cloak of darkness, they set out upon the Great Desert.

Close up, the desert was not as flat and unbroken as it had appeared from miles away and thousands of feet up. It was rough and cragged in places, and sometimes split apart by arroyos whose steep walls and dry bottoms were crossed only with difficulty.

At first light the desert was already warm. By the time the sun came into view the heat was unbearable. It reflected off the sand as it would off glazed oven brick. Death Wind directed them to scrape stones and sand into a knee-high platform.

"Most heat, low. We stay above."

Then he took out a dried lizard-skin tarp and showed the others how to erect it. Stones weighted on the end facing the prevailing wind kept out most of the sand, while short sticks propped up the sides and the other end. The only shade available was that which they carried with them.

"Lie flat, stay cool. Move only when you must."

All day long they waited out the heat, sweating, and sleeping fitfully. Within hours Death Wind felt dreadful thirst, and knew that the others, although uncomplaining, must also be feeling it. He passed around a canteen.

"Take only mouthful, hold on tongue, then swallow."

The hours of discomfort stretched on interminably. When the sun was at the zenith each tarp became a furnace. By late afternoon the heat reached its peak. Finally, when the sun dipped below the tall mountains to the west, Death Wind got up and folded his tarp. The heat lingered on for hours while they marched ever eastward. The first day passed uneventfully.

Under a rising star field, the desert was cast in bright relief. Life abounded in this rocky desert, from great fields of scrub to the many varieties of cactus, agave, ocotilla, yucca, and the strangely gnarled joshua trees. Warm-blooded lizards that lived underground or in the floral shade dashed about with energy to spare. When the moon rose the land was nearly as bright as day.

Along the way they passed more than one trail of glazed sand and burnt smudges. "These very old. See how sand start to cover. Another moon and the desert will swallow them."

On the third night they came to a river. It was not as large as the one by their last campsite, but it was too wide and deep to swim or wade.

"Gather driftwood. We build raft."

Twisted timber was lashed together with vine, and made large enough for the packs. Then it was launched into the slow-moving water and pushed across to the opposite bank. There Death Wind called a halt.

"Whenever we find water, we rest."

They spent the rest of the night and all that day by the river, drinking water like camels, replenishing food supplies from what they could scrounge. Death Wind collected salamanders and crayfish from under rocks, and roasted them whole in the fire.

"This is good. You eat, make you strong." He tossed an unskinned salamander into his mouth, then broke open the shells of the crayfish and sucked out the innards. But Rusty had clubbed an unnamed lizard with his spear, and after it was cooked he shared it with Scott and Sandra.

"Good," Death Wind said. "More for me."

Days later, Death Wind called a halt at a dry streambed. "We dig hole, find water in ground."

They had to dig three feet down, but the water was there just as the Nomad said it would be. He put his mouth to the sand, sucked through his lips until his mouth was full, and spit it into the pouch. They all took turns at the task.

Then they lay under their tarps, constantly harassed by ants and other biting insects. Death Wind had a unique solution to marauding bugs—he ate them.

"Listen!" cried Rusty.

The muted thrumming sound of a flyer vibrated the air. But the golden ship was a long ways off, paralleling their course.

"Do not worry. Our tarps cannot be seen from the air."

Scott shaded his eyes and watched the flyer disappear to the east. "Well, it looks like the slimy lizards are going to lead us right to the gate."

"I sure would like to fly in one of those things," Sandra said. "It beats walking in this heat."

"Can't say much for the company, though," Scott said.

Death Wind concentrated on finding water. With his long knife he lopped the top off a large barrel cactus, then beat the pith with the blunt end of Rusty's spear until it was a mass of juicy pulp. This could be sucked out with a hollowed stem, or the whole plant could be chopped down and the precious liquid poured out into a tarp and funneled into the canteens.

After that, Death Wind indicated a fracture line in the rock. "Shade make water. It roll down hard surface into small pool. There you drink with tongue." The amount was small, but in the desert no source of water was overlooked.

When they had started their journey across the Great Desert the moon was nearly full, a white beacon in the sky. Each night it appeared later, and smaller, until now the thin crescent disappeared altogether. And still there was no end of the desert in sight.

The food ran out. The oddly horned chameleons that scampered across the sand were fast and hard to catch. Vegetation grew sparsely, and the cactus smaller and harder to find. The few streambeds they crossed had not carried water in years, possibly decades.

"I—I'm feeling so weak." Sandra paused for a rest, and Death Wind relieved her of the bandoliers. He stuffed them in his now empty pack.

Scott licked lips that were dry and cracked. "How much

farther?" But there was no way of knowing, and no answer forthcoming.

"I'll take your small pack." Rusty shrugged off the straps, and helped Scott get rid of the fanny pack. He tucked it inside his own, so Scott would only have to carry the beamer and its power pack. Rusty used his spear as a staff, to pole him across the wasteland.

Death Wind too felt the terrible toll the desert was taking. His shoulders sagged, his steps grew shorter. He struggled to observe through filmy eyes. "Over there. You see?"

They all looked up at a lizard the size of a small chicken. Scott aimed and fired. The laser beam was on target, but its energy had fanned out in the distance. The creature leaped up on hind legs and darted off with little more than a hot foot.

Sandra dropped immediately to one knee, led the lizard with the sights, and brought it down with a bullet through the head.

"Way to go," Scott shouted.

Death Wind ran and picked it up before the precious blood dripped out of the severed neck. Then he closed his lips over the still pumping artery and drew out a mouthful of warm, red, life-giving liquid. He handed the prize to the others. Now there was no squeamishness as they partook of the sacrificial bloodletting.

They ate the lizard on the spot—raw.

The blood provided much needed salt, but it also made them thirsty for more. Death Wind spent hours digging a deep hole. The result was a layer of slightly damp sand. He covered it with a shred of material torn from Sandra's burnoose. When it became moist he sucked on the upper side. It did little more than wet his tongue, but it assuaged the craving that was driving him mad. He shared his technique with the others.

It was too dry for grubs, but insects crawled in the cracks and crevices. Death Wind ate them with glee, unmindful of the still-working mandibles and the flailing, tickling legs. First Scott, then Sandra, and finally Rusty followed his example.

Death Wind handed out round pebbles. "Put in mouth, roll over tongue. It make you feel better." The pebbles gave them no water, but the false sense of comfort kept them going—for a while.

Sandra collapsed, and three pairs of arms helped her to her feet.

"We rest now."

"No." Sandra shrugged off the men. "Just point me in the right direction, and let's keep going."

When she succumbed the second time Death Wind let her lie where she fell. "We rest." Scott and Rusty dropped their weary bodies to the ground and fell asleep, while Death Wind stood watch.

As far as he could see there was nothing but flat, rolling desert. He barely had the energy to suck in the air to fill his lungs. Every breath was pain—but pain, at least, was life. And because of his own weakness he feared for the others to whom this was more than torture.

After an hour he roused them. "Five-minute rest do us good. Sandra, you lead."

With the weakest in front, Death Wind concentrated on his own footsteps, putting one foot in front of the other, over and over, again, and again, and again, and . . .

Sandra he half carried: one slender arm hung limply over his broad shoulder, and her long hair mingled with his. Rusty could no longer hold onto his spear, so he tied it to his pack and let it drag behind him. Scott kept walking off on a tangent, apparently unaware of where he was going. Only Death Wind's constant shouting kept him oriented.

Rusty swooned, and sank to the ground. He opened his eyes and stared up at Death Wind. "Go on without me. I can't make it."

"We go together—or not at all." The savage lifted Rusty to his feet, let him lean on his other shoulder. Scott held onto the straps of Rusty's pack, so that he was half led, half dragged in the right direction. Sandra's eyes rolled loosely in their sockets, and she mumbled deliriously.

"Keep walking. We find water soon." Death Wind was the nucleus of an eight-legged creature that slithered across the rocky desert, supporting two people and towing one.

A tiny cactus offered relief from thirst. A snake caught unawares lent its body. A cache of lizard eggs gave them all some liquid and a small amount of energy. They walked, and still nothing was before them but more desert. They moved ever slower, but they moved.

A foot-long lizard scuttled out from under Death Wind's foot, but so befuddled was his brain that by the time he drew his bow it climbed up on two legs and ran off. He notched his bow anyway, and held it ready for the next time. When it came he was ready for it, and a two-foot-long specimen fell writhing to the ground.

Death Wind skinned it, and the blood and meat brought them out of the depths of despair. He ate none himself.

With this extra bit of energy Sandra unlimbered her rifle. The next lizard that popped up in front of them went down severely wounded. Death Wind crushed its skull with his foot. They ate again, and rested among some loose boulders, looking like a group of desiccated mummies.

Only Death Wind had the volition to go on. He hoisted Scott up and left him standing with his eyes closed. Then he pulled up Rusty and Sandra. The four walked abreast. Scott supported Rusty who leaned against Death Wind who held up Sandra.

A lizard appeared, but so entangled were the four warriors that it escaped by the time Death Wind freed an arm and pulled an arrow from his quiver. It was hours before they saw the next one. Death Wind stepped aside to shoot and, without his support, all three of his companions fell to the ground. He only nicked his target, but then Scott got out his beamer and, from the prone position, fired at the retreating animal. By that time it was so far away that instead of burning a hole in the beast it was only cooked. But it did not get away, and the hot meal helped to revive them from their lethargy.

Death Wind saw a lone shrub planted incongruously where there was nothing else but sand and rock. He pulled it up out of the ground, shook off the clinging dirt, and handed out the roots to his companions. They sucked off the slender shoots and got minute portions of moisture.

Then there were desert wildflowers, and they ate the blossoms and sucked the roots. A small cactus fell to Death Wind's knife, and nurtured them all. He wrenched it free of the earth and pulled squirmy blobs out of the tangle of dirt around the roots. Rusty and Sandra fought over the slimy grubs.

The sun appeared, and on the horizon there was a blur. Death Wind's weakened eyes could not tell if it was an hallucination, or a line of cliffs. He hoped it was a rock wall where they could spend the day, for the saving of a few degrees of temperature could mean the difference between life and death.

The blur was not a cliff face—it was a stand of stunted trees. There was also grass, and cactus, and insects by the hundreds. Death Wind broke off stems from an ephedra shrub, which had hollowed tubes, and showed the others how to suck up ants as they crawled over the ground. They feasted on grubs and roots, and were happy to have them.

Scott managed a grin. "I never thought I'd be so happy to see a grub." He plopped another one into his mouth.

Rusty turned over a log and gathered wood lice. "I'll trade you a louse for a grub."

Sandra pushed Rusty out of the way. "You idiot, you almost let that earthworm get away." She clawed the dirt until she was able to pinch the end and pull it out. She swallowed it without even thinking.

Despite the growing heat Death Wind urged them on. Now the wide hat brims brought some comfort. The grass grew thicker, the shrubs more plentiful. Small lizards abounded. They were fast, but the warriors were desperate. Death Wind showed them how to kill their prey instantly by biting the neck.

A trickle of water an inch wide and scant fractions deep carved a muddy path through thin underbrush. Groveling on their bellies, they slurped greedily until Death Wind pushed them away.

"No need to hurry when food and water plentiful. Drink now, drink later. We build our strength slowly. When strong, we fight."

CHAPTER 12

"This is a fine pickle you've gotten us into."

Death Wind was unperturbed by Sandra's words. He parted the branches in front of him and thrust out his head. From the top of the giant willow tree he looked down at the fifteen-foot-tall iguanodon as it pulled leaves off the lower branches and stuffed them into its cavernous mouth. The harmless vegetarian was interested only in browse, but any dinosaur had instinctive defense mechanisms and it was best to stay out of its way.

"Why didn't you let me shoot it?"

"Kill for food, run for life."

"Next time, you run. I'm not gonna let an old fossil that shoulda been dead for a million years chase me around like a rabbit."

Rusty balanced on the limb next to her. "More like a hundred million years."

Sandra glared at him. The iguanodon wandered off on business of its own, and Scott climbed down from his retreat. "Come on, Sandra. That thing's too big to kill with our puny weapons."

"That's no reason to give up." She alighted on soil that was soft and loamy, and squished underfoot.

Death Wind hit the ground with a thud, his eyes ever on the alert and following the direction of the animal's departure. Scott took the packs that Rusty lowered to him. "Why can't you live and let live? Is there some reason you need to slaughter everything that gets in your way?"

"You shut up, you, or I'll feed you to the dinosaurs." She pulled back the bolt and made sure a round was chambered.

"Does that mean you don't like me anymore?"

"It means I'm gonna bump off anything that resembles a dragon until I get my mother back."

Death Wind started off toward a grove of magnolias. "Lizard not dragon."

99

When Rusty retrieved his spear from a thick patch of laurel and sassafras he fell behind. He ran to catch up, his packs only half on. "Besides, you'd be wasting ammunition we'll need against the dragons."

Scott plucked a white blossom from a dogwood, and sniffed it. "Sandra, you just don't like Death Wind telling you to go climb a tree."

"I told you to shut up or I'll— Oh, forget it. But the next time I'm not running. I came here to fight."

"We fight when the time come. For now, save strength."

Scott lagged back for a moment and broke off a sprig full of dogwood flowers. "Yes, save your urge to kill for the dragons."

"I'm not listening to you."

His hand reached out. "I bet you'd listen if I—"

The cracking sound that interrupted him could have been a tree splitting, or two rocks crashing together sharply. A moment later two more cracks were followed by a muted shout that was unmistakably human.

"Let's go." Scott was off and running even before Death Wind. He plowed through dense foliage, then over a field of tall grass toward a grove of stately palm trees. The spreading leaves blocked out much of the sun, and some of the heat. A faint breeze cooled the air. He saw what he was getting into long before he reached the area of conflict. A lone man in a loose tunic of olive drab cloth was being pursued by a hulking monstrosity that was cousin to the triceratops.

Rusty matched his pace and uttered a groan. "A styracosaurus."

The splayed shield that protected the neck was ringed with tiny, daggerlike projections that could stab at the face of any predator that tried to bite its leathery nape. The two horns above the eye ridges were short and stubby while the one on the nose stuck out like a long, squat sword. And that sword was being wielded by ten tons of flesh and bone.

With hair and beard as white as snow streaming over hunched shoulders, the lone man limped for the sanctuary of a group of head-high boulders. As he squeezed among them the wily styracosaurus felt no hesitation in climbing right over the top and taking swipes at the old man. For something that size, it moved with an amazingly fawnlike grace.

A long, rapierlike tongue darted out, reaching into a crevice where the clawed forelimbs could not fit. One bullet skipped past the nose and spun off the curved shield into the air, another was swallowed up by the raging mouth. The beast subsided, licking its wounds. But the tiny pistol bullets were little more than bee stings.

Death Wind charged past and loosed a flint-tipped arrow. It hit the dinosaur in the rump, in the sensitive area under the swishing tail. The thick appendage swept from side to side. The shaft snapped off like a reed, but the point was still deeply imbedded. The styracosaurus pivoted in rage. It caught another arrow full in the face, but it was harmlessly absorbed by the horny material of the neck shield.

Before he could draw another arrow, Death Wind was almost caught in a crossfire as a lightning bolt seared past him on one side and a burst of rifle bullets sang dangerously close by on the other. Neither seemed to show any immediate effect other than to further provoke the beast. The beamer blackened the thick hide, and the bullets spanged uselessly off the orna-mented skull.

The styracosaurus charged, and the trio scattered like frightened doves. Momentum carried the dinosaur far past where they were standing before it comprehended that there was nothing in its path but a palm tree. It gored the sloping trunk, shredding bark as if it had gone through a sawmill. Its red, beady eyes fell on Rusty.

Armed with only a spear, Rusty hung back. Now, as he turned to run, his feet twisted around the shaft and he toppled over in the waving grass. The dinosaur lunged at this new two-legged foe.

Death Wind broke the beast's concentration with a well-placed arrow right behind the neck shield. Sandra's bullets pricked the coarse hide like so much rock salt. Scott kept firing the beamer. If there was enough time he might be able to erode the beast away.

The bright blasts of light attracted the dinosaur's attention. The small brain could not hold more than one thought at a time, so it swung toward Scott. But as the animal swept through the grass, Rusty sprang up from the ground and lunged with his spear. The hand-hewn weapon, molded so far away and carried with so much travail, now earned its worth. Rusty was almost bowled over as he imbedded the fire-hardened tip just behind the foreleg in such a position that when the blunt end gouged into the soft earth the beast's own momentum forced it straight into its vital organs.

The styracosaurus blundered to a stop. Rusty, now defenseless, ran toward the boulders where even now the old man was emerging from cover. Scott let go a couple of beamer blasts that befuddled the dinosaur enough to keep it tracking in circles.

"Get outa my way! You're in my line of fire." Sandra danced for a new position.

Scott pivoted as the girl put the rifle to her shoulder, and fired. Rusty and the old man met in the knee-high grass. Blue eyes peered out from under bushy white eyebrows as he spoke with throaty precision. "I think we've met our match."

Scott scuttled by them, yelling, "Run for cover. We'll hold him off."

Death Wind ran around the styracosaurus whooping and waving his arms. Sandra merged with Rusty and the old man, and ripped out the spent magazine. The dinosaur narrowed its gaze on the threesome; this was something on which its puny brain could concentrate. With arrows nipping at its heels and beamer blasts tanning its hide, it snorted and charged with the determination of a speeding freight train.

"Aim for the eyes." The old man held his gun out at arm's length and fired his last two cartridges.

Sandra crouched professionally on one knee. She slammed a full clip into the breech and pulled back the bolt, chambering a round. The styracosaurus came on like ten tons of locomotive destruction. With cool deliberation she aimed for the horned, shielded face and the two gleaming eyes.

"The eyes," the old man breathed, with religious fervor.

Sandra squeezed the trigger, and kept squeezing. A stream of bullets only split seconds apart stitched a zigzag line across the armored face, splintering horn and pinging off bone.

The beast was twenty feet away and closing fast. Sandra looked over the sights, then put the rifle across her bent knee. The thundering forelegs crumpled suddenly and the styracosaurus hit the ground like a bulldozer, plowing up great rows of dirt and grass. The furrow made by the long front horn stopped at Sandra's feet. With a single convulsive gasp it sank to the ground with its legs spread-eagled, and expired.

Sandra brushed loose hair from her face. "It was dead as soon as my first bullet went through the eye and into the brain. But it takes 'em a little while to figure it out."

CHAPTER 13

The old man looked at Sandra with a mixture of awe, respect, and surprise. "Oh, my," he uttered in a voice that was somewhat creaky but full of intonation. "This comes as quite a shock."

Scott helped steady the old man while he dusted himself off. "Are you all right?"

He shoved the rusted pistol into a brown leather holster that was cracked and faded with age. Casting his steel-gray eyes around the group of warriors, he studied their odd attire and anachronistic assortment of weaponry. His bushy eyebrows arched sharply. "Yes, I'm quite unscathed thanks to you and your arsenal. I'm glad you happened along."

"Men stick together. It is code."

"Ah, a member of the Nomads." The old man's smile slowly turned into a frown. "But tell me, what are you doing so far east? You people travel along the Rio Grande."

"Come kill dragon."

"I see." The old man pursed his thin lips. "An admirable goal, if only it were practical. I admire the courage of your venture if only for its boldness. How close is the rest of the tribe?"

Death Wind hesitated. "People all dead. Killed by dragon."

The old man's features contorted wryly, caught between pain and disbelief. His gray eyes veered off and stared sightlessly into the forest. "Oh. Oh, my. That is a pity. This unexpected increase in dragon activity must be to blame. What was your tribe?"

"Sintu."

Now the old man was horror-struck. "I—I can't tell you how—sorry I am to hear that. And the other tribes?"

Death Wind shrugged. "They are south. We come alone. We fight to the death."

"And have you forgotten the Nomad ethic to kill only when necessary—and practical? Rabbits live long because they hide." Silence was Death Wind's only reply. Now the old man swept the motley crew with eyes that had lost their sparkle. "And you four are all that's left of a once noble tribe?" There was sadness in his voice.

"Oh, we're not Nomads," Scott said, pointing. "Rusty, and Sandra, and me. I'm Scott. We just sort of met on the way, and tagged along."

"I see. And what's your name?"

The Nomad folded his arms across his chest. "I am called Death Wind."

The old man was quite taken aback. "That's—that's quite different. And why did you choose that particular name?"

"To become a warrior, I killed a dragon."

"Ah, then the name is well deserved. Anyone who manages to kill a dragon is quite a warrior in my book. I honor your choice."

Death Wind gestured to the others. "These are warriors, too."

"Even my little girl, here?"

Sandra recoiled like a viper. "I'm not your little girl. I'm not anyone's little girl. I don't belong to anyone." She slung the rifle onto her shoulder, pulled the shawl tight, and pushed out her chest. "And I'm not little, either."

"Yes, I can see that. But you are a feisty one, though."

Rusty said, "She knocked out a whole squad of dragons—single-handed."

"I'm impressed." The snowy eyebrows launched high into the deeply etched forehead. To Sandra, he said, "But let me point out, my dear, that the possessive pronoun may be used to denote relationship or connections, not just ownership. Now, what say we repair to my humble abode and celebrate this fortuitous meeting? The drinks, such as they are, are on the house."

So saying, the old man turned and hobbled toward the pile of boulders, where he searched until he found a carved stick that served him as a cane. He leaned heavily on it, and waited while the others retrieved their packs from where they had left them before the fight. Already flies and numerous insects were gathering around the body of the styracosaurus, for in this jungle terrain and steamy atmosphere flying bugs abounded.

"Excuse me, sir," Rusty said when they began walking after the old man. "But, you haven't told us your name."

The old man smiled. "Well, I've gone under quite a few titles and appellations in my day, but most of the time I'm just called Doc. I am, you know. A doctor, that is." He tapped his bent left leg with the cane. "The last doctoring I did was to set this bone. Didn't do a very good job of it, I'm afraid. But then, there *were* mitigating circumstances."

"I set an arm once," Sandra said. "It wasn't so hard."

Doc was unperturbed. "Yes, the trick is to do it as soon as possible, before healing begins. In my case, I was buried under a rock slide for two days, nearly delirious with fever. By the time I dug myself out it was too late. It needed to be broken and reset, and I couldn't do it myself. I've always hated pain, you know."

Scott was awed. "Didn't you have any—friends?"

"All killed by the dragons. The only reason they botched the job in my case was because they didn't know I was under that pile of rocks they had beamed down on us. You see, I was in charge of a spying party that kept an eye on the dragons, and their city. Now, instead of seeking them out, I am forced to hide from them—an exigency of which I'm not exceptionally proud. I'm afraid my spying days are pretty much at an end. Now, I can barely manage to get around enough to shoot some fresh meat."

"You mean, you go out after dinosaurs with that thing?" Rusty pointed to the holstered pistol.

Doc laughed heartily. "No, I stay away from the big ones. Rabbit-sized dinosaurs are about all I can handle with this peashooter. Mostly, I live out of cans, but the diet gets so humdrum after a while. I assure you, I'm not senile enough yet to think I can attack a styracosaurus and get away with it. No, I stumbled on that one quite by accident. Or, should I say, it stumbled on me? It must have broken out of the pens."

"Pens?"

"You don't seem to know much about your enemy. Knowledge of one's foe is important in any war. You see, those beasts are cattle to the dragons. They're herd animals, and they graze them out here in the reclaimed jungle. Of course, it wouldn't do to have them wandering all over the place, so they have them fenced in. The one you killed is what you might call a stray cow."

Sandra whistled. "That's some cow. I'd hate to meet the cowboy who lassoes it."

Doc laughed. "The dragons don't use lassoes, naturally— they use slaves. And they don't seem to mind much if they lose a few. They can always hatch more. On the other hand, all the dinosaurs relocated here are vegetarians—plant eaters, that is—and fight only defensively."

"You mean, we don't have to worry about running into an allosaurus?" Rusty said.

"You wouldn't be likely to find an allosaurus in any event. Besides the fact that the dragons wouldn't bring any carnivorous competitors with them, the allosaurs are from the wrong period. They lived in the Jurassic. All the dinosaurs you find nowadays came from the Cretaceous."

Scott scratched his head. "I don't understand. No matter what period the dinosaurs are from, how did the dragons get them all here in their spaceships?"

Sandra said, "Because, stupid, the dragons didn't come out of space. They came out of time."

Doc looked startled. "Oh, my, we do have a strange group here: two who are ignorant, one who knows all, and a silent Nomad who keeps his own council. And all traveling together."

The forest opened out into a field, acres in size, with the ruins of a one-story concrete building in the center. Waist-high grass wafted silently in the breeze, while a wood slat nailed diagonally across the splintered opening in the cement wall clattered haphazardly.

"Well, here's home."

Doc followed a narrow path beaten through the grass. It passed over a couple of six-foot-diameter clearings where nothing grew. The thin layer of dirt was tinged red at the edges.

"Rusty!" Scott stopped in his tracks, staring down at the ground.

"I—I see it."

Scott dropped to his knees and quickly wiped the dirt away with his hands. In seconds he revealed an ancient iron surface. He scrubbed more. The rusting iron plate had six straight cracks radiating out from the center, like pie wedges. "It can't be."

"But, it is. These are missile silos."

Doc stared at Scott and Rusty as if they were ghosts from the past. "Oh, my. I think perhaps we'd better have a *long* talk."

CHAPTER 14

The copper kettle whistled on the makeshift metal stove. Doc removed the boiling water from the heat and blew out the flame in the dish of dinosaur fat. He spread an odd assortment of cups on the slab of wood that served as a table. Into each he dropped a handful of finely chopped leaves and stems, then added the water. He passed out the cups of steaming brew.

"I'm not used to having company, as you can see." He reserved the only chair in the room for himself, as well as the crate parked next to it on which he propped his aching leg. "So you must excuse my housekeeping. By the way, this is my own special blend, collected fresh every week. I hope you like it."

The concrete building was surprisingly cool, and drinking the hot, flavored water had a soothing effect that plain, cold water did not have. Death Wind sliced meat from a slab in his pack.

Doc spread out a hand-drawn map on the tottering table. "Now, Death Wind, can you tell me approximately where you picked up these two itinerants?" He traced a line along the brown parchment with his index finger. "This is the Rio Grande, what your people call the River of Life. Here is your southern camp, and up here is the northern extremity of your summer migration. The other tribes are farther west and south."

Doc held an oil lamp over the middle of the map. Four others sat in the corners, casting weird, yellow, flickering shadows in the messy room. Wooden boxes and cans of rations had been hastily pushed aside to allow space for the guests.

A dark finger stabbed the paper. "Here."

"Hmmmn. That would seem to put them in the western quadrant. Yes, I can see how that would happen. And Sandra?"

"Here."

"Yes, that makes sense. It's along one of the old highway routes—probably covered with sand for quite some time.

107

Hmmmn." Doc moved the lamp over the map, and studied the surrounding areas. "I find it remarkable that your people have been living in complete isolation for more than a century. But considering the circumstances I guess it was the only viable option. You're lucky that your ancestors were trained to operate a command center instead of a missile base, otherwise you probably would not be here."

Doc sat back in his chair and propped up his leg. "You see, my predecessors were also opportunely stationed in an underground installation, near a place called the District of Columbia."

"The capital," Rusty said.

Doc nodded in an aside to Death Wind. "Yes, it's what you would call the chief hogan of this once great country. It seems that in the old days men had some very queer notions. They believed in something called specialization. Everyone studied a particular branch of knowledge and strived to learn as much as possible about as little as possible. Now, there was really nothing drastically wrong with this because technology had become so complicated that it was the only way one could learn a sufficient quantity about certain complex jobs—although it did leave one ignorant of other facets of contemporary disciplines. Compartmentalization of the vast store of human knowledge was necessary in order to carry civilization onward, and upward—so to speak.

"Unfortunately, due to certain carryovers from prehistoric times, when mankind lived as an animal instead of as a society, not everyone had the choice of where he stood in this great maze of aristocracy. There were restrictions placed upon people because of artificial and wholly imaginary boundaries such as race, creed, political persuasion—and sex.

"To make a long story short, very few women were allowed to reach high enough stations in the military hierarchy to be assigned to the highly classified missile sites. So even though many underground installations survived the coming of the dragons, the survivors died out through attrition. In an old manner of speaking, it takes two to tango."

Rusty was enthusiastic. "Boy, you really know your history."

"It's all boring to me," Sandra said. "Get to the point."

"Yes. Well, from what you've told me of Maccam City, my guess is that your home was at one time the main control center for the entire United States. In military parlance that would be Missile Control Center—Main. Appropriately abbreviated to MCCM, this would have come down as the acronym Maccam."

"Wow, I never came across that in any of the history disks."

Scott nodded slowly. "It seems logical."

Doc sipped his tea. "And, I would also guess that because of the many functions required for coordination and administration, and the inherent clerical work involved, a proportionately large secretarial contingent must have been necessary for efficient operation. Thus, in addition to individual survival, Maccam City was granted racial continuance as well."

Sandra was still skeptical. "So how come you know so much—or think you do?"

Doc sighed patiently. Answering the question instead of the implication, he said, "I grew up in the main political structure situated under the now defunct city of Washington. It managed to survive under the same set of circumstances which I've just described. I had access to many disks, as well as a direct, word-of-mouth link to the past."

"But you lived on the surface," Rusty said. "Why didn't our ancestors ever come out of the ground?"

"Because they were scared," Sandra said.

Scott jumped to his feet. "That's a lie. My father wanted to leave the city years ago, but the council wouldn't let him."

"Whoa, please. Can we act a little more civilized. We really can't afford to fight among ourselves."

"But she said—"

"I heard what she said, and if you'll take my advice, young man, you'll ignore her vituperations. And you"—Doc pointed a gnarled finger at Sandra—"will stop trying to foment trouble. Do you want to fight dragons, or comrades?"

Sandra pouted, but remained silent. Scott sat down, glaring at her.

"Now, as I was about to say, from what you've told me my guess is that Maccam City was conceived as a self-contained emplacement designed to carry out a nuclear retaliatory war. Its personnel must have been instructed to remain hidden in such an event, and thereby remain safe from bombs and their resultant radiation. According to your own testimony, and in light of your presence, Maccam City was capable of functioning for many generations without external support. You were, in a manner of speaking, an ace in the hole."

Death Wind shuffled to his feet and looked down on the doctor. "You speak lies. Men do not fight men."

"Ah, my good friend, I can understand that to a Nomad the concept of internecine strife is repulsive as well as unbelievable. But a look at our two warring associates disagreeing because of differing beliefs is proof enough that men did not always, I'm ashamed to say, stick together."

Death Wind slowly sat down. After an uncomfortable silence Rusty said, "Well, let me ask you something else, Doc. Are you trying to say that for a hundred years we've been trained to counterstrike a nuclear attack that never took place?"

"Quite simply, yes."

"What a waste of time. You guys have sure been played for a coupla fools."

"Sandra, please dispense with the antagonism. To elucidate, Rusty, the best guess I can hazard is communications failure. Remember that the dragons' victory was as complete as it was instantaneous. Practically the entire human race was liquidated overnight. Without human guidance the electrical power systems failed. And while places like Maccam City were in a state of perpetual preparedness, trained and maintained like a well-oiled machine, the rest of the world came to a dead stop. Those who lived through the catastrophe had their hands full tying to survive. And no one, not even those in Washington, knew what had caused the plague."

Scott ignored his tea. "And all these years we've been waiting . . . waiting . . ."

"From generation to generation," Rusty finished.

"You guys are worse than fools, you're grade A, number one suckers."

"My dear, where did you learn such poor manners?"

"It wasn't from a namby-pamby like you."

"I'm glad to hear *that*." Doc got up and gazed at the map. "I was in that area ten or fifteen years ago, and I never knew . . ."

"Never knew what?" Rusty had to repeat his question, louder, before Doc snapped out of the imaginary world of his mind.

"Oh, I was just thinking." He leaned back into his seat, propped up his leg. "You see, the Washington complex retained a semblance of the civilization and technology of the bygone era. We had all the modern conveniences: generators that still worked, when we could find the fuel; operable computers; a storehouse of disks. As a youth I studied medicine, among other things. I was really quite a scholar, with a wide range of interests. But as I got older I realized that if mankind was going to reclaim his kingdom he had to expand. I went on many expeditions in search of other pockets of mankind that had survived the calamity. Inevitably, we found some. They were living in caves, in subways, even in sewers. And from each group of survivors I picked up stories, rumors, threads of information. First I heard about spaceships that flew on beams of destruction. Then I heard about a race of dragons that inhabited the bayou country. Then I saw my first dinosaur.

"The Washington shelter had been isolated for over fifty years, and we never knew, never even suspected, what had befallen mankind. What we had thought was a worldwide epidemic disease perpetrated by enemy biological warfare, we discovered to be a pogrom instituted by a race of lizardlike demons. More than that was conjecture.

"In order to ensure man's survival we spread out, so that all our eggs were not in the same basket. Runners maintained contact between groups, scouts explored new territory in search of hidden conclaves. Families and friends split up, perhaps never to see one another again.

"I did quite a bit of traveling in those days. I came across the tribes of the Nomads, learned their customs and ways of life. And possibly I helped impart in them the true knowledge of man's heritage. The Sintu, by the way, are descended from guides and concessioneers, perhaps even tourists, who happened to be in Carlsbad Caverns during the critical phase of the epidemic—something which might account for the American Indian influence on their descendants: their ritual, their habits, their closeness to the earth. Anyway, I'm straying from the point."

Doc brushed a leathery hand through his long, white hair, then ran it over his mouth to dry his lips. "Separated from my family, I joined a group of younger men. Our purpose was to keep an eye on the dragon city, learn what we could about them, follow their movements, discover their weaknesses. One day we were caught by dragon soldiers and wiped out. Only I survived. I had to crawl for miles to reach the safety of this silo. It was six months before I could get about, during which time I almost died of a fever that lasted for weeks. I lived on canned stores, some of it rotting. But I had no choice. Since then, I've lived here as a recluse, unable to observe the dragon city, unable to return to my people."

Doc's voice trailed off. He stared sightlessly up at the darkened ceiling, lost for the moment in the failures of his past. Visibly, he shrugged off nostalgic thoughts. "I've always hoped that one day mankind would win back this beautiful planet. And that he would take better care of it than he did before. But it's only a dream. Only a dream."

"That's what we're going to do," Scott said.

Doc snickered affably. "Four youths, against the whole dragon race?"

"Four warriors," Death Wind said.

"It's not exactly what you would call an army, is it?"

"But we can try," Scott said, with determination.

"Yes, and you can die trying. Ah, in my youth I had the same delusions of grandeur. Now it all seems so futile."

"You're just a has-been who doesn't have the guts to go out and fight."

Doc looked at Sandra sharply. "Sandra, I'll forgive you your harsh remarks on the assumption that the exuberance of your youth has overtaken the dictates of your humanity. You're sadly misunderstanding the severity of the situation if you think a spear, an arrow, a rifle, and a stolen beamer are going to topple the superior technology and the sheer mass of numbers the dragons have at their control. It's like attacking a stone wall with a toothpick."

"If you had done something years ago we wouldn't be in this mess now."

Doc's voice went up a note. "If we could have done something years ago we would have. But remember that it was over sixty years after the plague before we recognized our enemy. And by that time they had gained such a foothold that no weapons at our command could fight them off. We had lost the tools and the knowledge of our civilization. We were a primitive people struggling only to survive, and ill equipped to fight."

"So you're just gonna sit here an' die?"

"Ah, if all decisions were that simple." Doc stroked his bushy beard, recovering his composure. "As things are, we are powerless. The dragons have started a new expansion program, they have increased their numbers, augmented their food supplies, and expanded their grazing area. Their city is spreading, their dominance is growing ever farther. Your own stories attest to that. Dinosaurs now roam most of the country, and soon the jungles will catch up with them. Even my poor observation post is on the verge of being overtaken by encroaching ranch land. There is more aerial traffic than ever—six flyers if my observations are correct, each capable of carrying a hundred soldiers. And they are systematically seeking out man's last strongholds, destroying the vestiges of his architectural creations.

"I'm afraid, my young friends, that the time for stopping the dragons is already past. We are the dinosaurs of this new age, doomed to extinction while a stronger and more viable breed takes over. Man was once a great and noble race, and he was endowed with even greater potential. Now he is vermin only slightly tolerated by a mightier race. You see, in real life it is not the good and the righteous who survive, but the most ruthless."

Doc dropped his leg to the floor and pushed himself up out of the chair. He picked up his cane and an oil lamp, and hobbled for the doorway.

"Your hostility is well deserved, my dear, but I'm afraid it's just a little too late. Now, if you will excuse an old man, I must rest these weary bones."

The stooped and disillusioned patriarch retreated through the door to an adjacent room, and left the four youths with their thoughts.

CHAPTER 15

The oil lamps were out, the concrete bunker was clothed in darkness, and the old man lay serenely asleep on a silver disc covered with palm fronds. He snored smoothly until his dim world burst into brightness and his dreams recoiled into the fantasy land from which they had come.

He lurched up in his jury-rigged bed, with rusting metal vanes snapping loudly beneath the fronds. He was blinded by the intruding light, and for several moments groped around shielding his eyes against the glare. Then, as he adjusted to the brightness, he began to comprehend what had happened.

"Oh, my." He squinted up at the ceiling of the cubicle, unwilling to accept what he saw.

He clambered down from his circular bed and rushed out into the narrow, concrete hallway. Here, too, where there should have been utter darkness, the corridor was alive with a yellow, unflickering light. It was as if the roof had suddenly been peeled off and the sun shone down.

He heard a yell, and instinctively ran in that direction. He turned a corner just in time to see Death Wind swinging his hand wildly, as if shaking off a cloud of bees. Sandra, standing by his side, laughed at his antics.

Scott stepped out of a doorway wearing a tool pouch full of wrenches, pliers, and screwdrivers. "What's the trouble?"

"Our mighty warrior has never seen a light bulb before, and he just got stung when he touched it."

Death Wind blew on his fingers. "Hot."

"Hey, Scott," came a shout from inside the room. "The breakers are holding fine. All we have to do is check the switches and—oh. Hi, Doc. Did we wake you?"

Doc quickly regained control of himself. "You certainly did. Pray, tell me, what is going on?"

Scott said, "We just turned on the juice."

"But—how? I've searched every corner of this place, and there's no fuel for the generators."

Rusty wiped grease off his forehead. "Oh, we didn't bother with the generators. We turned on the reactor."

"The *nuclear* reactor?"

"You know of any other kind, gramps?"

"But, it takes uranium—and the proper knowhow."

"You forget, we're specialists. Scott and I have spent our whole lives in a place like this. Of course, this place could use a little maintenance to bring it up to snuff, but . . ."

"But how did you get the reactor going?"

"We pulled out the control rods," Scott said. "Of course, the damping motors won't run without the generators, so we switched to manual override and raised the rods by hand. But now that the reactor's supplying electricity we can run the dampers on reactor mode."

Doc put his jaw back in place. "Oh, my. I really must sit down. Would you boys help me back to my room? I seem to have forgotten my cane."

With Sandra and Death Wind leading the way, Scott and Rusty each grabbed an arm and escorted the limping man to his bed. They helped him onto the edge where he remained sitting with one foot dangling and one propped up. Doc looked around at the smiling faces.

"Perhaps you'd better explain."

Rusty took the initiative. "According to standard operating procedure, shut-down missile bases are left in Code Two condition: that is, with warheads on safe and primers removed. We did a little checking and found that everything was in order. The missile pods had been sealed, the control room had been locked, and the reactor plant had been evacuated and fully damped. We found the restarting checklist and turned everything back on. Of course, we still have to clean out the electrical cabinets and dust the contacts and check the circuitry, but so far everything works."

"Not only that," Scott added, "but I inspected the missiles. The warheads are still in place, with the fuses out. All we have to do is rearm them. They're ready to fly."

"But—how can that be after all these years?"

"The rockets run on solid propellant so it can't leak away. Remember, that was necessary in the old days because they were never really intended to be launched except in case of emergency. They were mostly a deterrent, a bluff against enemy attack."

Rusty took the ball. "We activated the computers, too, and plugged in a few disks. It's still operational, although there are a few bugs."

"And there aren't any old movie disks," Sandra complained.

"I'm pretty sure that with some routine maintenance we can have the whole installation back on line. Scott's the best there is in missile repair—"

"And nobody can beat Rusty when it comes to plotting trajectories. We're going to show those dragons a thing or two. We'll knock those flyers right out of the sky."

Doc ran crooked fingers through unkempt, snowy hair. "It seems that while I was asleep the whole world has changed. Uh, you wouldn't josh an old man, would you?"

"Not if that old man's willing to put his money where his mouth is. We're gonna fight those dragons with whatever we have, right down to the fingernails. I'll scratch their eyes out if I have to. I want my mother back."

"Child, revenge is sweet, but you can't bring back that which no longer exists."

"You shut up, you, or I'll—" Sandra flung her long hair over her shoulder. Her eyes narrowed. "My mother's not dead."

"I know what you said, but—"

"I'm telling you she was still kicking when those slimy beasts dragged her into the flyer." She stared defiantly at her companions' blank faces. "All right, I know you think I have an obsession about my mother. Well, maybe I do. But you guys all lost your families to the dragons, so don't try to kid yourselves that your motives are all that noble. You're as selfish as I am, only I'm willing to admit it."

"That sounds like an astute observation, one with which I would not care to argue."

"Good. Then let's go all the way and assume that, since I'm not crazy, there's a chance that my mother's still alive—and that we *can* rescue her."

Doc sighed. "Just don't get your hopes up." After a moment's silence, he went on, "Well, now that that's settled, let's get back to the business at hand. How about if I rustle up some chow?"

Scott removed his tool pouch. "I'm ready to eat."

"You're always ready to eat," Sandra said.

Doc found his cane and led the group to the other room. He had difficulty locating the light switches, but when he did and the bulbs glowed with yellow brilliance, he realized how easy life would be if he did not have to constantly refine dinosaur oil for the lamps.

He gestured with his hand. "Please excuse this. In the dark I had no idea I was such a messy housekeeper."

Sandra blew dust off a pile of plates. "Don't worry about it, as long as you can cook on an electric range."

"It's something I haven't done in quite a while, but I don't think I've lost the touch. You can be the judge of that."

Scott found a rag and started wiping out bowls. "Anything would be better than raw grubs."

Sandra laughed. "For once, you an' I agree on something."

Doc opened cans of meat and vegetables and mixed them in a saucepan with a quart of water. After more than a century they were slow to rehydrate.

Rusty set the table with silverware. "We've got practically all the lights on in the lower levels, and we found some nice rooms. You can move into deeper quarters if you want."

Doc stirred the mixture as it heated. "I almost hate to leave this squalor." The soup boiled rapidly on the red-hot elements, and soon Doc ladled out steaming portions to everyone. "Well, what do you think of it?"

Death Wind fumbled with the unfamiliar utensil. "Food," was his only comment.

"Ah, a man after my own heart. He understands the simple essentials of life."

"Definitely better than earthworms. And this tea of yours ain't too bad, either."

"I accept that as a compliment of the highest order." And in his mind, he could not help but add: considering the source. "Now that your bodies are being taken care of, I have some food for thought."

Doc sat in his chair and propped up his bad leg. "As I see it, now I've got no choice but to help you. Your skills need to be wedded with my knowledge, and your rashness needs to be tempered by my sagacity. With that combination I think there is a better chance of success. Besides, if I don't help you, you'll go ahead and do it on your own. And I'd like to be there at the finish line."

Scott and Rusty cheered. Sandra snorted. Death Wind, as usual, was silent.

Scott stopped slurping his soup for a moment. "That's great, Doc. But could you give us some background information? Rusty and I are still pretty much in the dark about the dragon invasion. And every time I ask Sandra she gives me a dirty look and says ask the old—well, she's pretty tight-lipped."

Doc played with his beard for a moment before speaking. With his leg up on the crate he appeared to be lounging, but it was only way he could stop the constant throbbing. "Most of what I know about the dragons is a careful blend of observation, word of mouth, and deduction, with a good bit of supposition thrown in to fill in the gaps. But I think it conforms fairly closely to the truth.

"The dragons came here from the past, the late Cretaceous I suspect, about sixty million years ago, through an artificial window they created in the space-time continuum and kept open by a power of unimaginable magnitude. To herald their coming they released into the atmosphere a bomb which disseminated a viral nerve gas that killed all breathing animals with a highly evolved central nervous system: mammals, birds, reptiles, amphibians, and fish, although most ocean dwellers escaped because the plague-producing virus could not exist for long in water. One bomb was dropped over each continent, and the virus spread by the wind. Within a week it was all over. When their hosts ceased to exist, the virus died out, and the dragons had virtually a virgin planet all to themselves.

"Naturally, there were survivors. Burrowing animals, bats, possibly bears in hibernation, anything that had not breathed in the deadly virus during its short virulent stage, were spared, although many of them must have died anyway because of the changes brought about.

"Into this world empty of dominant life forms the dragons brought eggs from their own time, and began raising the saurian livestock on which they feed. Now they are spreading their influence even wider, even faster, although there is opinion that every ten years or so the dragons drop bombs on the other continents of the world, presumably to keep them sterile until they are prepared to expand from North America."

Rusty toyed with his food, finally pushing the bowl away. "But, Doc, if there was a civilization of intelligent—well— lizards in the past, why hadn't fossil evidence been dug up?"

"Who says it hasn't? Naturally, you wouldn't expect to find traces of cities, or machines, or artifacts. They would not survive in recognizable form throughout the millennia. But there are many examples of bird-hipped dinosaurs, such as the struthiomimes, which the dragons resemble. There must have been hundreds of skeletons in museums all over the world similar in form and size. But even an experienced paleontologist could not tell from bone fragments what kind of brain the bearer had."

"Yes, I can see that. But another point: didn't the dinosaurs die out around the end of the Cretaceous?"

"Right you are, my lad. Your profound knowledge never ceases to amaze me. At that time there was only one massive protocontinent, known as Pangea. For some unknown geological reason Pangea broke up into the individual land masses we recognize today. At the same time the little mammals, our very ancestors, took over the Earth, and the age of the 'thunder lizards' came to a rather abrupt end. The theory has been advanced that it was the appearance of these early mammals which spelled the end of the dinosaurs' reign, perhaps because they were smarter than their predecessors, or ate their eggs, or were more adaptable to changing climatic conditions. No one knows for sure. My guess is that in their own epoch the dragons are on the verge of dying out, and the discovery of the time transporter has offered them a way to a less troubled era: a place-time where they can expand their cold-blooded rule."

"That reminds me of something, Doc," Scott said. "Death Wind has told us that the dragons are cold-blooded, while the dinosaurs are warm-blooded. I don't quite remember it that way from the history disks."

"Yes, before the coming of the dragons it had only recently been theorized that the dinosaurs might in fact be warm-blooded animals, and that the mammals and birds are actually offshoots which then split and developed along different evolutionary lines. There was convincing experimental data that animals of such bulk could not have heated their bodies solely through the warmth of the sun, as true lizards do, and that they must therefore have had internal regulators.

"The dragons, on the other hand, are related to the true lizards. They can't stand the cold, and never go out at night. Instead, they huddle in enclaves for warmth. They are not only cold-blooded, but ruthless. They are completely without feeling, without sentiment, without love or affection. Their eggs are hatched in great nurseries, their wounded are dispatched, their dead left to rot. They are cold and calculating not just in body, but in mind. They have an urge to conquer which knows no bounds of humanity, if I may use the word in its broadest sense. We just happen to live in a territory which they wish to occupy, so they must exterminate us like pests—or parasites."

"Then we have to make sure they don't succeed," Scott said.

To which Death Wind added, "We will fight to the death."

"For revenge."

"For my mother."

"For our folks."

In the silence that followed Doc examined his newfound friends. He sensed a dedication among them that reminded him of times past. Working together, these four seemed to have become a unit that was far greater than the simple addition of four talents. His heart reached out for them, and for their goals. He felt a longing he had not felt in years.

"Your devotion to duty overwhelms me."

Scott said, "We didn't come all this way for nothing."

"And we ain't about to give up."

"I see that."

"And if the dragons are expanding their sphere of influence, as you said, this may be our last chance," Rusty said. "But why have they waited so long?"

"Another astute observation, my friend. For that you must understand *how* the dragons arrive here. Some thirty years ago a certain restless and wayward, and I must say bold, scout sneaked into the city and spent many days exploring, making maps, and learning dragon ways. From him we learned that the temporal opening through which the dragons and all their belongings must pass is extremely small: hardly larger, in fact, than a closet. Besides this, another limiting factor is the energy requirement for each transfer. The receiving end of the transporter, in our time, is powered by a huge capacitor bank which is constantly being recharged. But I think that the energy level here is insignificant when compared to the amount of power required at the transmitting end, where the actual warp machine is located. They can transmit, of course, without a receiving apparatus, but not as often or as efficiently, and not, I suspect, as accurately. The machinery at this end is a fine tuner, an anchor which designates the exact time to which things are sent.

"Lately, I believe, they have stepped up their power production in order to allow more transfers. With the aid of a spyglass I have watched the movements of their flyers. Recently, in addition to riding over man's ancient cities with their disruptor beams and dropping bombs which have unbelievable destructive power, they have been seeking out the last pockets of human resistance and stamping them out."

"My people?"

"My friend, the Sintu relied too much on stealth and movement, and did not impart enough variation into their migration route. The dragon warship may even have followed the path of your people to the vicinity of Maccam City, although they may have found it in any event.

"Now the dragons are expanding exponentially. With a larger base camp, with more supplies, with more personnel, they are burgeoning forth like a plague of locusts. As their influence increases, mankind's will lessen. At this moment we may represent one of the last vestiges of Homo sapiens, the hangers-on of the few who have escaped the dragons' clutches and have refused to give up."

"I thought you gave up a long time ago," Sandra said.

"Ah, that spiteful tongue again." Doc spoke without resentment. "My dear, before I met you I think I had given up. I was an old man, crippled and alone. But your spunk has inspired me. Your otherwise quixotic quest is doomed to failure without my assistance. Indeed, if you are going to attack the great city of the dragons as you intend, you will need my guidance. You will need to know the layout of the streets and buildings, how to get about without being seen, what to be wary of."

"Then you'll help us!" Scott said. "And do you still have the map that scout made?"

"That I have, young man. That I have." Tapping his gray temple with a crooked finger, Doc said with pride, "I keep that map right here where I can't lose it. For, you see, I was that scout. And I intend to go with you."

CHAPTER 16

"This is just an auxiliary testing station, with the mainframe computer acting as our fault detector," Rusty explained to Doc one afternoon. He flipped switches and showed how the gauges took readings on each circuit. "Since the lower levels were hermetically sealed, problems with moisture and oxygenation were eliminated. And with solid-state components time and nonuse is not a factor—by design, these printed circuit boards will last forever. Malfunctions occur only during use. But we're experiencing a lot of insulation breakdown on the high voltage lines. There's also been some drying and cracking of dielectric material in transformer and motor windings: we've got shorts all over the place."

Doc gazed reverently at the vast array of dials and switches, and the blinking lights of the annunciator panel. "What about that roomful of spare parts on the launch deck level?"

"We'll use them if we need them, but with triple redundancy we've been able to reroute all the circuits we need. Remember, we're not fixing this up for a standby emergency. This is a one-shot deal, so what we want is immediate firing capability. Most of the equipment we're not even trying to fix, such as the air conditioning, telecommunications, and remote control servo motors. We're going to open the silo lids by hand and leave them open."

Doc leaned on his cane and tugged at his beard. "But won't you have the same percentage of electrical failures in the missiles themselves? How can you know in advance that they'll perform satisfactorily?"

Rusty smiled. "Let's go down to the control room and see how Scott's making out. After all, he's the missile man. All I do is set trajectories and push the firing button."

They found Scott sitting at a console surrounded by video screens, flush-mounted gages, and seemingly endless rows of toggles, each of which was tagged and numbered. When he

123

heard Doc's question he leaned back in the chair and arched his back. Then he rubbed his eyes.

"Thanks, I can use a break to answer questions. Well, missiles have very few moving parts. With a solid rocket propellant there's no motor and no fuel feed: once it's ignited it keeps on burning until it either reaches its target or runs out of fuel. All the sensing devices and telemetering equipment are made with silicon chips and solid-state circuitry. The only real maintenance problem is from auxiliary engines that control guidance and attitude. Each missile has four, and these have to be in perfect working order or it won't track. So far, I've condemned two missiles as irreparable, but I'm going to cannibalize them for spare parts. That still gives us eight working missiles that we can count on."

Doc shook his head in admiration. "And you have the knowledge of all this? Why, you're mere children."

Scott laughed. "You're showing your age. But, to answer your question, I don't have all this knowledge—but the computer does. Here, let me show you."

Leaning forward in his seat he keyed the input panel and began typing instructions into the computer. The display screen lit up with an intricate pattern of interconnected dots and lines.

"Each missile has a computer access terminal. Once the cable's plugged into it any malfunctions are automatically registered. Most of them can be corrected from right here, by computer rerouting. If it can't, then I have to perform a physical check. But the computer still guides my work, like an electronic overseer. Of course, I have to be familiar with the circuitry, but mostly I have to be able to read computer lingo."

"I see." Doc studied the diagram on the display screen. It showed blowups of circuit diagrams, and highlighted in red those areas where trouble existed. Then, to show that he did understand, he said, "And those yellow lines indicate probabilities where failures might be."

"Exactly. Of course, the computer can do only so much. When it comes to nuts and bolts, or screwdrivers and wrenches, then it's up to me. But the computer also monitors my work so if I goof up it'll tell me I did something wrong."

"This is completely different from the computer we had back in Washington. That was really only a very complicated storage bank. It could do calculations and repeat stored material, but this—this computer actually does something creative."

"It's not as creative as you think," Rusty said. "It's just making calculations according to its program. It has limited applicability, since it's designed to do one particular job. Outside of that, it's useless."

Doc snorted. "And you boys feel certain that you can activate these missiles and knock down those flyers?"

"Once we entered the codes we gained unlimited access to the command and ballistic channels," Rusty said.

"It's simple mathematics. Six flyers, eight missiles. We can't lose." Scott leaned back again. "And it's unlikely they'll have any antimissile systems, or forms of electronic evasion. They've never needed any defense mechanisms. No, we've got them cold, Doc. We've got a weapon they're not prepared for. They've been fighting vegetables for a hundred years. Now those vegetables have suddenly grown teeth, and they're going to bite."

"Don't let your contention get the better of you. Revenge is an awful monster. It can make you take chances you would not otherwise take."

"And win against odds you wouldn't otherwise bet against," Rusty said.

"Yes, that too."

"Besides, we've got nothing to live for but revenge," Scott said. "And if what you say about the dragons expanding their territory is true, we've got nothing to lose. They want to wipe us out, and unless we fight back they're going to do it."

Doc nodded his gray head. "You speak with logic."

"However, we're missing one essential piece of equipment—we need a radar antenna. Without it all this fancy electronic apparatus is useless."

"Oh, my, that could prove to be a problem. The hills around here are so overgrown with Cretaceous fern that I don't suppose the original is still standing. At least, I've never come across it."

"The original didn't stand," Rusty said. "It flew. It was part of a network of orbiting satellites. But every station was equipped with emergency low-range antennas for close order surveillance. For what we need we could wire through those, if they still existed. There should be spares in stores, but we haven't been able to find any. Do you have any idea where one might be?"

Doc scratched his head. "I did some rummaging when I first moved in here—that's how I found these clothes. But that was a long time ago . . . I saw so many unfamiliar items." He pursed his lips. His cane clattered up the corridor, but he said over his shoulder, "I'll have to sleep on it for a while."

Work was going well until several days later when Scott divulged a serious problem during dinner, when the whole company was together.

"As you know, these are conventional ground-to-air missiles. That is, they're non-nuclear warheads intended for anti-insurgence from the Gulf of Mexico quadrant. They have a range of about five hundred miles—assuming we have radar pickup with that range—" His voice trailed off as he cast a glance at Doc.

"I'm—uh—still sleeping on it."

"Right. The attack computer can't lock onto a target without a dish antenna. Rusty and I have talked it over and we may be able to build one. But what I'm getting at is this. The proximity fuses are filled with a highly sensitive explosive. In accordance with shut-down procedures they've been removed and put into storage. We've found them, but after a hundred years they could be unstable. It's going to be touch and go resetting them on the warheads."

There was a moment of silence before Doc intervened with a question. "I know this must be overtly obvious to you, but tell me: what happens if this primer goes off when it's being set?"

Scott explained, "The missile explodes on the launch pad—along with the rocket propellant. We won't lose the whole base, just the one silo—and the person who sets it. Rusty and I have already discussed it and, well, my work will be done at that point. Setting the fuses will be the last thing I'll do. If anything goes wrong . . ."

There was a collective gasp that lasted for no more than two seconds before Death Wind jumped up and said, "I set."

A general hubbub ensued, which Doc did his best to quell. "Very commendable of you to volunteer, but in light of the fact that I'm the oldest and therefore the most expendable I think I should be the one to take the task to hand."

Now there was more jabbering and disorder. Scott had to shout to be heard. "You can't, Doc. We need your experience when we attack the city. Once I get the missiles in working order Rusty can handle the programming."

"Now, wait a minute, Scott. If you had to you could work out the computations."

"Oh, sure, I can fumble through and maybe get it right, but can we afford to take that chance? You're the one who tutored *me*, remember? We can count on you to get it right the first time. And we can't let Death Wind try it because we need him to get us to the city—through that jungle."

"All of a sudden everybody's a hero." Sandra banged her spoon on her plate. "You'd think they were giving away gold stars, or something, the way you guys are jumping at the chance to get yourselves blown up. Why don't we decide this democratically?"

"What do you have in mind, my dear?"

"Obviously, you'll have to let me do it. I'm the only one who's not indispensable. I can't do anything but shoot a gun and run my mouth. And nobody likes me anyway, so there won't be any hard feelings if I go sky-high."

"There is no doubt about your querulousness," Doc said dryly, "but that is no reason to say that we don't love you, each in our own way. I, myself, am quite fond of you—in a grandfatherly fashion. And I'm sure these young men all feel a certain, shall we say, attachment, toward you. Am I right?" But he went on quickly before either of them could agree—or object. "Besides, the ultimate success of our venture rests more with you than with any one of us. There is one task that only you can perform, one that will require a great amount of courage on your part."

"Oh, yeah? And what's that?"

"You can have children."

For the first time since he had known her, Sandra was struck dumb. Red with embarrassment, she spit and sputtered and gesticulated wildly—but not a word would come out. Finally, all dignity fled, she ran out of the room in a rage.

Then the four men laughed uproariously. There was room for humor no matter how serious the situation.

Eventually, Death Wind had the most winning argument. It was not because he was any less valuable, but because no one could find any fault in his reasoning. He merely pulled his long-bladed knife out of its sheath, held it threateningly before their faces, and said, "I set."

He got the job.

CHAPTER 17

"Doc, don't move." Doc opened his eyes and saw Rusty creeping slowly toward him. He had grown so used to his two ground-floor rooms that he disdained against moving to another sleeping cubicle in the lower levels. "I think I've found it."

"Found what?" He sat bolt upright and shook himself free of his lethargy.

"The spare radar antenna." Rusty put his hand on Doc's shoulder and prevented him from moving.

"I knew it would turn up. Where was it?"

Rusty brushed away some of the palm fronds that comprised Doc's mattress and exposed the gleaming metal underneath. "You've been sleeping on it."

"Oh, my." He looked down between his legs and saw the overlapping vanes, the edges tinged with rust.

Rusty helped him out of bed. "Careful. We don't want to bend the metal."

"I knew I was close to the solution, but . . ."

"It's all right." Rusty lifted it up and shook the dried matting to the concrete floor. "It's not damaged—you had it padded pretty well. I found the receiver down below in an open crate, so I knew you had been in it."

"It must have been when I first found this haven." By that time Rusty was already out the door with his prize. Since he no longer had a bed, Doc decided it was time to get up and help.

Later, while Doc supervised the setting up of the antenna, Death Wind and Sandra did the actual labor. Several hundred yards from the missile complex Death Wind climbed the highest tree on the highest hill and sheared away the upper branches. To this he lashed a metal conduit, like stepping a mast, on which was mounted an electric motor with a coupling.

On the ground the receiving horn was attached to the parabolic reflector, where Sandra spliced the electrical leads. Ropes were strung from the antenna to the tops of the adjacent

trees. Then Scott and Rusty turned out to help hoist it into
position. Death Wind climbed up the tree that was to be the
tower, and with the others pulling on the ropes from the side,
the whole affair, including a short spar and the trailing wires,
was lifted to the uppermost point. With three guide wires
maintaining its vertical attitude, Death Wind wrapped his legs
around the peeling trunk and with well-toned arm and shoulder
muscles he pushed it straight overhead and let the spar down
into the rotor aperture. Once the power leads were connected,
the antenna could be rotated three hundred sixty degrees to give
full coverage.

While the control work was being attended to by the
electronic wizards, Doc, Death Wind, and Sandra concentrated
on the silo doors. With lubricating oil and elbow grease, they
worked open the rusted glide plates. After pounding and prying
with hammers and chisels, crowbars and come-alongs, all eight
missiles were eventually laid open to the sky. Now it remained
only to attach the proximity fuses.

"Do you want to do this again?" Under Scott's direction,
Death Wind performed the practice maneuver faultlessly for
the fifth time in a row. "I just want you to be sure."

The savage shook his head and handed the mock-up fuse to
Scott. "I am sure." He took a real fuse from its wooden storage
crate and cradled it in the sling around his neck.

Scott slapped him on the shoulder. "Okay. Good luck."

Death Wind put his foot on the upper rung of the maintenance ladder inside the silo. Sandra ran up and knelt in front of
him. "Please be careful." She kissed him lightly on the
forehead, then joined the others and went below to watch the
delicate operation from the control room. The video camera
was set up so in case something went wrong they could learn
from Death Wind's mistakes.

"I'm praying for you, lad." Doc felt his own tension
mounting, as if he were right in there with the Nomad, setting
the fuse. He looked incongruous wearing a tool pouch over his
loincloth, and working on a sophisticated device that might be
the cause of his immolation, when until recently he had never
seen any weapon more advanced than a bow and arrow.

From the staging platform Death Wind manipulated the
various nuts, bolts, springs, and cotter pins with a deftness
learned in the wilds. He was a natural mechanic; tools seemed
to fit into his hand as an extension of his body.

Doc practically jumped out of his seat when he heard the savage's war whoops echoing from the chamber. He disappeared from the video screen in a way that made Doc catch his breath. Then a door burst open down the corridor, and a moment later Death Wind was standing among them.

Sandra was the first to throw her arms around him, followed by Scott and Rusty, laughing and cheering.

Death Wind grinned from ear to ear. He cast a wry face at Sandra. "It was—piece of cake."

After that, the other seven were easy.

"Are you sure this thing works?" Sandra said in a bored tone.

After six days of monitoring the radar screen, Doc was beginning to wonder too if it was functioning. "It must be doing something, or we wouldn't have seen that storm that got Scott so upset."

"Yes, they didn't have those in the training manuals. I didn't know what was going on with all that snow on the screen, and we never had hurricanes in Maccam City." Scott fingered a mode switch for computer verification. "Everything checks out okay. Doc, you've been watching these flyers for years. Is there any pattern to their schedule?"

"None that I've ever been able to determine. Like I said, the average is one or two passages per week. The only thing I know for certain is that they always use the Mississippi River. They either go south to the Gulf, then west to Mexico and north from there; or they go north until they come to a prominent landmark. I suspect they have no navigational aids, so rivers and mountains must be quite useful to them."

Rusty squinted at the dials. "Well, assuming we knock down one of their machines, how soon would they be able to replace it?"

"I would guess at least a year. You see, the temporal transporter has very a small scope. It's not a—box, or anything you would recognize. It's a focal point where a vast amount of energy is discharged in such a way as to rip open the fabric of time. The field of influence is some eight feet in diameter and, from what I've seen, one simply walks into this focal point where the presence of matter causes an instantaneous discharge in the capacitor bank. The capacitors need to be recharged before it can be used again."

"Did you say walked?" Sandra said.

"Once, I saw what I believe was a delegation from the home world—er, time. These were very fat dragons, four of them, wearing capes inlaid with braid and jewels, and they appeared out of nothing in the middle of the warp field. All the capacitors instantly discharged, and it was more than a day before it was used again. I followed these characters around all that time while they made their inspection of the city. Then, they simply walked into the transporter field and vanished— gone back to their own time, to report to their superiors. Although, while I think of it, the terms *backward* and *forward* may have no real meaning in the Einsteinian sense of space-time."

"So what you're saying," Rusty said, "is that anything bigger than eight feet across has to be sent here piecemeal."

"And in addition to all the other necessities that are already scheduled for transport. In order to maintain the status quo—"

"The screen," Death Wind said calmly.

All eyes were instantly riveted to the radar screen. With each sweep of the electronic hand there was a splash of blurry patterns. But now there was one very solid image moving slowly near the perimeter.

Rusty grabbed a chair and threw some switches. "That's no storm front—it's a real target."

"Take it away, Rusty." Scott let him slide his chair in front of the console where he could reach all the controls. The computer viewscreen spewed out distances, altitudes, speeds, course projections, time delays, and coordinates. Rusty's fingers flashed across the keyboard. Scott threw one massive hand switch. "Missile Number One is ready for launch."

"Eat 'em up," Sandra said. Only Doc groaned.

While Rusty was making computations, Scott explained, "In the past all this would have been done automatically. Satellite scanners would compute a continuous intercept program that could be fed into the missile guidance systems with only a thousandth of a second delay. But we have to—"

"It's ready, Scott."

Scott wiped his hands on his tunic. "Well, here goes." He flipped up the protector cap on the red firing button, paused to look once more at Rusty, received a grim nod, and pressed the button home.

The annunciator panel came alive with green lights—the go

ahead. Almost immediately a red light blinked on, flashing a
warning for mechanical override. There was a grinding sound
as of the clashing of gears while the computer waited the
programmed ten-second delay for cancellation of the order.
When it did not come it was forced to carry out its instructions.
The concrete foundations began to vibrate. Ancient plaster
dropped off the walls and ceiling. A roaring explosion reverberated throughout the complex.

Then there was a strange, preternatural silence.

Scott threw up his hands. "It's off. The missile's on its
way."

Amid cheering, Rusty typed instructions that would cause
the computer to print on one of its video screens an overlay of
the area. He pointed to a meandering, snakelike dot matrix
pattern. "That's the Mississippi. And the flyer is coming right
down the middle. The missile will show up as soon as it attains
enough altitude to—"

"There it is! And look at that sucker go." The blip that was
the missile raced across the screen with ever-increasing speed
as its flight path leveled out and more of its fuel expenditure
went to pushing it horizontally. The two electronic signals were
converging rapidly.

There was nothing to do now but sit back and watch, but
Rusty leaned forward and gripped the console tightly. "This is
just like the simulators back home. We've done this a hundred
times, haven't we, Scott? As soon as the two blips touch they'll
disappear. That's the destruct signal."

"There's no evasive action," Scott said.

"They don't even know it's coming." Rusty's fingers
hovered over the keyboard in case the automatic tracing
sensors gave out.

"It appears that the altitude signals have matched," Doc
noticed.

The blips were only a hairsbreadth apart. Quickly they
merged into one, the smaller missile signal swallowed up by
the snowy flyer. Tension gripped Doc's stomach, then·knotted
into despair as the flyer blip continued unabated along the
Mississippi.

"The warhead didn't go off," Scott groaned. "It was a dud."

Rusty sat back heavily. "And we've lost the advantage of
surprise."

Feeling their disappointment, Doc placed a heavy hand on

Rusty's shoulder, and tousled Scott's golden crewcut, now growing long. "You did your best, I'm sure."

Sandra pounded the console top. "Well, don't just sit there. Arm another one. Quick.".

"Wait!" Rusty leaped up out of his seat. All eyes went back to the screen, as if the collective willpower could bring down the craft. And as they watched, the blip slowly faded. With each sweep of the antenna its image became less intense until it disappeared altogether.

"What happened?" Scott said.

"I'll check for a malfunction." Rusty played with the keyboard, his fingers a blur. "Oh, no. I don't believe it." He sat back and stared up at the ceiling, his eyes dancing from the fluorescent lights.

"What is it?" Sandra thwacked him on the back of the head. "Speak up."

Rusty laughed, and shook his head. "There's no malfunction. It's just that I'm used to working on simulated displays, with instantaneous feedback. But in real life the enemy craft doesn't blow up and vanish—it crashes. And the ship stays in contact until it drops below detection range. We made a direct hit, and the flyer sank in the river. Whoopee."

The room burst into a bedlam of cheers, whoops, and backslaps. Even the stoic savage joined the fun. If the flyer held its usual compliment of troops, a hundred dragon soldiers had just been sent to their happy hunting ground.

"I congratulate you all, my young friends."

Scott grinned, and rubbed his hands together. "And this is only the beginning."

CHAPTER 18

"Here comes another one," Scott said smoothly.

Rusty jerked upright in his seat, not even aware that he had fallen asleep. He rubbed his eyes and took control of the attack computer while Scott readied another missile.

"I've got a go on pad two."

Very soon afterward, Rusty lifted his hands from the keyboard. "Fire when ready."

Scott lifted the protector cap. "Do we have time to call the others?"

"I have a hunch they'll be here as soon as the walls of Jericho start tumbling down."

"Okay. Then, here goes." He pressed the button. The warning light flashed, giving them ten seconds to abort the flight. When the time was up the familiar rumbling sound started, and more plaster rained down from the crumbling ceiling. Almost immediately, Death Wind and Sandra ran breathlessly through the open door, followed a few moments later by Doc, hobbling on his cane.

The scene that followed was virtually a replay of the previous occasion. It was almost anticlimactic. The dragon flyer followed the same course up the river.

Doc said, "They are undoubtedly looking for the wreckage of their other machine."

The missile whipped across the screen with extreme speed and unerring accuracy, and intersected the flyer in almost the same place. As before, the blip stayed on the screen a few anxious seconds before fading away. The computer graphics indicated another success.

"Just like a turkey shoot," Sandra said.

"Two down, four to go," Scott said dryly.

Rusty swelled with pride. "If this keeps up the skies will be clear inside of a week. Then we can plan our assault on the city."

"You boys have sure put new spirit into these old bones. In

135

all the years of dragon domination I've never seen such
triumph. I never in my wildest dreams imagined—
imagined . . ." Doc's voice broke off with a tremor, and his
eyes grew glassy.

Rusty's lanky arm encircled the sagging shoulders. "Don't
worry, Doc. This time we've got them on the run."

"I'm beginning to believe you."

It took longer for the next contact. It happened three days
later when Sandra ran into the missile complex screaming,
crying, and bleeding from a nasty gash on her hip.

"They've got Death Wind. They've got him cornered.
You've got to go help him." Fainting from the pain of the
wound, she keeled over and slid down the cement wall.

Doc caught her in his arms. "Oh, my."

Scott got up so fast he knocked his chair over backward.
"Let's go." Rusty ran out after him. He stopped in Doc's
ground-level room long enough to pick up the forty-five, while
Scott donned the power pack. Already beamer blasts could be
heard outside.

Just as they got outside a tree on the perimeter of the clearing
burst into flames. Fire raced up the trunk as palm leaves
crackled into ash. Death Wind leaped from behind it and
charged for the protection of a nearby depression. A bolt of
lightning flashed over his head and discharged its energy
uselessly in the grass a hundred feet beyond. He leaped up and
loosed another arrow, straight into the breast of a soldier
dragon. But the lizard was undaunted, and plucked at the shaft
with its forepaws while hissing in anger and pain. The distance
had been too long for a killing shot.

Coming upon them unawares, Scott and Rusty had the
advantage. The dragon never knew what blew its head off. But
a dozen yards away another dragon returned Scott's beamer
blast with one of its own. It scorched the earth next to Rusty,
but he had not forgotten Death Wind's training and kept in
motion.

Rusty emptied a cartridge into the flank of the dragon. While
it groped wildly in the air, hissing in pain, Scott severed its
neck with a well-aimed shot. Death Wind had already ac-
counted for four dragons with his deadly arrows. One still
moved, and the savage sank another flint-tipped shaft into its
throat. Then it lay still.

The forest was a charnel house of dead bodies and smoldering vegetation. Smoke rose up from the ground where the tall grass had been singed, but the flames were dying out. This jungle was far too damp to support a fire for long. Even the burning tree had been quenched: now its bark smoldered, and black wreaths slowly curled skyward. Death Wind stepped close to the last dragon he had shot and recovered his arrows from the still warm corpse.

Scott looked down at the elongated neck, bent around backward so the top of the scaly skull touched the bony protuberance of the back. "What happened?"

"Dragon lie in wait. Sandra and I walk, pick flower. Then they shoot. We dodge, and shoot back. I cover for Sandra while she go for help. You arrive in time."

"I think you would have taken care of them anyway."

"How is Sandra?"

Rusty blew on the hot barrel. "She's got a pretty nasty burn on the—"

Before Rusty could finish a titanic explosion rent the forest, knocking all three of them backward. Metal shrapnel, slivers of wood, and chunks of bloody gore flew up in all directions, and dropped back down.

"What the heck—" Rusty uncovered his face, but another explosion cut him off. This time they all fell to the ground in a heap. When the debris settled Rusty saw his companions covered with blood. "Scott! Death Wind! What happened? How badly are you hurt?"

"I'm not hurt at all, but you are."

Rusty looked down at his own body, and gasped. He was covered with blood, but a finger wipe revealed that it was not his own. It was dragon blood!

Scott got to his feet. "Hey, somebody's dropping bombs on us. Let's get out of—"

Another explosion took place, this time farther away.

Death Wind took the others by the collar and dragged them back to the bunker. "Dragon blow up."

"They haven't hit anything but their own soldiers."

Rusty stopped by the door. "No, don't you see." Two more explosions went off almost simultaneously. A tall palmetto dropped to the ground as if it had been felled by the blow of a giant's axe. "It's the power packs. They're blowing up."

As they watched, the last dragon warrior that had died with

Death Wind's arrow in its throat burst apart in a fury of blood
and guts.

"But how?"

"I don't know, but there's not enough of them left to find
out. Maybe Doc can tell us."

Scott paused at the doorway. "Death Wind, did any get
away?"

"They are all dead."

Rusty scowled. "What troubles me is, I don't think they
found us by accident."

Inside, Sandra lay on the cot Doc was using as a replacement
for the confiscated radar antenna. He put the finishing touches
on her wound when they walked in.

"Don't make such a fuss, girl. It's a superficial burn that
took off a few dermal layers."

"That's easy for you to say, old man. You're only looking at
it."

"Is she going to be all right?" Scott said.

"Where's Death Wind?" As soon as she saw him step
through the doorway she cried, "Death Wind," and pushed
Doc aside as she jumped to her feet. She threw her arms around
the savage, and sobbed softly.

"She must be all right, Scott."

"Of course I'm all right. But, what happened to you?" In
disgust she drew her hands away from Death Wind. They were
wet and gory. "You look awful."

"How about if you lie down and let me put a bandage on that
wound?" Doc pulled Sandra back to the cot and eased her
down. He took up his ministrations where he had left off.

"Well, what are you guys gaping at? Haven't you ever seen
a girl's skin before?" Doc had cut away the dinosaur hide all
the way up the side.

Scott stifled a snicker. "Not that part of it."

"Oh, you men!"

"My dear, would you please control your temper. The
increased blood pressure is likely to prevent the necessary
clotting."

"I can't help it. I'm mad. I should have known better than to
go out without my gun. Next thing I know a beamer blast hits
me below the belt and sets my clothes on fire. While I'm
rolling on the ground to put out the flames Death Wind has to
tackle a whole squad single-handed. I was about as much help

as a barnacle. I had to get up and run for help. Me, running away."

"The practical thing to do, under the circumstances. Even if it did leave Death Wind in a somewhat vulnerable position."

She shoved Doc away. "Yeah, well, what did you expect me to do, lay there and fry."

"Ah, the beamer must have affected your hearing, too, since you heard something other than what I said. I repeat for your benefit: it was the practical thing to do under the circumstances."

"Yeah, well, I don't like your tone of voice."

"Please do not read into my statement meanings that stray from what I've said. Now, may I please get this bandage on?"

Her eyes burned like fire, but she let Doc place the gauze across the burn. She redirected her anger at Scott. "I'm glad to see you two could drag yourselves away from your precious computer."

"It was safer out there than it is in here," Scott said.

"You shut up, you, or I'll launch one of those missiles down your throat."

"Why don't you let the doctor handle the tonsillectomies?"

"Please, please, please." Doc smoothed adhesive tape over Sandra's thigh. "Can we put an end to this banter and try to evaluate the situation? My dear, you can get up now, but don't do any obtuse bending. The glue on these bandages is long since out-of-date. Now, tell me what has occurred, other than that you successfully vanquished the enemy."

As Sandra vacated the cot to stand by Death Wind's side, Doc sat down and swung his bad leg into a comfortable position. Without interruption he listened as Scott and Rusty cleaned themselves off with rags and outlined the incidents of the fight. When they were done he sat quietly for many minutes, stroking his white beard. His eyes became narrow, coal-black discs, his lips a tautly drawn line. When he spoke, it was with a deep, reproachful voice.

"I must apologize for a grievous error in judgment. I've underestimated these devils, and now they've stolen a march on us. I did not anticipate such shrewdness, perspicacity, or adaptability in the plodding dragon brain. Slow thinking they may be, but stupid they are not."

Sandra leaned back against Death Wind and stared up at the ceiling. "Can you speak plain English for once?"

Doc pursed his lips. "Yes, well, it seems that while we've been sitting here waiting for them to put up another target for us, they've taken the initiative to investigate the demise of their machines. The fact that they discovered us so quickly and so easily demonstrates both their understanding of the situation and the capability of their science. Once their suspicions were aroused they triangulated our position and dispatched a patrol to probe the area in question. The booby-trapped beamers proves the precautionary measures they've developed. I would not be surprised now if a signal were also sent back to their high command."

"To make a long story short, it's time to hit the road."

"I'm afraid that sums it up. After all, we're fighting a guerrilla war, and the task of a guerrilla is to hit and run: mobility is the key to success. I haven't thought along those terms for so long that I've let it slip my mind."

"But we can't leave now," Scott said. "The greatest weapon we have is at our fingertips. If we lose it we may never have another chance."

"An unfortunate circumstance, my friend, but perhaps the only viable one."

"Good. Let's stop playing computer games and go in for the kill."

"My dear, please try to constrain your vivacity. Let's think this thing through before we jump from the frying pan into the fire."

"I think she's right," Rusty said. "I think we should attack."

"What did you do, pick up an extra backbone out there?"

Rusty ignored her. "For the last few days I've been—well—playing computer games. I've been trying to work out a self-operating program. The problem is that with only one radar antenna I only have single line feedback. But now I know something else: all the flyers, sooner or later, must enter or leave the city. By having the radar stationary, and aimed at the city, I can have the computer launch a missile automatically as soon as one of them tries to take off, or comes within range.

"But wait! I can also design an auxiliary program that will fire the missiles at will, and I can rig up a homing beacon that the guidance control will respond to. We can launch our two extra missiles directly at the city—*and blow up the time transporter!*"

There was a moment of dazed silence while this idea was

digested. The result of such a plan, however, was obvious: for then no more supplies, weapons, or dragons could be sent from the past. The outpost would be isolated.

Doc raised bushy eyebrows. "Please excuse my ignorance but, how does this homing beacon work?"

Rusty was nonchalant. "Well, it's really very simple. It's just a radio transmitter set on a preselected wavelength. When it's actuated the computer will treat it as a target and home in on it. I've got enough spare electronics from storage to—"

"I don't think I understand. How does it inform the computer where the target is? How do you point it?"

"You don't point it, you place it. You have to put it *on* the target."

"Now we're talking turkey. Let's bust into that city and show 'em we mean business."

Doc was still cautious. "It's not as easy as it sounds."

"I don't care. Rusty's plan gives us the chance to get in there and find my mother."

Doc sighed. "Tell me, what is the explosive force of these warheads? How much earth and rock can it blast through?"

This was Scott's department. "These missiles are designed to knock down opposing aircraft or missiles. It doesn't have to obliterate its target, just make it aerodynamically unstable enough to cause it to crash. I'd say it won't penetrate more than a few feet of rock. Why?"

"Because the time warp equipment, and the transporter room, are conveniently located inside a mountain, with only a narrow tunnel entrance."

Rusty thought for a moment, and tried not to show his dejection. "Well, we can still drop two missiles on the city and cause some damage."

"Not until we find out where my mother is."

Doc used his best bedside manner. "Child, would you please listen to me. It grieves me to have to say this to you, but for your own good I must. You can't keep thinking of your mother as being alive."

"She *is* alive. I know what I saw."

"She may have been alive when you saw her last, but remember who are her captors. I'm afraid the best you can hope for—is that she died quickly."

Sandra stared at him with daggers in her eyes. Torture was something no one wanted to think about, but why else would the dragons want to capture an enemy they had tried so hard to annihilate? Perhaps they were using human subjects for some inhuman experiments.

Scott interrupted. "Wait a minute. I've got an idea."

Doc looked at him, sighing again. "Whenever one of you boys comes up with an idea I get the strangest feeling in the pit of my stomach. I know this is going to scare me, but please proceed."

"Well, we've got two missiles that are nonfunctional—at least as far as missiles. But there's nothing wrong with the warheads. We can take out the explosive canisters, drop the other two missiles somewhere else in the city to create a diversion, then sneak into the cave with the time transporter, and set off the charges electrically."

"And while we're in the city we can look for my mother— *before* we set off any bombs."

"You know, you boys are forcing me to think like a warrior again. And to think that I used to plan raids against the dragons."

"You—a fighter." Sandra laughed. "I don't believe it."

"It's true, my dear. That's the only reason I agreed to go along with your schemes in the first place. It takes me back to my own deeds of daring, in my younger years. Killed a dragon or two in my time. But I thought I had retired from all of that. Now it looks as if I'll have to do more than take you *to* the city—I'll have to guide you *through* it."

"All we need is the map," Rusty said. "You can draw it for us."

"No, I must do more than that. As I stated before, I would like to be there at the finish. I feel—I feel the old scout in me resurfacing. After listening to you two my heart is full of the old enthusiasm, my mind is full of ideas. I—I want to do something. I've fought against the dragons all my life, but never before have I had such an opportunity as this."

Doc paused for a moment, put his leg down on the floor, then stood up and tested his weight on it. "Even the pain is gone, now that I no longer need it as an excuse. Yes, and I'm beginning to think along the old lines." He lowered his voice to a confidential whisper. "Listen to me, this is what we're going to do. . . ."

CHAPTER 19

Scott held a small battery in his hands, to which he attached two wires, while Rusty unraveled the extension cord that led to the switch. They both nodded to Doc at the same time; Doc nodded back. Rusty closed the knife switch.

Several hundred yards away a thunderous explosion blew dirt, plaster, and several tons of reinforced concrete into the air. When the roar subsided and the dust settled the only thing left of the above-ground bunker, the entrance to the missile complex, was a mound of unrecognizable rubble.

"That should cover our tracks fairly well," Doc said. "When they send their army out here the next time they'll find nothing but ruins."

Scott coiled the wire over his arm. "Let's hope they don't decide to dig through the debris, or they may find more than they bargained for."

"I certainly hope not, or that would ruin my well-laid plans."

Sandra huffed. "You've already got a lame leg. Try not to break your arm patting yourself on the back."

"I promise to be more reserved in the future. Death Wind, Scott, check all the silo coverings for damage. Sandra, check the antenna."

"I've checked it three times already."

"Thank you, but please check it once more. I know it's well hidden, but I want to make sure the explosion didn't loosen any connections. And make sure the cables are out of sight."

Sandra grumbled, but went anyway.

"Rusty, how is reception?"

Rusty picked up the control box. It was twelve inches square and six inches high. The top panel held a double row of toggle switches and indicator lights, and a ten-keyed numerically assigned input board. He punched in a sequencing code and watched as the tiny globes lit up.

"All my readings are affirmative. And the green light means I'm receiving the signal from the antenna."

"With the radar dish in the thicket, will you still be able to pick it up from the city? Doesn't the drop in elevation affect its range and sensitivity?"

"It depends on the frequency, but we should get atmospheric bouncing like a shortwave radio. And I still have manual control."

"And you're sure it will stay dry in there?"

Rusty placed the control box in a clear plastic container and snapped it shut. "Absolutely. The rubber gasket makes it airtight. It's standard equipment for spare electronic components." When it was securely stuffed in his pack and the straps were cinched tightly, he put the battery and cords in a similar container and put it in Scott's fanny pack.

"What about the explosive canisters?"

"Water won't affect them one way or the other. They're completely stable and can only be set off with a blasting cap."

"Hey, Doc," Scott called out, returning from his errand. "We walked right on top of them and they didn't even creak. Death Wind did a terrific job covering the openings with sticks and brush. Those dragons will need second sight to find the silo openings."

Sandra returned at the same time. "That's what lizards use the other brain for."

"Yes, they say two heads are better than one." Doc climbed to his feet and hoisted up his pack. Now that everything was checked out he was anxious to get underway. "And I guess that goes for brains as well. They may be retarded in hand-to-hand combat, but they are particularly shrewd when given the time to think things through." To Sandra he added, "I take it the antenna survived the concussion?"

Sandra merely scowled. Doc accepted this as an affirmative. The rest donned their packs. Death Wind carried the heavy explosive canisters from the dismantled missiles. Around his waist he knotted a rope which would shift some of the weight off his shoulders and onto his hips.

Doc took the lead, not only because he knew the way but because he had to set the pace within his limits. Rusty settled the delicate electronic equipment more comfortably on his back. "How long will it take us to reach the city?"

"As a young scout, traveling light, I could make it in two

days—swimming part of the way. But now—we've got to take a circuitous route in order to avoid possible dragon war parties; we have heavy loads; we have lakes to cross; and then, we've got an old man not in the best of health. I'd say four days at least."

Hobbling forward on his cane in a rambling, uneasy gait, Doc took a bearing with his compass and set the course. The brush was thick, and clinging vines barred the way. "Death Wind, I think you had better break trail for a while. I'm only carrying the medical kit and already I'm exhausted."

Once pointed in the right direction the savage needed no further bearings, for he steered by the sun. Even in the dense jungle he simply followed the shadows, altering course periodically to make up for the fifteen degree change per hour as the day star traversed the sky.

Scott hung back to talk with Doc. "What's this about the double brains?"

With the cane he knocked limbs and vines out of his path. "It's probably a misnomer to call the spinal enlargements brains. All large dinosaurs have a thickened bundle of nerves at the base of the spinal column, but it was not a thinking brain: it merely controlled movement of the hind legs and tail. Some, like the Jurassic stegosaurus, had three brains, the third being in the shoulder."

Sandra, carrying most of the food, the rifle, and the remaining two hundred rounds of ammunition, stayed close to Death Wind. "Doc, look at these trees with flowers on them."

"They're dogwoods, my dear." They were only a few minutes on their way and already the jungle was becoming denser, more luxuriant, and more tropical. "The dragons come from a magnificent era in Earth's history, for it was a time of change. Conifers still ruled the plant world, but deciduous trees and flowering plants were coming into their own. The age of ferns was giving way to laurel and sassafras, magnolias, and dogwood. It was what you might call the best of both worlds."

Death Wind had his knife out now, and used it like a machete to cut through the thickening vegetation. Underfoot, the ground became soft and squishy. Logs and tree trunks were dotted with large crawling insects. Flying bugs buzzed everywhere, and high in the treetops lizard birds cawed raucously from their sanctuary.

"Doc, what about the brains?"

"What? Oh, yes. Well, I've dissected more than one dragon in my time: their carcasses were always left to rot when we managed a kill and returned several days later. They have a thinking brain that is quite a bit smaller than ours, although just as complex. But since they have two other brains to handle motor coordination it can all be used for cogitation and interpreting the senses. It's very concise in that respect, and accounts for their rise above the beasts of the time. But it lacks efficiency because of the time lag while messages are being passed between the fore brain and the secondary brains.

"It's like a military chain of command, where the general tells the colonel who tells the major who tells the captain who tells the lieutenant who tells the sergeant who tells the corporal who tells the private. By the time the message reaches the worker the information is outdated. Dragons have the same trouble catching you in their sights as you have in trying to catch a butterfly. Your eyes can follow the insect, but by the time you instruct your hand where to grab, it's no longer there."

The land dipped considerably, and the dense mass slurped at every step. Their moccasins soaked through, but it did not matter. They waded knee deep through a bog with an oozing, muddy bottom. The water was stagnant, and stank with marsh grass. Rotting logs and stumps blocked their way. And the insects grew larger.

"Halt." Death Wind's command was soft, but urgent. Sandra unslung her rifle and crouched beside him. She chambered a round and thumbed the safety. Death Wind forced the barrel down into the ground. "Do not shoot."

"What is it?" Doc drew up behind the savage. He looked out over the pond, but saw nothing. Scott and Rusty likewise peered over his shoulder, scanning the water. There was not so much as a ripple.

On the other side of the pond, a scant hundred feet away, the trees parted. Out stepped a bipedal dinosaur, fifteen feet in height and counterbalanced by a long, thick tail. With jerky motions of its stocky forepaws it pulled leaves off a willow tree and stuffed them into its drooling mouth. The sun shone down and reflected off smooth, brown skin. The curious skull was a rounded, bony knob two feet long, half of which was forehead. Around the eyes protruded a collection of nasty-looking spines and bumps.

"A bonehead," Doc whispered. "Not particularly dangerous unless you happen to frighten it."

"Will it run if we make some noise?" Scott asked.

"Probably not. Generally speaking, dinosaurs with armor attack anything that threatens them. It's a survival instinct that protects them from the carnivorous predators of their own time."

Sandra fingered the trigger. "So what do we do? Sit here like boobs and wait for it to go away?"

Doc was unruffled. "Either that, or walk around it. Experience has taught me never to attack them unnecessarily. It is that warlike aggression you harbor that has caused mankind so much discontent in his internecine past."

"Cut with the philosophy and let's do something."

"Well, if you won't accept my advice, why don't you ask Death Wind for his opinion."

She did. Death Wind's curt comment was, "Wait." So, they waited. It seemed as if the bone-headed dinosaur would never fill its monstrous stomach. It browsed noisily, ripping and tearing limbs off trees with its paws, then chewing off the leaves with long, flattened teeth. After a half hour it had eaten its way through enough jungle so that it was out of sight, although not out of hearing. Cautiously, the war party made its way around the pond and veered off diagonally away from the feeding animal. Sandra grumbled the whole time.

Rusty slapped at his face. "Ouch!" Grimacing comically, he pulled away a two-inch-long, partly squashed beetle that had dropped on him from above. A sticky ichor oozed out of the crushed abdomen. He tossed it away as if it were poisonous. "I don't think I'm going to like this."

"I think you're going to hate it." Scott laughed, then slapped his arm. "Beetles I can live with, but I don't like all these mosquitoes."

"Here, let me show you a trick." Doc looked around until he found a bright green, treelike plant with a broad, flat leaf that was a tiny parasol some eighteen inches in diameter. Breaking it off at the stem, he crumpled it up in his hands until they were coated with a sickly green liquid. Then he rubbed his hands over his face, neck, and exposed portions of his lower legs, and around his waist where his shirt left a gap. "It's not exactly the scent of perfume, but take my word for it that most of the insects will like it even less."

Following his example, they all applied a generous portion to their bodies. "Need any help?" Scott said to Sandra, while she was rubbing it on her midriff.

"If you lay a hand on me you'll regret it. Yeech!" She pulled a multi-legged creature resembling a toy tank from under her blouse, and hurled it to the ground. "I don't mind dragons or dinosaurs, but these things give me the creeps."

As the sun dropped lower in the sky and the jungle grew darker, the fauna grew louder and more bold. The air was filled with a cacophony of barks, howls, and shrieks. Four-legged dinosaurs abounded. Some were the size of squirrels, and lived in the trees. Others were the size of alligators. Some danced rapidly out of the way, others squatted, or clung vertically to the smooth bark of trees with needlelike claws, and watched with apparent unconcern as the people walked by.

Doc arched his neck and peered up at the purple, cloudless sky. "I think we'd better look for a place to camp."

Sandra said, "I haven't seen a place flat enough or dry enough to stand on, much less lie down."

"You haven't been looking in the right places. It isn't safe to spend the night on the ground. What we need is a nice, comfortable perch."

CHAPTER 20

"This is for the birds." Sandra straddled two thick boughs a hundred feet above the jungle floor. While Death Wind busily cut off branches with his knife, the others tied them with vines athwart a framework of heftier, parallel branches.

"I thought you liked living out on a limb." Scott leaned against the trunk of the giant oak and twisted several creepers together to make a stout rope.

"Can't you do anything without making wisecracks?"

"Someone has to make up for your gloom. Say, did anyone ever show you how to smile?"

Sandra flashed a mouthful of even, white teeth with something more like a grimace than a grin. She brushed her silky hair out of her face and shoved a hacked-off branch at Scott, thwacking him in the abdomen.

"If you two are done trading witticisms, and have completed your work on the upper berths, you can come down for some food." Doc looked up from a lower limb, where he felt his climbing expertise had been sufficiently strained.

"Be right down." Scott drew a tight knot around the last set of branches, and put the finishing touches on the sleeping platform. Now it was ready for a makeshift mattress of soft leaves. That was soon accomplished, and the three of them climbed down to where Doc and Rusty sat on a lower platform. He had the food out and ready for distribution.

"Ah, just like the good old days." Using a small penknife he sliced off several pieces of meat, passed them around, and chomped into a large chunk he left for himself.

The climbing had not bothered him as much as he had thought it would: there was still plenty of strength left in those old arms, and he delighted in the exertion of pulling himself upward. His leg was propped up perfunctorily, but exercise and incentive had done much to ease the pain.

Dark clouds were rolling in, eclipsing the low sun even more

than the tall trees and dense foliage. A welcome coolness
accompanied the early dusk.

"We'll have to be careful from here on in. We're near the
stockades where the domesticated dinosaurs are kept. And that
means there will be guards around the perimeter; only a few,
but they'll be armed." Doc looked directly at Sandra. "We
don't want to announce our presence, so we'll do everything
we can to avoid trouble."

Sandra ignored him, but Scott said, "Hey, did you hear
that?" There was a plopping sound overhead, then another,
then many. "What's going on?" The pattering increased in
intensity for a minute. Scott looked up. "Hey, something's
dripping on me."

Rusty held out his hand. "It's—water. The leaves up there
must be leaking."

Sandra let out a loud guffaw. "Don't tell me you guys have
never seen rain before?"

"Well, uh, as a matter of fact—" Scott caught some of the
large drops in his mouth.

"I would heartily suggest that we seek the protection of our
beds, or we're likely to get very wet—and cold." Doc crawled
into his aerie with the rest of his meal, where the broad leaves
of the mattress quickly became umbrellas. There he spent the
rest of the night shivering slightly from the sudden drop in
temperature—and scratching from the number of insects that
desired to share his shelter.

He awoke stiff and cold, and was happy to get underway.
The ground was soggier than ever, and the air clammy. It took
an hour for him to warm up. Then they stopped at a small
rivulet of fresh water for breakfast.

Doc smelled the green, algae-filled liquid. "We have to be
careful what we drink now. Much of the water is polluted by
the outflow of the pens." He pointed a quivering finger at a
structure that was barely visible through the moss-covered
trees.

At first it looked like a wall of gold, but that was just a trick
of the sun. Without the glare it was dull orange. Ten feet high,
and broader at the base than at the top, it wound sinuously
through the jungle without true definition. It was made of a
material that was basically amorphous, but covered with ropy
contours.

"Plastic. It's extruded from nozzles and poured without a

mold until it conforms approximately to the shape they want. The dragons do not care about art or architecture—only form and function."

As they walked along the wall the squeaks and bellows of dinosaurs on the other side could be heard. Doc led them away from the alien structure.

"There used to be houses and highways here a hundred years ago—even a few good-sized towns. Now, there's no trace of human habitation. What time hasn't destroyed, the dragons have demolished. They level an area with their disruptor beams, let the wind cover it with sand and dirt, then seed it according to their own specifications." His voice took on a tone of sadness. "They've not only exterminated mankind, they've obliterated every vestige of his civilization."

"And we're gonna take it back. They'll be sorry they ever set foot in *this* time."

"My dear, why do you have such pent-up—hatred?"

"What should I have—love for what they've done to me, and my life. Do you think I like skulking around in this jungle, in this heat, in this filthy water? Do you think I like having to fight to survive? Well, damn it, I don't. I hate the dragons, and I hate everything about them. And I'd like to blow every damn reptile off the face of the earth."

"Surely you don't mean that? Remember that our enemies are the dragons, not a herd of dull-witted dinosaurs."

"Yeah? Maybe you should remember it yourself. A little hatred wouldn't hurt you. It might even make you more dedicated."

Doc's voice showed no anger. "My loyalty is not in question. Nevertheless, I don't hate the dragons any more than I hate a growth of cancerous cells. I recognize that they must be removed in order to ensure my own survival. They are merely a force to be reckoned with."

"Then let's stop arguing and start reckoning."

Scott said, "Sandra, I think you and I agree again."

"Good. Then let's go."

"Yes. Let's." Doc knew that the dispute was futile. They both had the same aims, but their motivations were different. Still, he would rather have her on his side than against him.

As they trudged along the jungle thinned out until it was more of a swamp: watery lowlands with aquatic plant life interspersed with slightly elevated drylands on which abounded groves of oak and willow, with a few palms at the water's edge.

The procession continued on a course parallel with the orange, plastic wall. Several times they stopped and climbed up the massive oak trunks in order to peer over the top. Subdivisions kept different kinds of dinosaurs apart. Doc named a few of them, but many were species unknown to human paleontology. It was as strange an array of animal life as one could possibly imagine.

When the sun was straight overhead Death Wind raised his hand and called a halt. There were noises from in front, and he moved up alone to investigate. When he came back, he said, "Big water ahead. Many lizards swim. We need to build raft."

Scott and Rusty started hauling in logs, while Doc hacked vines off nearby trees and dragged them to the bank. Sandra helped Death Wind with the lashings. The lake was half a mile across, and dotted with small, tree-covered islands.

Suddenly Sandra screamed. When Doc looked around, his hackles raised, he saw a huge monster rising up out of the water only a few feet from where Sandra had fallen back. Water dripped off an enormous arched head with a duck-billed mouth. Dull eyes opened and transfixed the girl as she scrambled backward, tripping over a pile of rotting sticks.

She rolled to where she had leaned her rifle against a tree, swung it around, and was tightening her grip on the trigger when Doc plopped down beside her. He pushed the barrel up into the air.

"Don't waste your ammunition. It's only a harmless tracodon."

With a flurry of leaves and underbrush Scott arrived with the beamer trained on the fearful head. Death Wind had drawn his bow, but at Doc's command lowered it slowly.

"They're not usually belligerent. When caught on land they tend to run away. And in the water they're safe from their natural predators. It's only curious."

"Yeah, well, its curiosity scared the daylights outa me."

The massive head moved toward them as if on a conveyor belt. It rose higher out of the green water until the neck appeared, then the thickened body. Small hands came into view, but the beast then started submerging until only the top of its head, its eyes, and the glossy upper surface of the flattened bill showed. It stared at them.

"I used to swim across these lakes, and never had one bother me. They're really very docile, and sometimes quite playful. They have powerful hind legs with webbed feet, which they use for swimming. They used to glide gracefully alongside me, like ducklings after their mother."

"Thanks for the nature talk, but I'm not swimming in this lake with that thing in there."

The tracodon backed away and when it reached deeper water it submerged so slowly that only the barest trace of a ripple showed where it had gone.

"Of course you're not, my dear. We can't afford to let that wound get wet or it will become infected, so you'll have to ride on the raft with the rest of the baggage."

And that is what she did. Sitting astride the packs and weapons, she acted as lookout while Death Wind, Scott, and Rusty paddled alongside and pushed the raft. Doc trailed off the rear of a long vine: he was not up to pushing, but neither did he want to be a drag. He was able to swim for himself.

During the crossing they were not bothered at all by tracodons, although several smaller swimming reptiles left wakes under the surface. Once away from the banks, where the green algae tended to grow thick, like a sludge on the water, the lake became bright blue and crystal clear. Logs and stumps could be seen on the bottom, as well as some of the larger denizens.

"Remember, the dragons brought no carnivorous dinosaurs with them," Doc said, to instill confidence. "Unless some sneaked through, of course."

They camped that night on a dry, raised knoll, where Doc assured them they would be safe. The more hostile dinosaurs, like the triceratops and styracosaurs, liked the dry, open plains. The scurrying reptiles of the lush jungle were behind them, while those that inhabited the swamps lurked in solitude, avoiding contact.

The stars came out and lit up the sky with their silvery, twinkling brilliance. And later, the waxing moon arose, casting long shadows on the ground. They could not afford themselves a fire because it might be spotted by dragon guards. Yet, they experienced a tranquility and warmth that could only come from close companionship. There was a serenity of thought that belied their differences of opinion, and the seriousness of their mission.

Doc was almost asleep when he heard Sandra yelp. "Hey, what did you mean by 'the rest of the baggage'?"

CHAPTER 21

For two days the party prowled through the marsh: swatting insects, rubbing on leaf sap, sweating it off, and swatting more insects. The water became more and more polluted as they neared the city, so whenever they could they ascended to high ground, and dry ground. But so did many of the smaller reptiles, and they became an increasing problem by their sheer numbers.

On the final approach there lay a series of wooded hills that were rough and cragged, and separated by long shallow lakes which, because of their elevation, had escaped the contamination of the lowlands. While the clean water was welcome, each crossing meant the time-consuming construction of another raft.

One of these lakes was bordered by a low cliff line some ten feet high, with no beach on which to land. Finding a place where the rocks created a broken ledge a body's length above the algae-filmed surface, Sandra held the raft close while one by one the others climbed out of the water, onto the raft, and up the rock face. Death Wind let Sandra climb up before him so he could pass up the packs.

Once the raft was emptied, the Nomad severed the vines that held the logs together and let the timbers float away. It would not do to have something so obviously manmade discovered by dragon patrols.

Doc surveyed the area. "I believe we are very near, perhaps just over the next rise."

They rested for several minutes in the tall grass, picking leeches off their skin and squeezing their clothes dry. Sandra peered ahead, always on guard. Then they donned their packs and prepared to move on.

A stick cracked in the forest. Doc heard a faint hiss. In the fading light from a setting, orange sun shadows moved softly behind a line of trees. Thick bodies and long necks were vague silhouettes moving through green foliage.

"Dragons," Sandra whispered. They dropped flat into the cover of the waving green blades.

Doc heard the click of the safety. "Careful. Let them pass."

"No way. This is what I came here to do."

Doc reached over and deftly disengaged the cartridge clip from the rifle. But Sandra always had one round chambered, and that shot would be enough to give them away.

Sandra rolled out of his reach. "Damn you." By this time the dragons had withdrawn into the protection of the trees. She pulled another clip from the bandolier.

Death Wind loomed over the top of her, bent slightly under the weight of his pack. With fingers like steel springs he wrenched the rifle out of her hands. Sandra was too startled to do anything more than grunt. When she recovered from her surprise she reached out for the gun and kicked with her powerful legs.

The moccasined feet struck the savage in the solar plexus. Caught off guard, air puffed from his lungs as if from a bellows. He stumbled backward and caught his heel, the weight of the explosive canisters in his pack bringing him down. As he twisted sideways and placed a hand on the ground for support, the pack was still levering him over. He slipped on the moss and in an instant he tumbled over the brink and cartwheeled into the water with a resounding splash.

Doc scrambled through the grass to peer over the edge. There was no sign of Death Wind, only the sloshing, stirred-up algae. The pack dragged the savage right down to the bottom. The splashing stopped and settled down. Ripples cascaded gently against the base of the rock wall. The water became still. Nothing moved.

"Do something!" Sandra screamed, heedless of the retreating dragons.

Without thinking, Scott wriggled out of his pack straps, stood up on the top of the cliff, and dove. He carved a small hole in the smooth surface of the lake, then was gone. Long moments passed with no further movement other than dying ripples. Doc strained his eyes, but could see nothing below. It was as if the lake had swallowed them both.

Anxious moments later, as the water cleared, a dark shape could be seen through the patchy algae. As it grew larger Doc could make out flailing arms. Then a blond head broke the surface and sputtered for air.

Scott splashed from side to side. "Where's Death Wind?" Without waiting for an answer he took a quick, deep breath, and dived again. This time the water had not had time to settle before he reappeared, clutching the savage's inert body. Cradling his head so it was out of the water, Scott did a one-sided dog paddle until he came to the rock wall. But from this level it was impossible to climb up—and the raft had already been broken up.

"I can't hold him," Scott said between gasps. He coughed and sank, then clawed his way to the surface again. Rusty jumped into the water and grabbed hold of Scott. "Get him, not me."

Rusty paddled around and took Death Wind by the shoulder. Together they kept him up. Then a vine dropped into the water and fell across the savage's unmoving chest.

"Tie it under his arms," Doc ordered.

Rusty found a finger grip on the smooth rock and held on tightly enough to take the burden from Scott. He immediately began looping the vine around Death Wind's chest, under the armpits, and in a knot in front. He fumbled more than he should have, kicking and staying afloat at the same time.

"Pull him up," Scott shouted.

Death Wind's face lost its ruddy hue, and was slowly purpling. It was obvious to Doc that he had stopped breathing. He and Sandra pulled, Scott and Rusty pushed. The body came up out of the water by inches: far too slowly, and with far too much effort. Doc knew that he and the girl did not have the strength necessary to haul up the weight of a fully grown man.

"This isn't working. Let him down," Doc said. He wasted no more time. As soon as he was sure that Sandra had a good grip on the vine, he held his nose and leaped into the water. He came up right away, and one stroke put him in touch with the struggling trio. Now Scott and Rusty held onto the vine for additional support. They kept Death Wind's face out of the water.

Doc floated between Scott and the savage. Pinching Death Wind's nose with his fingers and tilting his head, he placed his mouth over the other's. He blew deeply, watched the bronze chest expand, released his mouth, and felt warm air expel slowly from the lungs. He blew into Death Wind's mouth again, watched the chest expand, let him exhale. He did it again—and again—and again, while the rest waited in anguish for some result, for some sign of life.

"The water's full of blood," Sandra shrieked. Then, she snugged the rope around a rock outcrop.

Doc wondered only briefly about the noise they had made, and the proximity of the dragons. Then Death Wind went into convulsions, his body jerked spasmodically, and almost pulled him underwater. But Doc held him up, and turned his head to one side as water and vomit spurted from his mouth. The surface of the lake was a witch's brew of bile and green algae stained red with blood.

Death Wind stopped convulsing, and merely gagged. But at least he kept breathing. His body suddenly went limp. His eyes opened to a narrow slit, but rolled up inside their sockets. The constricture cleared itself from his throat, and he passed out, breathing lightly.

"Climb up the vine," Doc said. Scott scaled the wall easily. Rusty had a little more trouble, but as soon as he got within reach Scott extended a hand and pulled him up the rest of the way. Doc pulled the rope up under Death Wind's arms so it would not tighten on the chest. "All right, now pull."

Pulling together, they hauled him up the ten-foot rock wall until he was almost at the top. Leaving Sandra holding the vine, Scott and Rusty grabbed the limp form and dragged him onto the soft grass.

Doc waited awhile before calling out. "Excuse me, but could someone please throw me a line?" He calmly treaded water and awaited his rescue. Scott slipped the vine from around the savage's body and dropped it to the doctor. He climbed into the loop and allowed himself to be hauled up the rock face while he scrabbled for footholds. Then he squirmed over the brink. "Are there—any dragons—about?"

"I forgot all about them," Scott said.

"They'd have been here by now if they had heard anything," Rusty said.

"Doc." Sandra cradled Death Wind's head in her lap, and combed the matted hair from his forehead. There were tears in her eyes. "He's got blood all over him."

Doc crawled on hands and knees, and lifted the savage's eyelid. "It's all right, my dear. It's not internal." With practiced fingers he examined the gash on Death Wind's abdomen. "It's not deep, but it will take some tending to."

"It was the waist rope," Scott said. "He couldn't get out of the pack, so he cut the knot with his knife. I got there in time to help him out of the shoulder harness and push him to the surface, but he must have passed out on the way up."

Lying restfully in the warmth of Sandra's lap, Death Wind's eyes flickered open for a moment. He coughed, spitting up water. Then he rolled over and tried to climb to his feet.

Sandra clung to him, and Doc gently pushed him back. So weak was the Nomad that he could not resist Doc's gentle pressure. "Rest now. Just rest."

"I'm sorry. I—I'm sorry." A tear fell from Sandra's eye, rolled down her cheek, and dripped onto Death Wind's broad, naked chest. "I didn't mean to—please forgive me."

Death Wind nodded faintly, closed his eyes, and fell asleep. Sandra continued to cry. "I didn't mean to. I didn't mean to—now I've ruined everything."

"My dear, life is like a soap bubble: a thin and tenuous film buoyed up by a moving, unstable force. It is the most fragile thing in the universe and, once burst, can never be repaired. But his life force is strong. His bubble is safe." Doc patted him on the arm, as if to share a secret between them. "Let us all be thankful for that."

They made camp where they were, while Doc dressed the laceration with first-aid supplies from his pack.

Sandra was inconsolable: she would not allow Death Wind to be moved from her lap. She spent the entire night in a crouched, uncomfortable position, dozing fitfully, and awakening whenever her patient moved. She stroked his hair absently.

"I'm so sorry."

CHAPTER 22

The morning sun had barely cleared the sky of its reddish glow when Scott dived off the rock ledge with a coil of freshly cut vine peeling out behind him. He cleaved the water with a splash, and started kicking.

He held his breath during the descent, working quickly on the bottom to locate his objective and perform his job. The water was still for almost a minute before he casually came to the surface and shook his head clear. Triumphantly, for all to see, he held up in one hand a bow and a quiver of arrows. "And the knife." He held up the other hand and let the sun glint off the steel blade. Then he slung the bow and quiver over one shoulder, put the long blade between his teeth, and scampered up the vine like an agile monkey after a banana.

Scott dropped his treasures to the ground. "I've got the vine through both straps." It took but a moment to haul the pack full of explosives to the surface, over the rock face, and onto the grass.

The pack was still dripping as Death Wind lifted it to his shoulders. "I will carry." He grimaced in pain, and slowly twisted to the side and sank to his knees. Scott took the weight of the pack and set it down. The Nomad rubbed his side where Doc had applied some salve and taped on a string of compresses. "Too much pain. I cannot carry."

Sandra bit her lip. The packs were shuffled around so that Scott wound up with the heaviest, carrying the explosive canisters; Rusty took the beamer; and Death Wind took the instrument package.

Doc put a finger to his lips. "We'd better go quietly from here on. I've never seen patrols so far out, so I suspect something must have them stirred up. Losing two flyers must have hit them in a sensitive spot."

Like snakes in the grass they slunk through the forest: toward the city, toward the dragons, toward their destiny.

* * *

Doc stood on the very edge of the rocky bluff, and let the binoculars drop slowly down his face. "It hasn't changed as much as I would have thought." He handed the glasses to Rusty. "It's grown some, but mostly in the other direction, on the other side of the central mountain. That's where the transporter is housed."

The dragon city had no tall spires, no majestic landscapes, no architectural wonders. Instead, it was more like a rough cast Roman village: cluttered streets lined with two- and three-story buildings, uneven walls that bordered not-quite-rectilinear atria, parapets that were blobs of frozen magma. The whole fortification looked like something a child might build out of clay.

Rusty put down the glasses. "It's plastic! Orange plastic, just like the stockade walls in the jungle."

"Dragons are not known for their artistic design," Doc said.

Scott tussled with Rusty for the binoculars. After a moment of viewing, he said, "It's like an anthill down there. There must be thousands of them, scurrying all over the place as if someone had disturbed their nest."

"They have a caste system much like the hive insects, with three different ranks which I've named leaders, technicians, and workers. The workers are the most numerous. Less than slaves, they are more like beasts of burden. They are raised like livestock, live in corrals, receive no education, wear no clothes, and are expendable. Their soldiers come from that group.

"The technicians are superior in dragon hierarchy in that they live in barracks and are highly educated. They are transported here already schooled in their specialties. And they are distinguishable by the litheness of their bodies as well as by the tool vests they wear. The leaders are the elite: they do no manual labor, but direct the course of others. They'll be the fat ones in the highly ornamental capes."

"Hey, I can see three flyers over there." Scott pointed to the high-walled revetments, with black-stained decks.

"I've seen them land. The disruptor beam melts the landing pad if the craft is brought in by unfamiliar hands. The plastic becomes malleable, but resolidifies quickly after the beam is turned off. The ramparts prevent the molten plastic from running off. But an experienced pilot can land it quickly without damage."

Doc took a step closer to the cliff edge and peered down over the jagged precipice. He saw something, then nodded slowly to himself.

"Where's the hatchery?" Scott said.

"Toward the eastern end of the city."

Scott panned the binoculars. "Yes, I see it. And the nursery, too."

"Hey, do you mind sharing the peepers?" Sandra jerked the glasses out of Scott's hands. Behind her, Death Wind scrutinized the city with eagle-sharp eyes.

"Anybody hungry?" Scott reached for the food pack. "As long as we have the afternoon to kill—"

"My palate can be twisted, but that does not mean that we have time to waste."

Rusty took a slice of meat. "We can't enter the city in broad daylight."

"And besides, you said the dragons don't come out at night."

"What I said was that lizards become extremely sluggish in the cold because they have no thermo-regulatory system: they rely on the sun for heat. The only way they can raise their own body temperature is by the friction of muscles. Ambient temperature is—"

"Hey, there are people down there," Sandra screamed.

Scott said, "I don't think dragons are civilized enough to be called people."

"No, you fool. I mean real people." She shoved the glasses back at Doc. "Human beings. There!"

Doc put the binoculars to his eyes, aimed them where Sandra was pointing, and stared for a long time. He gasped once or twice before he found the ability to speak.

"Oh, my. I do believe you're right." His eyes were still riveted to the lenses. "I—I just don't—understand it." When he passed the glasses on his face was as white as a sheet. "Damn. I keep underestimating those devils. Their tactics are—changing drastically."

There was triumph in Sandra's voice. "Now you'll believe me when I say my mother's down there."

Doc stroked his snowy beard, clearly disturbed. "My dear, I understand your plight, but remember too that the mission is all important. We can't afford to endanger our chances of success. This may be our last opportunity to beat those devils at their own game. This may be—"

"Screw the mission. I'm going after my mother."

"Child, I truly empathize with the depth of your concern. In your moccasins I'm sure I would feel quite as strongly, but—"

"Shut up, old man."

"—there is more at stake here than the life of one individual, or even a host of people. We're fighting for the survival of the human race as an entity. It would do us no good—"

"I'm not listening."

"—to save your mother at the expense of the greater sacrifice. It would only ensure her death at a later and not too distant time. But I promise you this: as soon as our main objective is attained I will turn all my energies to the rescue of your mother, and all the helpless prisoners with her."

"Promise anything you want, old man." Sandra's face was twisted into an agonized caricature. "*I'm* going after my mother—with or without your help. But either way, that's what I'm doing. And you can't stop me."

"Oh, dear, I *was* hoping you would be a little more reasonable."

"It's my neurosis. Take it or leave it."

Doc sighed heavily, and surveyed the other three faces. They were looking to him for advice. Slowly, he nodded consent. "All right, we'll go after your mother. *But*, we'll have to do it my way. I see no reason why we can't think of some manner in which to accomplish both objectives at the same time."

"Don't lie to me—"

Doc held up his hand, and looked hurt. "I promise. Just leave everything up to me. So finish up your food and let's get started."

Scott started wrapping up the meat. "I still don't see how we're going to walk across this city in broad daylight."

A sardonic grin spread across Doc's leathery face. "I must have forgotten to mention. We're not going to walk *across* the city, we're going to walk *under* it—through the sewers."

CHAPTER 23

•

Viscid, green liquid dribbled out of the eight-foot-high rectangular tunnel and fought to get into an evil-smelling, scumcovered pool. A bluish-green smoke ebbed in and out of the entrance, like an ocean surge, carrying with it the effluvium and carrion. Willows surrounding the outflow drooped more than usual, and the lower bark was eaten off at the waterline. Nearby fallen trunks were etched, as if with acid. And where the pool drained off into the forest there was a distinct perimeter of death.

Stifling the urge to puke, Scott pointed to something lying in the shallows. It was a thick bone, bleached by the organic soup in which it lay half submerged.

Doc nodded grimly. "That is how they dispose of their old, their sick, their infirm. They're cup up into small chunks and shoved down the culverts."

"You gotta be kidding." Sandra waved her hand in front of her face, warding off fetid fumes. "You're not gonna get me in there."

Doc maintained a straight face. "You *do* want to see your mother again, don't you?" Sandra rolled her eyes, but said nothing. Doc pointed to the plastic grate that barred their entrance. "Burn a small opening down by the water."

Rusty held the weapon awkwardly, stood back, squinted his eyes, and pressed the firing stud. A bolt of lightning arced into the grate, melting a sizable hole but one not large enough to climb through. He fired again, wincing at the thunderclap the beamer made.

"I think that'll do." Scott plunged into the foul water. He sank almost knee deep into a sticky ooze underneath the grate, stooped, and crawled under with his face a fraction of an inch from the floating stench. He stood up inside the sewer and resumed breathing. "It doesn't smell as bad in here. And there's some high ground out of the water."

Doc waded in next. He had a little more difficulty crouching through the low opening: his back was not as limber as it used to be. "Death Wind, bring those torches in." His voice reverberated strangely in the tunnel.

The savage ducked in, careful of his wound. He found the sand ledge on which Doc and Scott were waiting, unlimbered his pack, and struck a flint at one of the homemade torches. In the yellow light they could see Sandra, holding her long hair in a knot in order to keep it out of the putrid water. Rusty was right behind her.

Sandra let her hair fall back over her shoulders. "I think I'm gonna be sick."

Doc took the flaming brand and held it high. "Death Wind, get the rest of those torches going. Scott, Rusty, take some of this silt and build up a mound by the hole. I don't want to give away our entrance. Sandra, is that bandage still dry?"

Sandra mumbled in assent. The savage took the loose bundles of sticks, tied with vine, and dipped them into a bladder containing dinosaur oil. He lighted each one from the first, and stuck them into the island of sand and silt.

With the opening covered, Scott washed his hands in the foul water. "Doc, that beamer didn't seem to have the punch it used to. I think it may be running out of power."

"Yes, well, I'm rather surprised it lasted this long. We should try to go easy with it."

Now they congregated on the island. The vagaries of flood and run-off left half the tunnel sanded in, and half carrying the current. In the flickering light of the five torches, weird shadows seemed to jump about on the orange, plastic walls.

"This is the main tunnel, running right up the middle of the city. In order to get to any of our assigned destinations we'll have to take side pipes."

Rusty was a stickler for details. "Are you sure you'll remember which pipes to take? After all, it's been a long time since you've been here."

"I put markings on the walls when I made my original survey. And I used a code I'd not be likely to forget." With great effort he extracted his cane from the muck, peered dubiously as globs of mud stretched like cotton candy from the end and fell off. Then he started slurping down the embankment. Soon he was padding in shallow water where the walking was easier. The rest followed.

Very soon they came to a mud bank more than waist high

and choked with strange, organic remains: stripped bones, bent limbs, and laughing skulls. There was also a flurry of motion as rat-sized reptiles with long tails, dazzled by the incursive light, ducked into their burrows.

"Carrion eaters." Doc's voice sounded priestlike in the hollow echo chamber of the sewer. With the mud taking up so much of the tunnel, the water became deeper. "They're afraid of the light." Using the openings of their holes as footholds, he climbed onto the sticky mound and continued up the tunnel. Inquisitive, beaked snouts and beady eyes peered out in the flickering, yellow light. "Come on. They won't hurt you."

"This place gives me the creeps." Sandra's whisper was hardly audible. Undaunted, Doc was far in front.

For fifteen minutes they sloshed through the ooze. With only four feet of clearance they had to walk hunched over like gnomes. There was an eroded pathway through the middle of the tunnel, winding like an ancient river, but that was where the carrion-eating reptiles were the thickest. They made no outcries, but could be heard scurrying about in the shadows. Finally, the mud bank receded, and they were able to take a more upright posture. Doc groaned as he stretched his aching back.

The stink, if anything, was worse. Half-seen, gooey objects floated by in the underground soup. Long strips of plastic hung down from the ceiling like stalactites, where the once soft compound had dripped between molds during construction. The walls were overgrown with slick, glistening mold.

"I need a rest." Scott panted under the weight of the pack. A small circular tube intersecting the main tunnel at waist height trickled with black, viscous liquid; a drooling tongue. He backed up to it and let it take the weight off him. He wriggled out of the straps and stretched upright. Faint scratching sounds emitted from the pipe. "How much farther?"

"It's another quarter mile before the first main cutoff. At this speed it should be dark by the time we're ready to go to work, so we won't have to sit it out until sunset."

"You're crazy if you think I'm going to sit in this stuff." Sandra stayed in the middle of the channel, far away from both mildewed walls.

"Merely a matter of speech. What I meant was that our timing is going perfectly. We'll be able to complete all our topside work before the moon rises."

"Less chance of being shot at."

"Oh, my, no. Never fear being fired upon, my boy. This city has been without incident of enemy attack in its hundred-year history. There are no guards. And during the night, except for a few technicians wandering the streets on wayward missions, the dragons are securely hidden in their quarters like chickens in a coop. They don't like the dark, or the cold."

Death Wind passed around his water pouch. Sandra rinsed out her mouth. "You mean in all your trips into this city you never had the urge to stick a spear into one of those sleeping demons?"

"I can't go as far as to say that, but the purpose of my excursions was strictly exploratory. If I had yielded to such temptation the dragons would have been put on their guard, and we would not be able to enter this city today with the ease with which it has been accomplished. Of course, I always had in the back of my mind a general assault of this nature, but I never had the arms or the manpower."

"So you did nothing instead."

"Killing individuals does not win wars, only battles. Shall we proceed?"

Without waiting for a reply, he slurped on through the muddy tunnel. Death Wind repacked his canteen, and the four youths started out after the aging scout. There was a spring in his step, a purpose, which the rest found hard to match. The mud that slogged them down seemed to leap out of his way.

Still, Doc leaned on his cane with every step. His renascence was more mental than physical.

Fifteen minutes later Doc stopped beside a four-foot-high side passage that veered off to the right. "Well, here it is." A torch cast into it did not shed light very far, but it was enough to send the local denizens scurrying away. The walls were wet with condensation, and an unsightly trickle of effluence flowed down the middle. It did not look very inviting.

"Are you sure this is the right one?" Scott said.

"My mark is still on the wall." Doc held his torch high so they could all see it above the entrance. Rough-hewn letters were cut into the orange plastic.

"No mistaking that code," Rusty allowed.

Death Wind leaned close, and read with newly acquired knowledge, "To airport."

"Nice going, Death Wind," Scott said.

"The dragons do not read English. Nor would I expect them to come down here to look for engravings." Doc grinned at his own wit. "Now, if you'll excuse me for being a perfectionist, let me go over this with you two again. You'll pass under half a dozen street accesses with ladder rungs. Look for a slightly smaller tube on your right, with the words *to flyers* printed above it. That will take you to an access near the flight bay. It's pretty open up top, with very few walls for protection, but it's usually not guarded, either. But don't loll around too close in case they turn on the disruptor beam. There may be some technicians about getting ready for a night flight. It's rare, but it happens."

Scott shrugged off the pack and laid the explosive canisters by the entrance. "Got it."

Rusty transferred the beamer to Scott. "Where will we meet you?"

"About half a mile up the main tunnel, on the left, is the tube leading to the hatchery. After we set our homing beacons we'll stay there and wait for you."

"When do we rescue my mother?"

"That's farther up the tunnel. But I want to make sure we're all together, and safe, before we make another move. It's important that all the homing beacons be set so we can do the most damage and have the optimum amount of diversion when we make our attack on the transporter."

"Yeah, well, what happens if one of those flyers takes off in the meantime and triggers the computer automatically—aside from the fact that our little experts get fried?"

Rusty swung Death Wind around and removed the plastic utility box. He took out three homing beacons, then returned the box and cinched down the straps. "You'll have the control box with you. All you have to do is push the button, and when the red light comes on you're home free. Doc knows how."

"So if we get cooked, you still get your mother," Scott added. "But don't worry about those flyers getting away. If they try to take off, the missiles will launch as soon as the flyers gain enough altitude to reach scanning height. So we'll get them one way or another."

"You guys have really thought of everything."

Scott flashed a smile. "You forget, we're experts in our field. Sarcasm isn't the only profession."

Sandra glared. Doc passed over his pistol to Rusty. "And

boys, do be careful." He squeezed their hands warmly. "I don't want to lose you—even for the world. I've grown to love you too much."

"Uh, thanks."

"Yes, we'll watch our step."

They ducked into the tube with torches out in front, and started off half stooping, while Doc, Death Wind, and Sandra turned toward the hatchery.

CHAPTER 24

"Doc forgot to tell us this tunnel got smaller," Scott groaned. He did a duck waddle and at the same time tried to straddle the flow of fetid water that ran down the middle of the plastic conduit.

"Ouch!" Rusty surged ahead, then stopped several feet away and looked back by tucking his head between his legs. "Don't get so close with the torch, will you?" He swatted at the bottom of his lizard-skin shorts, where they had been singed.

"Sorry." Scott held the torch back a respectable distance. He tried not to slip on the slimy floor. More than once they passed patches of unidentifiable goo. Smaller side pipes brought in fresh streams of putrid liquid stained red with chemicals so they looked like gushes of blood. And always, beyond the feeble glow of light, there was the scrabbling sound of tiny reptilian feet.

At last they reached the first street access. If Rusty had not been standing up in it, Scott would have missed it. It was already nighttime so no light shone through the small holes in the grate. Scott stood up in the narrow vertical shaft and leaned against the ladder rungs to take the weight of the power pack off his back. Rusty's face was only inches away. Looking up, he could see stars through the grating, twinkling in the hot summer sky.

The next moment the stars were blotted out, and the lid crunched overhead. They both crouched as a large leg stepped off the grating; a tail dragged by behind it. Torches were thrust into the horizontal tunnel.

After a moment of breathless silence, Rusty said, "Let's get going."

Scott did not argue. Back in the lame-duck position, they plowed on. Scott had crawled through many maintenance tunnels in his day, but never any as revolting as this. It was quite a few minutes before they passed under another grating. This one was sticky with goo.

171

Rusty went by without pausing. "If this keeps up we'll be hours getting to the airport."

Carrying the heavy power pack in this unnatural position was becoming a strain for Scott. "I think Doc's memory for distances is a little off."

Fortunately for his aching back, the next three accesses passed by in quick succession. There was only one more to go when, impossibly, the tunnel shrank again. Now, instead of doing a duck waddle, they were forced to crawl on hands and knees. Scott had to stoop even lower because of the pack, and his face was practically in the viscous liquid.

At last they reached the sixth access. The torches were already growing dimmer, but with the conduit so small it was hardly noticeable. Out in front, and closing in behind them, the scampering carrion reptiles stayed out of the cone of light. Sharp claws clicked dully against the plastic. They lived in the multitudes of small inlet pipes, only inches in diameter, lining the sides.

Rusty stopped and turned around. He faced a side passage that was barely two feet across.

"I hope you're kidding," Scott said.

Rusty pointed with the torch. Inscribed in the plastic at the junction were the words: *to flyers*. "At least Doc got the number of accesses right."

Scott worked his arms out of the beamer straps. "Yes, but I wish he was more explicit on size. I'll never get the beamer through there."

Rusty shoved the torch into the pipe. A gentle breeze bent the flames back. "Leave it. The soldiers should all be cuddled up in some nice warm place. The technicians won't be armed. And besides, I've got the forty-five."

Scott set the beamer upright on the floor. "You don't have to twist my arm."

Rusty slithered forward on elbows and knees, holding the torch out in front. "Don't get too close." Scott could not answer: he was holding his torch in his teeth.

The air in the small pipe was thick. The fumes were not noxious, but there did not seem to be quite enough oxygen to go around. Soon they were both gasping. The smell alone was enough to make Scott pass out. And it appeared hotter than before, but that was probably due to his own exertions.

Scott opened his mouth and let the torch fall out. "Hey, hold up."

"What is it?"

Scott jerked his thumb in the semidarkness. "You missed it." With his face down Scott almost had not seen it himself. Because there was no room to turn around, Rusty had to crawl backward.

Scott wedged his torch behind the lowest rung and climbed up ten feet to the grating. He listened intently for several seconds, heard nothing, then pushed gently on the grimy cover. It did not budge.

"It's stuck." But being close to fresh air quickly renewed his strength. He braced his back against the wall and shoved hard. The lid popped off so easily that it clattered and rolled away before Scott could reach up to grab it.

Rusty's voice echoed from below. "What are you trying to do, make a formal announcement?"

"It was an accident. Leave the torch and come on up." Scott climbed out of the manhole—as he called it in his mind—and recovered the lid.

Rusty poked his head up, but kept it at street level. He glanced around in the starlight. "I don't see anything."

Scott plastered himself against the base of a seven-foot-high wall that ran along the edge of the street. On the opposite side was a two-story structure that extended a hundred feet in either direction. It must have been a tenement house, for it was lined with doorways, although there were no actual doors. "I thought we were supposed to be at the docking pens."

Rusty climbed out and joined Scott by the wall, where the shadow seemed to offer protection. "We are."

Through gritted teeth, Scott said, "What makes you so sure?"

"He hasn't been wrong yet."

"His distances haven't been too close."

"All right, so we look around." Rusty slipped out of the slender pack and looked up and down the empty street. "It must be around here somewhere." He studied the wall at Scott's back. Then he sprang up and grabbed the lip with his hands, and pulled himself up until he could see over the top. He stayed there for several seconds, then dropped back down. "I guess he *has* forgotten a few details. But we're only twenty feet from the edge of a flyer."

Scott rolled his eyes at his own stupidity. When he stepped away from the wall he could see all three flyers. "Did you see anybody?"

Rusty shook his head. "Not a soul."

"Forget religion. Did you see any dragons?" Scott flashed a set of teeth that shone whitely in the dark.

"No, but you'd better take this anyway." He took the gun out of his pack and handed it to Scott. Then he grabbed the three homing beacons and tucked them under his belt. He dropped the pack down the shaft, and fitted the lid over the hole. "All right. Let's do it."

With athletic ease Scott vaulted to the top of the wall and balanced on the foot-wide, rounded ledge while he lent Rusty a hand. Rusty jumped up, allowed himself to be pulled onto his stomach, then pivoted around and dropped off the other side. Scott alighted beside him.

Like a giant toadstool, the flyer was an immense disc resting on a tall central column which was open on one side where a ramp descended. The hundred-foot-diameter underbelly was covered with gleaming nozzles that protruded down like stalactites: exhausts of the disruptor beam. They were dark cones eight feet in length.

"Cover me." Scott nodded, and held out the gun so its smooth surface glinted in the starlight. In the light of the stars Rusty inched toward the supporting column that was a retractile part of the flyer. His lizard-skin moccasins made no sound on the plastic landing pad.

When he reached the ramp his body was outlined in a weak cone of light that spread out from inside. He glanced briefly upward. Then he slipped a homing beacon from under his belt and slid it out of sight under the edge of the metal ramp.

A moment later he was back at Scott's side, smiling confidently. "One down, two to go."

Scott returned the grin. "This is almost too easy."

They sidled along the wall toward the next flyer pen. A rampart separated the two, and probably had a door in it somewhere. But Scott did not want to waste time looking for it. After a quick glance over the top, he clambered onto the wall and dragged Rusty after him.

"There's not even a sign of a dragon," Scott said. The docking bay was dark and quiet, yet he looked around warily. He followed Rusty while he planted the beacon, then together they continued right on to the other side. They repeated the wall-climbing procedure.

Scott was trying not to make the mistake of overconfidence. Yet it all seemed so simple. They approached the ramp. Rusty took the last beacon and shoved it under the bottom step. Metal groaned overhead. Scott lifted his eyes and saw a dragon's clawed foot on the top step, and another one descending.

He grabbed Rusty's tunic and pulled him out of the light. Then they dashed to the far wall and crouched in the shadow. By that time the dragon was halfway down the ramp. Its head was bent down on its snakelike neck, and red eyes squinted through nictitating eyelids at the inside of the revetment. Scott wished he were a turtle so he could cringe into his shell. He willed the creature to look the other way.

The dragon reached the plastic deck and rotated ponderously, its tail swinging in a slow arc. The gray vest it wore identified it as a technician. It was unarmed.

Scott held the forty-five in a hand that shook slightly. The dragon peered myopically around the compound once, then a second time. It seemed to sense that something was wrong. It stopped with its lanky body pointed at Scott and Rusty.

Then, with curiosity, it started walking toward them.

"Here it is." Doc pointed with his torch to the side passage. He held the light close to the wall where years ago, as a lone scout, he had first entered the city, mapped out its complex tunnel system, and scratched street signs at the intersections. The opening was only slightly smaller than the main tube. A noxious, yellow muck flowed slowly, like molasses. Ugly reptiles ran for the darkness.

"To hatchery," Death Wind pronounced.

Sandra screwed up her face. "What do they do, drop their bad eggs down the drain?"

"The sulfur smell is more likely from chemical waste than rotten eggs. The plastic manufacturing plant is on the other side of the hatchery."

Death Wind stepped into the circular side passage and set the instrument pack in a dry spot high on the curve. He let slip a grimace of pain, which brought Sandra in after him. She placed a hand on his side, but said nothing.

Doc took the two remaining beacons from the protective housing and put them in a pocket. "My dear, I think it would be most propitious if you would wait here for Scott and Rusty, in case we're not back before they arrive."

"Not me. I wanna go where I can shoot some dragons."

"And that's precisely why I want you to wait here. We're not going to shoot anything: stealth is our prerequisite. We want to do more than kill a few stray slaves—we want to clean out the nest."

"I always was a good housekeeper, so I'd be glad to help with the spring cleaning."

Doc took off his pack and laid it beside the other. "My dear, I understand the vengeance you feel, but if you want to do the best for your mother you'll see to it that everything goes according to plan."

"Don't start pulling that stuff on me. I'll—"

She was cut off as Death Wind squeezed her arm. "Sandra, it is best this way."

Sandra scowled as she peered into Death Wind's eyes. After a moment she spoke in a lowered voice. "Well, okay. But I don't like the idea of being left alone with these creepy lizard rats."

Doc knocked caked-on mud off his cane. "Just keep the torch brightly lit and they won't bother you. They abhor light. Well, then, are we ready?"

Death Wind gave his usual single nod. He readjusted his bow and quiver, squeezed Sandra's arm again, then followed Doc's sucking footsteps.

The stench grew worse as the old doctor and the young Nomad, men of two different worlds yet bound together by heredity, penetrated deeper into the black sewer. The torches did little to dispel the gloom, for the walls were stained with ooze that absorbed the feeble flames. They waded through muck that was several inches deep, and cold and unctuous to the touch as it seeped through shoes and moccasins.

After several minutes they came to a fork where the tunnel split into two smaller passages. Without reading the signpost Doc automatically veered to the right. Here the atmosphere was too noxious even for the carrion eaters. The remains of tiny dragon dolls lay scatted in the mud in various states of decomposition. Some of the dolls were perfectly formed, others wildly distorted.

"The dragons dispose of their malformed and unwanted without proper burial. They are merely discarded, sometimes still living. Sandra's opinion of their barbarous nature is vile enough without her having to see further evidence."

Death Wind nodded. "Dragons do not care about the ones, only the many."

"Yes, that's true. But there were also nations of men who cared nothing about the individual—to them it was the state that was sacred. Individuality and personal happiness were sacrificed for the goals of the government. Let us hope we can learn something from this. We cannot change our past, but given the opportunity we can use our knowledge to shape the future."

With torches held high they skirted around the decaying bodies. But there were more ahead. And from the sides smaller conduits were choked with pieces of rotting flesh, skinny white bones, and strips of skin like parchment. A sticky fluid as thick as paste tried to fall to the mud-covered floor. The odor was nauseating.

Doc swooned, and would have collapsed had not Death Wind caught him. He held the older man in his arms for a moment while he recovered.

"I'm not as young as I used to be," Doc rasped. "I'm afraid that my scouting days are numbered."

"I will help you. Lean on my shoulder."

"Yes, thank you, son. I do need your help. I—I'm having difficulty breathing, but we must go on. It's only a little farther."

It was with difficulty that Doc pulled his feet from the thick, clinging mire. He allowed Death Wind to pull him along, and ease his exhaustion.

"This is it. I'm sure of it." The tunnel constricted ahead, and a side passage went off to the left. Doc stopped on his own. "It's only a few more feet."

The starlight did not penetrate through the grating, but the rungs were visible in the torchlight. Doc ducked down, leaning forward on his cane, and waddled the few feet to the shaft. Death Wind kept one hand on his belt to steady him.

Doc stared at the engraved arrow that pointed up. "From here on we travel the alleys and corridors. Up you go."

Death Wind left his torch on the floor and climbed up the filthy rungs. The lid slipped aside easily, and in a jiffy he was out and motioning Doc to climb up after him. Doc put his torch next to the Nomad's. A moment later he emerged into a

courtyard bounded on four sides by twenty-foot-high walls
which were inset with doorways and window openings.

While Death Wind replaced the cover, Doc sucked in the
cool night air and regained his composure. He wiped sweat off
his forehead. Slowly the color came back to his face and he
breathed more easily. After a five-minute rest, he was ready to
continue. Again he took the lead, stepping through an arched
doorway that emerged into utter darkness.

"Use your ears," Doc whispered. As his eyes adjusted he
could see that the room was furnished with low stools, each
with a circular groove on one side of the seat. "An indoctri-
nation center. Baby dragons sit in these chairs, and their tails
fit comfortably in the grooves."

They passed through the room in a few seconds, into a large
yard that was a playground. It was empty now, and they used
the hundred-yard-long plastic field as a way of reaching the
building at the far end. This had several rooms in it, each of
which was crammed with stools and tables. They passed
through this into another playground, but stopped halfway
across.

"Look over this wall and tell me what you see."

Death Wind's fingers wrapped over the seven-foot-high
parapet. He hoisted himself up. He stayed only for a second,
then dropped back down. His expression was quizzical. "Many
dragon babies. They look—innocent."

Doc nodded wearily. "You'd better let me see." Death Wind
interlaced his fingers and made a step. Doc put his foot into the
cupped hands and allowed the savage to lift him up.

He saw hundreds, possibly thousands, of baby dragons,
from hatchlings to puppy size, crowded together for warmth.
Each one was a tiny ball, with long neck bent and head tucked
under tail. Like babies of any kind they jerked and moved
spasmodically, rolled in their sleep, and kicked their siblings
when their legs twitched. Every now and then a sloe-eyed,
reptilian head arched on its long neck as a half-aroused infant
hissed in discontent.

Doc stepped down. "Ah, yes, I understand your sentiment,
my friend. They are the unsuspecting children of the future:
without sin, without evil intent, but waiting to be imprinted.
Nevertheless, by the nature of their heredity they are our
enemies."

Doc fumbled inside his shirt and brought out a hand-sized homing beacon. "Place it on top of the wall. I couldn't bear to see their faces again."

As soon as the simple task was performed they moved to the other end of the courtyard, and into the next building. Here there was no furniture, but an odd variety of, for lack of a better word, playthings. They were models of simple hand tools, designed to fit the miniature alien paws. Doc did not give Death Wind time to look around, but immediately mounted a flight of plastic stairs.

In the second level a long corridor stretched interminably toward a pinpoint of light at the farthest end. It seemed to Doc that he was looking through the wrong end of a telescope. They passed room after room, with only the faint glow of the stars peering in through tiny portholes. It took a full minute to pass all these classrooms, and when they did they found themselves on a walled parapet.

"The hatchery." Doc swept the scene before them with his wrinkled but still strong arm.

Below was a network of cubicles, a virtual maze of tiny, roofless rooms, extending hundreds of feet in all directions. The walls that separated the cubicles were wide, like platforms, and in between was filled with a dry, strawlike vegetation. Here and there white ovals showed through where they were insufficiently covered.

"At night the eggs are covered up to prevent heat loss. During the day, workers pluck them out with rakes so they can have the full benefit of the sun."

Death Wind nodded dumbly. After a long surveillance he turned to Doc. "They are still the enemy, for when they grow, they will kill."

"Yes, I'm afraid it's true. They are our potential foes of the future." He stared out over the thousands of living but unborn usurpers. "We do what we must—but let us do it with remorse."

Doc leaned over the low wall, found a suitable niche in the uneven plastic wall, and secreted the other beacon.

From behind came a loud hiss, like the sound of escaping steam. Doc snapped around. Death Wind stood between him and a leering dragon's head that strode forward quickly on a stout, strangely clad reptilian body.

The mouth gaped wide, revealing double rows of gleaming white teeth and a menacing, darting tongue. It was so close that drooling saliva stained Death Wind's hair as taloned paws reached out for his throat. . . .

CHAPTER 25

Scott slowly, and silently, pushed the safety lever into the off position. He was reasonably certain that a well-placed slug would kill the inquisitive beast on the spot. But the resultant pandemonium might not only compromise their escape, it might ruin all they had planned for.

Before he was forced to pull the trigger, the curious dragon's attention wandered, and it veered off to inspect some other imaginary disturbance. For several minutes it poked around the revetment in a seemingly random pattern. Then, with broad tail swaying, it ascended the ramp and entered the flyer.

Scott breathed a sigh of relief and tucked the gun away. Without a word, Rusty sidled along the wall back the way they had come. Scott tailed along behind. But the night was not as quiet as it had been.

There seemed to be some commotion in the other landing pad, so Rusty pulled himself up cautiously and peered over the partition. After a quick look he dropped down beside Scott. "Five dragons—technicians—prowling around."

"Do you think they found the beacon?" Rusty shrugged. Scott said, "Well, we can't stay here. Our friend may get restless again. Let's assume they're just making a routine check—" He clamped his mouth shut when he heard another tread upon the flyer's ramp. A clawed foot appeared in the light. "We can't stay here and wait to get caught."

"The street. It's our only chance."

Without waiting for Scott's confirmation, Rusty leaped to the top of the wall and squirmed to get over. Scott gave him a shove from below that tossed him clear over and into a pile on the plastic road surface. Then he leaped over after him almost without touching the top. He crashed into the street and rolled over.

"Are you all right?"

Rusty sat up and dusted himself off. "A few broken bones is all."

"Better than a laser beam." Scott looked hastily up and down the avenue. "You know, I thought Doc said they never come out at night."

"He said they *seldom* come out at night. But still, it does seem funny that—"

Scott suddenly slammed him against the partition, then pointed with his chin up the wall-lined street. "Here come some more seldoms."

A whole squad of dragon soldiers was marching toward them, claws clicking on the plastic. They were carrying beamers, and they were holding the triggering mechanisms in their reptilian paws.

"I think they mean business."

"Time to go." Rusty took off, running crouched and keeping close to the wall. Scott ran along expecting any moment that a beamer blast would cut them down. But it seemed as if the soldiers had not observed them—yet.

"Hold up. I think we passed it."

Rusty stopped and looked beyond Scott. They had outdistanced the plodding dragons. "No, it's right up ahead. I can see it." He crawled out into the middle of the street and removed the lid. An instant later he was at the bottom of the shaft, and Scott climbed down the ladder far enough to ease the cover back in place.

"The torches are almost out." Rusty held them both upside down, nursing the flames. Scott descended the rest of the way and took one. "They're not going to last much longer."

Scott blew meager life into the dying reeds. "Neither are we if we don't get out of here. I'm not sure they didn't see us."

Rusty ducked down and entered the narrow conduit. He backed out a second later. "Hey, the pack's gone."

"What do you mean, it's gone?"

Rusty remained in a crouch. "I dropped it straight down the shaft, but it's not here."

"It's got to be here. It didn't get up and walk away."

Rusty parted Scott's legs and thrust his torch in the other direction. "It's not here either."

"Well, come on. We haven't got time to look for it."

"But it's got our spare torches in it."

Scott said, "If we hurry we won't need them. Now let's get moving. I don't want to be here if someone decides to look down."

Rusty swung back and started slithering along the pipe. "Maybe it floated away."

Scott ducked in right behind him. "Or maybe the scavengers dragged it away."

Rusty added a sigh to his grunts. "I can do without the moral support." There was a hiss, followed by, "Darn, I dropped my torch in the water."

"Where did the water come from," Scott said sarcastically as he kept his elbows and knees out of the sludge that seeped down the middle of the pipe. "Do you want mine?"

"Never mind. I don't want it passed up under my legs." A moment later, he screamed. "Aaaagh."

"What is it?"

"I bumped into something."

"Maybe it's the pack." There was not much flame left in his torch, but Scott held it low so the light would pass under Rusty's body.

"Yeech." Rusty crawled back a step. "It's not the pack." He hunched his back and cringed past the object.

"I see what you mean." Scott clambered over the torn limbs and ripped body of a carrion-eating reptile that was still oozing warm blood. He tried not to touch it, or to breathe as he passed over it.

"Hey, here's the beamer." Rusty entered the larger pipe and stood up. Scott crawled out behind him and felt the cool plastic of the power pack. "And there's what's left of the pack."

Tatters of material, pieces of strapping, and a chunk of flint were all that remained. "I guess the reptiles got it after all. And that one back there lost the fight."

"The torches are gone."

Scott grunted resignedly. "Well, at least we can't get lost. It's a straight shot from here to the main tunnel." He handed the torch to Rusty and in the fading light slipped the power pack harness over his shoulders. When he felt the bulge of the forty-five in his belt, he took it out and handed it to Rusty. "Here, you hang onto this."

Rusty nodded, and tucked it in his own belt. Then, holding the dying torch out in front, he scuttled down the sewer like a racing spider. By the time the pipe broadened, and they reached the first street access, the torch was reduced to little more than a glowing ember. Scott was happy to be able to stand up for a moment, despite the prospect of coming darkness.

But Rusty allowed him no rest. "All we can do is keep moving." He ducked into the tunnel. Scott arched his back, but was forced to follow. A few minutes later the torch went out. Blackness hammered in with a tangible clap.

"I can hear noises up ahead." There was a slight tremor in Rusty's voice. One thing Scott had not banked on was that the light was all that was keeping back the hordes of carrion-eating reptiles.

"Yes, and they're behind us, too." Scott knew that they were also on every side, peering out of the small drain pipes. "If they get too close I'm going to turn around and kick them." He tried not to let his imagination run wild. It was all too easy to picture in his mind the darting tongues and leering faces that were probably only inches away in the Stygian darkness. He held onto the stub of the burned-out torch, ready to stab at anything that touched him.

With agonizing slowness they passed under the accesses, and reveled in the brief amount of light each one offered. The clicking noises were getting louder, the reptiles more bold. They were beginning to close in on them.

When they stopped under the next access, Scott took the lead. "I've got an idea. Let me go first."

"Be my guest." Rusty trailed along so close to his friend that whenever Scott made a misstep he bumped into him. In front the noises grew louder, as if the carrion eaters were licking their lizard lips. Finally, Scott decided it was time to put his plan into action.

Bending low, he leveled the laser gun and let loose with a bolt of lightning that arced down the sewer with blinding brilliance. In the strobelike flash Scott saw scores of little lizards walking on the slimy floor or clinging to the curved wall. In the ensuing darkness he could hear the frenzied motion of clawed feet scurrying for cover.

"I guess that will show them."

He picked up his pace. With his legs spread wide he straddled the ichorous fluid that collected in the middle of the tube. The curvature helped guide him through the inky dark. Whenever the reptiles became too audacious Scott let loose with the beamer and sent them scampering for cover.

As they passed under the sixth access, counting backward, Rusty tapped Scott on the shoulder. "Even though I don't think the warheads will go off, I don't think it would be a good idea to burn through the canisters."

"Right." Now that he could stand straight, Scott did not mind kicking the scurrilous beasts out of the way—until he encounted something more solid. "Hey, I think this is it."

In the pitch-black he felt the contour of the explosives pack. By feel, Scott handed the beamer back to Rusty while he threw the other pack over his shoulders.

"Now what?"

Scott stepped into the main tunnel. "Now we just head upstream until we see a light. It's not likely there will be anyone else down here."

"Suppose there's no light? We might get to the junction before they get back."

Scott nodded, forgetting that Rusty could not see the gesture in the dark. "All right. You walk up this side and I'll walk up the other side. Just keep dragging your hand along the wall."

"Through this crud?"

Scott thought about the slimy covering on the sides of the passageway. "Do you have a better idea?"

"I wish I did."

Instead of dragging his hand, Scott just touched the wall with one finger at each step. Often he heard the scurrying reptiles, but they were not as profuse as they had been in the smaller pipe. Separated by the width of the tunnel, Scott listened for Rusty's footsteps in the slurpy mud to keep abreast of him. He did not want to talk because of the eerie echo effect. He searched for a glimmer other than the coruscating points that haunted his eyes in the total absence of light.

Time passed.

Suddenly the darkness in front burst into dots of fire, punctuated almost instantly by the hammering of explosions that reverberated deafeningly in the long chamber. The air was full of flying debris that ripped past Scott's face, thudded hollowly into the walls, and plowed furrows unseen in the mud.

They were blind, alone, and under attack!

If the dragons had a slow reaction time during the heat of the day, their responses were that much more sluggish at night when their blood thickened and their muscles were stiff. Death

Wind, acting with trained Nomadic impulse, ducked and stepped aside. Reptilian paws clapped on empty air.

At the same time Doc's cane swept up from ground level and smashed into the beast's lower jaw, breaking bone and snapping off teeth. Hissing with pain, the dragon backed away with its paws to its face. Doc swung again, and the dragon was unable to ward off the blow.

Death Wind took but a moment to unsheath his long knife. He lunged under the flailing paws and stabbed hard through the clothing and into the massive chest where the two-chambered heart pumped torpidly. With an overhand swing Doc's cane crashed across the skull. The knife was whipped out of the savage's hand when the wailing beast twisted away. This gained it no respite.

With the knife buried in its chest, and Doc still beating it about the head, the dragon technician died in stages. While the neck slowly drooped, the oversized hind legs kept walking back in retreat. When the paws dropped and the head literally hung on its belly, it was already dead. Still it moved back, until it bumped into the wall of the corridor and could go no farther. Then it finally stopped moving.

"Quick! Help me drag it into one of these rooms." In the adrenaline flow Doc forgot all about his pain and fatigue.

The creature had died on its feet, in a squat. Together they upended it and dragged it on its back into a dark corner of the room. Death Wind recovered his knife while Doc picked up his cane.

Doc was breathing hard. "Whew. That happened so fast that I quite forgot to limp." He wiped sweat off his brow. In the aftermath of the fight he did not forget to scan the area for other insomniac dragons. "I think it's time we withdrew, before another mentor is awakened by the clamor."

As quickly as they dared, they retraced their steps along the darkened corridor, downstairs, through the courtyards, to the tunnel access. There was no further incident.

They found their torches going dim, so before they started out they took spares out of the pack and lighted them from the still-burning brands. The used ones were doused in the water and buried in the fetid muck.

They moved fast through the melange of tiny, rotting bodies and the thick, noxious atmosphere. With a lungful of clean, topside air Doc was able to get through the worst of it easily.

Then there was nothing to bar their return but mud and distance.

The faint light from Sandra's torch was already in view when the tunnel ahead erupted into a cacophony of loud gunshots that came so quickly because of the echo effect that it sounded like one continuous roar.

"Sandra!" Death Wind did not wait for the older man, but charged ahead stringing his bow as he ran. By the time Doc reached the pair Sandra was crying hysterically, and from down the tunnel came the frantic shouts of Scott and Rusty. Death Wind held the girl to his breast and brushed her hair with his hand.

"Sandra, what's wrong? What happened?" She was sobbing so hard that she could not answer Doc's question—or even return to a rational state of mind. Doc stepped into the main tunnel with his torch held out. "Scott. Rusty. Are you all right?"

"We will be if you can keep that madwoman from shooting at us." There was no mistaking Scott's furious voice.

"It—It's all right." Doc waved the torch. "But, what are you doing there in the dark?"

Rusty moved cautiously into view. "Our torches went out and we lost our spares."

"What's gotten into that crazy girl? We've got enough problems without having a trigger-happy kid on the loose."

Sandra tore free from Death Wind and stepped out of the side pipe. "What the hell's the idea of sneaking up on me in the dark? This place is creepy enough without you two playing hide-and-seek."

Scott tried to match Sandra decibel for decibel. "We weren't playing games. Rusty already said we lost our torches."

"And how did you do a stupid thing like that?"

"It's not as stupid as screaming and losing your head."

"I didn't scream. I never scream."

"Yeah, and how do you think we heard you that day in the ruins? Because you were whispering for help?"

"You shut up, you, or I'll jam this rifle right—"

Doc chose drastic measures and clamped a hand over her mouth. "Please, please, please. Can we calm down before we wake up the whole city?"

"What does she think, that we were out for a moonless stroll in the sewers?"

Sandra pulled Doc's hand from her face. "Get off my back, will you?" She tried to strike Scott, but Doc prevented her.

"Children, please." Gently he pushed Sandra back to Death Wind. The savage held her tightly. "Scott, please control yourself. Now, Rusty, can you tell me how this eventuality occurred?"

Rusty gave a concise account of their activities. Doc harumphed. "Yes, we had a slight altercation ourselves." He tendered a brief account of their own foray. "And the beast was wearing clothes. Unheard of. Something is afoot, or our presence is compromised. Now, if you two can reconcile your differences, at least temporarily, we are a wee bit behind schedule. . . ."

Neither combatant said a word, or even deigned to exchange glances.

"Fine, well, now that that's settled we can continue. But I must warn you—I'm somewhat concerned about the midnight peregrinations of our reptilian counterparts. We must exercise utmost caution." Then he added, for Scott's and Sandra's benefit, "And quiet."

The patrol started out again, deeper into the hostile city.

CHAPTER 26

"This is where we split up." Doc held his torch against the sharp angle that formed the base of a Y, where the sewer split. "This way lies the stockade, that way the time transporter."

Rusty handed his torch to Scott and helped take the instrument package off Death Wind's back. "Time to shift gear."

Scott dropped the explosives in the inch-deep water and reached for the beamer that Rusty was still wearing. "I hope this thing doesn't die on us."

With deft fingers Rusty unlatched the clear plastic storage box and flipped open the lid. He pressed the switch that connected the battery circuit. Stored-up power surged through the wiring to the roughly soldered electronic components. He placed the toggles in the ready position, punched in the sequencing code for a quick check, and sat back on his haunches.

"Seems to be all right. All I have to do is push this button and the missiles will be on their way."

"How can you be sure?" Sandra asked, more with reproach than with concern.

"This 'signal received' light will come on. Then, as the missiles leave their silos the annunciator lights will change from green to red."

"How far are we from our target areas?" Scott asked Doc.

Doc tugged on his beard; it had stayed amazingly white during his perambulations. "I should say not more than fifteen minutes to either one. We should be in position before the missiles arrive."

"Then let's cut the gab and get a move on. Push that damn button."

"Okay." Rusty pressed down his index finger. In the flickering torchlight it was difficult to see the glass lenses because of the glare. Rusty tilted the box into the shadow and pressed the button again.

"Is something wrong?" Doc inquired softly.

Rusty lifted the block of components out of the plastic housing and inspected the wiring. He pressed the button a third time, shaking his head. "I'm not getting a positive return."

"That's just great," Sandra said. "All dressed up and nowhere to go."

"Could there be something wrong with the filament?" Doc said.

Rusty shrugged. "Well, there could be—if the bulb got broken in transit. But most likely the signal's not getting through. I think these plastic walls are damping the broadcast. We've got to get topside."

"I'll start looking for an access," Scott said.

Death Wind pointed with his torch. "We pass access one, two minutes ago."

"One can always trust a Nomad for constant vigilance. I suggest we retrace our steps." Doc let Death Wind lead the way. Rusty picked up the instrument package and hand carried it as they backtracked down the sewer. The savage entered a large side passage where, only a few feet in, a faint glimmer of light shone down.

"The moon might be up by now," Doc said. "I'm afraid we may have lost our cover of total darkness."

Rusty looked up at the pattern of dots filtering through the grate. "Let me try it from the top of the shaft. That might be all it needs." He cradled the instrument package in the crook of his arm as he climbed up the plastic rungs with one hand. At the top he wedged himself tight so he could fiddle with the box. A moment later he was back down.

"It's no use. The signal's too weak to get through all this plastic. It must be an almost perfect insulator. I've got to get above where there's no interference." He jerked his head upward. "And I couldn't get the cover off. It's stuck."

Doc issued orders. "Death Wind, go up first and see if the coast is clear. Scott, cover him. Rusty, get ready to follow."

"Hey, what about me?"

"You hold the torches."

Death Wind beat against the grating with his massive shoulders until it broke free and rolled away. "Clear." Then he leaped into the street and notched his bow.

Scott clambered out right behind him, and took up a station

facing the opposite direction. Rusty climbed out awkwardly with the instrument package.

Right behind him came Sandra. Scott said, "Hey, what are you doing here?"

"Hell, I'm not gonna stay down there an' miss the action."

Doc poked his head and shoulders out of the hold. "Head-strong lass."

The quarter moon had risen, and shed a stark light over the dull orange architecture. This street, like all the others, was bounded on both sides either by buildings, or walls that enclosed courtyards. The entire city seemed to be one vast molded plastic model: without relief of color or style, without art, without trees or flowers, without any form that was not strictly functional.

"It's still not working," Rusty murmured, more to himself than to Doc. "I'm going to have to get higher—above these walls."

"How about that watchtower?" Scott gestured with his chin toward a structure which rose three stories high. The walk-around porch on each level was connected by external steps.

"That should do."

Doc looked nervously up and down the street. "Do you realize that this is a public thoroughfare?"

Sandra stood with legs spread apart and the rifle butt resting on her hip, the barrel pointed skyward. "If any dragons come this way they're gonna hafta pay a toll."

"Keep us covered." Scott escorted Rusty up the stairs to the first level.

Rusty pushed the button. "Higher." On the second level the moon sent silvery beams that lighted his features and cast shadows. Again he shook his head. On the third, where the porch was wider, a solid railing a body length high cast a dark umbra. Rusty pursed his lips and looked up at the roof some ten feet above. "I have to get higher."

Scott nodded, thinking about the antenna hidden in the bushes. It was low; very low. "Climb up on my shoulders." He stepped onto the orange railing and leaned inward so his hands were against the wall.

Rusty cradled the signaler under one arm, steadied himself with Scott's aid, and jumped first to the railing. Then he shinnied up Scott's back, using the power pack as a footstool.

When he got to Scott's shoulders he pushed the box onto the roof, then clambered after it.

Slowly, he stood up on the platform. His angular figure was silhouetted against white clouds drifting low across a purple sky. Standing on his toes, he held the box overhead in outstretched arms, as if he were supplicating to the gods. He could go no higher. He pushed the button.

Two things happened almost simultaneously: a tiny red annunciator light flashed on, and the plastic box with its delicate electronic components exploded in his hands with a burst of light and a loud report.

Rusty was thrown backward. He rolled off the edge of the platform, collided with Scott, and both of them fell into a snarled heap behind the solid railing.

For a span of about two seconds there was a stunned silence. Scott untangled himself and tried to see what was going on. The still of the night was again broken, this time by Sandra's burping rifle. She stitched a line of bullets so neatly across a dragon's neck that its head was practically severed from its trunk. The beamer it had fired at Rusty blasted twice more from the falling gun before the restless fingers got the message that it was dead.

As the creature slumped to the side another dragon's head appeared behind it, leering over the wall of an adjacent courtyard. But by the time its beamer rose high enough for a shot, Death Wind buried an arrow into its throat. Gurgling, it fell back and dropped from sight.

Scott pushed Rusty unceremoniously out of the way, and rushed toward the stairs. "Come on." He was not abandoning his friend, but joining the fight. On the second level he leaned out over the railing with the beamer in hand, and sent a blast at a dragon that was ambling up the street behind Sandra and Death Wind. Lightning burned a hole through the lizard hide into vital organs. The creature hissed as it fell, smoldering.

He fired again at its replacement, but the beamer refused to discharge its deadly bolt. Faintly, he could hear the drawn-out whine as the capacitor strove to reach full charge. By this time both Sandra and Death Wind, warned by Scott's beam, pivoted and fired. Another dragon hit the ground, dying from lead and flint.

Rusty, weaponless, fumbled past Scott and down the stairs.

From his vantage point Scott covered him until he reached the manhole from which Doc had just ducked out of sight.

Another dragon peered over the courtyard wall right below Scott. The beamer still would not discharge. "Death Wind!" The savage turned around and let loose an arrow into the gaping maw before the beast's gun came up. The reptilian head was so close that when the point of the arrow penetrated the neck, the feathers were touching the outstretched hand that held the bow. With unbelievable audacity the savage reached out and plucked the arrow from the wound, then turned and fired it at another dragon that was stepping out of the opposite doorway. Both dragons died in seconds.

Rusty dropped down the hole at the same time that Scott charged out into the street from the lower level of the tower. Beamer blasts came in from all angles as dragon patrols converged on the disturbance. Remembering Death Wind's training, he danced across the street faster than the soldiers could draw a bead on him. "Let's get out of here!"

Death Wind was closest, so he jumped into the manhole. Scott fired over his head and zapped a dragon slinking out of a doorway. Then he waited for the beamer to recharge. He skidded to the opening. "Sandra, come on."

But Sandra had ideas of her own. Her face was contorted into a leer, as if in the heat of battle she was being overtaken by primal blood lust. She picked off dragons left and right with well-aimed, single shots. Scott realized that she was having the time of her life, and had no intention of leaving.

Until her gun jammed.

Crouched right in front of the sewer access, she was a sitting target for the dragon soldiers. "Sandra!" She looked up, saw the danger, and dodged her head slightly to avoid a lightning bolt. Her hair was singed as the heat ignited the dark strands and burnt them away. Then she calmly pulled back the bolt of the rifle and cleared the round in the chamber.

Scott rammed into her and knocked her aside just as another laser beam would have transfixed her. Bracing on one knee, he raised his gun and aimed at the dragon that was approaching and getting ready for another shot. For an awkward few seconds Scott held his fire, until he saw the dragon drawing a bead. At the last possible second he fired. The dragon's hide sizzled, but the beast did not fall. Scott's beamer was running out of energy.

Dark, steellike fingers wrapped around Sandra's ankles and pulled her to the hole, then down the shaft. As soon as her head dropped out of sight Scott sprang after her. As he landed in the muck at the bottom of the sewer, Sandra was still struggling in Death Wind's arms.

"Whudja do that for?" she screamed. "There were more of 'em coming."

Scott appreciated Death Wind's knowing when to talk and when to act. The savage threw her over his shoulder, picked up two torches standing in the mud, and ran down the pipe. Sandra beat him on the back with clenched fists. "Put me down. Put me down."

Scott grabbed the last torch and chased after them. Doc and Rusty were waiting in the main tunnel. Then they all splashed through the water to the fork.

When Death Wind put her down, Sandra was still swinging and kicking like a tigress. "What the hell's the idea?"

Death Wind's eyes were ignited black pools. "We have mission."

"Our mission's to kill dragons."

"You not understand mission. You get us killed because you have no sense."

"Listen, buster, I have enough sense to know the more dragons we kill now, the less we hafta worry about later. And *I* didn't run out on *you*."

"Sandra, please calm down. Death Wind is right. Your foolhardiness is likely to compromise our lives as well as the mission—which, as you may recall, is to blow up the time transporter." As an afterthought, Doc added, "And to rescue your mother."

"The mission's already compromised because wonderboy's box didn't work. Now we gotta shoot our way through this burg."

"Oh, it worked," Rusty said matter-of-factly. "The light went on just before it got hit."

"So what? The box blew up."

"That doesn't matter. If the light went on it means the signal got through."

Scott added sarcastically, "The missiles are on their way."

Sandra clamped her mouth shut, and stared from eye to eye. After a long silence, she plucked a torch out of Death Wind's hand and stared into the flame. "Oh. Well, how was I supposed to know."

Slowly, the tension eased.

Scott smiled. "In a few minutes the dragons are going to have real egg on their faces."

Sandra looked up at him. Her face mellowed. "You know, you're really slinging my lingo."

"It's from hanging around in the wrong company."

Doc's chest finally stopped heaving. "If I can interject some commentary into this pleasant diatribe, I would like to mention the obvious—that it would seem we have lost the advantage of surprise. If, indeed, we ever had it."

"You think they knew we were coming?" Rusty said.

"I'm sure of it. I'm afraid I've underestimated their cunning again. That patrol on the outskirts of town was no accident, as I thought. They must have been expecting some kind of action, even if they did not know from which quarter it would come. I wonder what other precautionary measures they've taken."

Scott waved his torch to make it glow brighter. "Listen, Doc, I've got an idea."

Doc rolled his eyes. "Every time one of you boys gets an idea I have a premonition of fear."

Scott flashed a quirky smile. "Well, the beamer's almost dead—"

"So that's why you took so long," Sandra interrupted.

"—we're almost out of bullets, and pretty soon Death Wind's going to have to use his bow as a banjo. Why don't we get resupplied?"

Doc chewed his lip. "I'm afraid I don't follow you."

"Right now we don't have the firepower to assault an anthill. And the dragons are armed tooth and nail. If we split up we'll be practically defenseless. So, why don't we take over the armory—beamers for everybody?" For Sandra's benefit, he added, "Including the prisoners when we let them loose."

"Now we're talking turkey."

"Oh, dear. If I live through this I think I'll retire from scouting for good."

Rusty said, "I think it's got a chance."

"Plan is good," said Death Wind.

"But the armory is locked—and probably guarded," Doc said.

Sandra playfully punched Scott on the shoulder. "I'll bet it won't be guarded when those missiles start making scrambled eggs."

Doc shivered. "Levity at a time like this."

"You gotta keep your sense of humor."

Doc merely shook his head. "Far be it from me to stand in the way of—" He coughed once, then again. He seemed unable to catch his breath.

Scott slapped him between the shoulder blades when *he* started coughing. Among the putrid smells of the sewer he picked out one that sparked his memory and sent chills down his spine. In the flickering, yellow flames a green mist appeared, and a stinging sensation gripped him by the back of the neck.

The dragons had gassed the sewers!

CHAPTER 27

Scott braced himself with one hand on the rung of the ladder, and stared up the shaft that led to the surface of the dragon city. He could go no farther along the tunnel because he detected a whiff of gas coming from up ahead. The dragons were trying to seal them off.

Death Wind jogged up next, wearing the heavy explosives pack. The bandage on his side was tinted red, but if he felt any pain his face did not show it. Sandra, too, ignored her injuries, both the beamer blast that had burned her hip and the one that had singed her hair and blackened the side of her face.

"I'm going up." Scott started climbing as soon as Doc and Rusty were close enough to hear.

"Wait!" Sandra reached out and stopped him on the third rung. Scott had tucked the beamer gun in its holster; it was almost useless except for charring meat. She swung the rifle off her shoulder and thrust it at him. "Here, take this."

Scott summed up the significance of the act with a brief glance. "Thanks." He no sooner reached the top of the ladder when a shadow moved across the grating. Visible through the slots was a dragon's face so close to the cover that the forked tongue behind the mouthful of shiny teeth could be seen licking outward. Instinctively he brought up the rifle and sent three short bursts through the slots into the leering face.

The dragon was jerked up by the force of the bullets, away from the grating. With his head hunched forward, Scott rammed the manhole cover with the top of the power pack. The lid shot two feet into the air, crashed on its side, and spiraled away. He leaped out of the hole and rolled to the side just as a bolt of lightning seared the leading edge of the opening. The rifle burped again, followed by the thud of a body.

Death Wind, Sandra, and Rusty poured out of the hole like flies escaping a trap. All three turned to help Doc, whose strength had been severely sapped by the poisonous fumes.

A laser beam chased Scott across the street. The dragon that had fired the bolt was trying to adjust its sights to the rapidly moving youth. Scott wasted no time in firing two quick shots from the prone position into the tawny breast. The beast was dead, but the paw with the beamer was still moving in a slow arc—and firing. Scott jumped out of the way, trying to conserve ammunition, and watched as the dragon slowly heeled over and crashed into the street. There were no other soldiers visible, but the fight was sure to bring on a patrol to investigate.

Scott was afraid the battery pack was booby-trapped. "Let's get out of here. Quick!"

Sandra flung back her hair. Bits and pieces broke off where the strands had been seared. "Which way?"

Doc sat with his head between his legs, hyperventilating. He glanced up at the moon, still low on the horizon. "We have to go south and east. Let's follow this street and look for an intersecting alley." He pushed himself to his feet with his cane and hobbled off past the dead dragons.

They found an alley before being discovered by any dragon soldiers, but they could be seen in the distance. The seven-foot-high walls were tall enough to hide the skulking humans, but low enough for dragons to see over—and be seen.

"Do you mind if I rest for a moment?" Doc leaned heavily against the plastic. "I'm afraid I'm not as young as I used to be."

Rusty was fidgety. "We've only got a few minutes before the fireworks begin."

"And we've got to have those weapons so I can get my mother."

Scott said, "Give him some time, will you. He got us this far, he'll get us the rest of the way. A few more minutes won't matter one way or the other."

"That's easy for you to say. You don't have a mother—" She gritted her teeth. "I—I'm sorry. I didn't think—"

Scott ignored the tactless blunder. "Forget it."

"No need to argue. I'm ready." Doc straightened up. "And she's right. We have no time to waste."

At the end of the block Death Wind scrutinized the street in both directions, dashed across to where the alley continued on between two rows of three-story buildings, and motioned the others to follow.

"This is a barrack district." They passed many openings

leading into the black recesses where sleeping dragons undoubtedly lay. But so far only the soldiers had been aroused—the general populace was blissfully unaware that an invasion was going on. And the dragon leaders had no idea of the calamity of what was about to happen.

At the next street they had to wait in the shadows while a dragon patrol marched slowly by, dragging their tails. They were about to run across the street into the next alley when Doc gasped and fell back. Clutching his chest, he sagged to the ground writhing in pain.

"Doc, what's wrong?" Rusty's voice rang out too loud. Scott caught the man and watched helplessly as his face contorted horribly.

"I—can't—go—on," he said, through gritted teeth. Then, his face relaxed. Breathing hard, Doc bit his lip after each word. "The strain has been—too much. I'm too old for this kind of thing."

"What can we do?" Scott said.

"Complete the mission. Go on without me. Remember that it is not individual life that matters in the long run, but the survival of the race. We are ephemeral, but we live on in spirit in the hearts and minds of others."

"Keep your words of wisdom for later," Sandra said. "Scott's right, we need you."

"I'll only slow you down. And it's only a few hundred more feet—"

Sandra was adamant. "We don't have time to argue. You're coming with us even if we have to carry you. Right?" Sandra looked sharply at Scott and Death Wind, her large brown eyes flashing brightly in the moonlight.

Scott helped Doc to his feet while Death Wind approached from the other side. Together they lifted the white-haired man, each holding an arm and a leg as if he were a chair. Sandra led the way across the next street while Rusty brought up the rear. They jogged along the alley with their parcel as if he were nothing more than a sack of potatoes. They did not put him down until they reached the end of the alley.

"How ignominious," Doc huffed, dusting himself off. Then he pointed with his chin across the open expanse of a wide street. "There's the armory, and I don't see any guards."

The building was constructed of the same orange plastic of which the entire city was made. It had no windows, and only

one entrance—a ten-foot double door that glinted metallically.
A massive shackle held the two swinging portals together.

"How do we get in?" Sandra said to no one in particular.

Doc pointed to the beamer. "You'll have to melt off the
hasp."

"I don't know if there's enough power left in this thing. It
takes forever to recycle, and when it does the energy output is
weak."

"The missiles should be here any minute," Rusty said.

Sandra pushed him aside. "The hell with the missiles.
There's nobody here. I say let's get started *now*." She dragged
Scott by the harness into the deserted street. Death Wind and
Rusty followed, leaving Doc in the shadow of the alley.

The street was slanted, rising upward to the east and
descending slowly in the west to the mountain that housed the
time transporter. The quarter moon cast a white glow of
serenity over the dragon stronghold. The gently undulating
plastic streets and buildings had a look of surrealism as the low
orange shapes merged with the darker shadows. It was the calm
before the storm.

Rusty bent close to examine the lock. "I think it's steel—and
the hasp, too."

"All right, stand back." Wincing slightly, Scott aimed the
gun at the shackle of the alien mechanism. There was no way
of telling how the lock was supposed to work, but the idea of
a shackle was universal. As he pressed the firing stud an arc
stabbed out of the nozzle and hit the metal only a foot away.
There was a ball of lightning the size of an orange. When it
receded, the metal glowed a bright red.

"It melted a little." Rusty inspected the shackle, then jerked
on the recessed door handle. "Hold it closer this time."

On Scott's back the power pack was struggling to recharge
its capacitor. The firing circuit was temporarily deadened while
the storage battery was being sucked dry. A precious minute
passed.

"Hurry that thing," Sandra said.

Scott fired again. Barely more than a visible spark jumped
the gap between the nozzle and the still radiant shackle.

Rusty looked again. "One more might do it."

"Dragons come," said Death Wind calmly.

As all eyes looked up, Doc scurried across the street to join them. "I don't mean to rush you, but I think the enemy is precipitating an advance.

"Can't you ever say anything short?"

With a wry look, Doc said, "I promise to try to please your predilection for brevity in the future—if we have one."

Sandra rolled her eyes, but readied the rifle, too. She nudged Scott with the butt. "What're you waiting for—an invitation?"

"I can't help it. This thing's just about dead."

"And so are we if we don't get this door open right away." She looked up and down the high-walled street. The dragons were drawing nearer—from both directions. "I'll get them while they're still outa beamer range."

Dropping to a kneeling position, Sandra rested the rifle against her leg. She fired one round at the leading dragon on the downslope. The bullet went through its head and out the back, blasting away face and skull. Without waiting to see it fall, she spun around and fired at the first dragon on the upslope. She misjudged the rate of fall: the trajectory carried the bullet into the lower jaw where it tore out bone and muscle but did not kill.

Instantly the dragons started returning her fire. From several hundred feet away, on either side, laser beams with full potential lashed out. The air in front of the armory crackled with electric discharge.

Sandra burped off two more shots. "I can't hold them off forever."

"Flyer in air." Death Wind pointed northward with his bow. Everyone looked, including the dragons, as the flyer rose on a shimmering purple heat wave and began to move laterally out of its pen.

"It's going to get away," Sandra shrieked.

Rusty shook his head confidently. "No, it's not."

"Damn." Sandra threw down her rifle, seemingly in disgust.

"What are you doing?" Scott yelled.

"I'm outa lead. It's up to you now."

The dragon soldiers lumbered on like slow freight trains. The momentary distraction caused by the flyer taking to the air no longer held their attention. They were close enough now that the full power of their laser beams could be felt. Blobs of molten plastic were blown off the street and gouged out of the walls. They were uncontested as they moved in for the kill.

Death Wind notched his last arrow and prepared to let it

loose as a final challenge. The airborne flyer climbed for elevation along a well-worn track that had already been burned through the jungle hundreds of times over. A second flyer was rising slowly on its disruptor beam.

Scott put the point of the gun right on the shackle and pressed the firing stud. One last weak, almost ineffectual charge trickled through the mechanism and warmed the sagging steel.

A laser beam skittered overhead, then two more from the other side. The dragon soldiers were getting the range. Doc shoved Rusty aside and raised his cane in the air. A lightning bolt sheared it in half. Undaunted, he took the shortened stick and with all the force he could muster struck the shackle while the metal still glowed. The weakened steel snapped apart. Then, using the cane as a pry bar, he bent the connecting bolt out.

His shout was nearly drowned out by the crackling of beamer blasts. "Open it."

Scott grabbed the right-hand door while Rusty fought with the other. They were heavy, and moved ponderously on squeaky hinges. Laser beams ricocheted off the steel barriers as Doc ducked into the opening—

—right into the leveled beamer of a dragon guard!

In the next instant Doc knew he was going to die, for he had not the willpower or the strength to move his fatigued and aged body. But before the clawed hand could squeeze the trigger there was a twang close by his ear. Death Wind's last arrow buried itself triumphantly into the open mouth. Sandra tackled Doc, and as the two crashed to the ground the already dying dragon got off its last shot. The electric bolt burned the savage's bow in half.

Then the five of them fell, stumbled, and crawled into the armory with beamer blasts gouging large holes in the steel door. The wounded dragon, hissing madly, fell forward in its death throes and was immediately baked by a crossfire of hostile lightning bolts.

At the same time a streak of fire descended from the sky. An enormous explosion rent the air, and the flyer that was making for the river shuddered wildly. The disruptor beam winked out, and for long seconds the flyer continued on its course as an act of momentum. Then, it angled down sharply and crashed with a fiery blast that leveled a large area of jungle and set up small blazes.

Sandra jumped up and down. "You did it. You did it. You shot down the flyer."

Rusty peered out the door at the spectacle, with a look of smugness on his face. "You mean you doubted my word?"

Before Sandra could reply the second flyer cleared the landing field and exploded violently. It fell back and crashed into the adjacent buildings. Almost instantly the third flyer blew up in its revetment, sending flaming slivers of molten metal into the sky in a bright pyrotechnic display.

Rusty could hardly conceal the pride in his voice. "I had the computer set on automatic override. Even if the homing beacons got melted during takeoff the missiles were programmed to revert back to antiaircraft mode."

Scott threw off the dead power pack. "That's great. When you think you can get your hat back on, how about helping me get these beamers off the shelf."

Death Wind shrugged out of the pack with the explosive canisters and slid it close by the door. He spun a power pack around and backed into it. While the others were arming themselves he stepped into the street and fired an accurate and deadly volley at the stunned dragon soldiers. They were frozen in their tracks by the awesome spectacle of destruction. The savage cut them down like so much wheat. Sandra joined him and in moments the street was a smoldering wilderness of dead and dying dragons. The seriously wounded hissed horribly.

The armory was stacked from floor to ceiling, and along shelving in the middle of the room, with power packs. Doc walked all around the room, surveying its contents. He noticed that not all the power packs had pistols attached to them.

"You know, I think the dragons must use these modules to power all their portable equipment, whether it be weapons or tools. Depending on how the energy is released—in one full burst or with a trickle discharger and diffusing system—they can be used for many functions."

"Terrific, Doc. Can we discuss it later?" Scott rigged the straps of a power pack to fit his body, then drew the gun out of its holster.

Rusty checked through the pack carrying the explosive canisters. He pulled out coils of wire, blasting caps, and a handful of dried-up flowers. Death Wind must have been carrying them for some reason. He tucked everything back in, next to the battery. It was all he could do to get the pack on his back.

"How's it look?" Scott stepped outside behind Death Wind and Sandra. The battle was still raging, but the dragons were definitely on the rout. He shot down two dragons before he got an answer.

Sandra sent a beam of energized light into the street opposite. "Watch out for the alley."

Even as they talked two silver streaks dropped out of the velvet sky, like shooting stars, and impacted in the middle of the city. A huge cloud of fire and burning plastic globules erupted upward and outward. Streamers of flaming orange cascaded in the air, casting temporary daylight over the battlefield.

Cheers arose from the armory. Even the usually stoic Nomad laughed and issued war whoops. Sandra holstered her gun long enough to throw her arms around Rusty and plant a kiss on his freckled cheek. Rusty turned a shade of red that matched his hair. Then she hugged Scott unabashedly.

"The day I ran into you three turned out to be the most important day in my life—until today."

Scott showed mock surprise. "That's funny. The way I remember it *we* ran into *you*."

Sandra flashed a smile. "Have it your own way."

Doc stuck his head out long enough to take in the situation, then ducked back in and explored the rest of the armory. He puttered around the many strange devices, wishing for the time to study them. He rubbed his gnarled hand over the clear plastic casing of a cylindrical object that lay horizontally on a dolly. Seven feet long and half that in circumference, each end spouted brass end caps. Through the transparent plastic he saw a whirling, hypnotic maelstrom, a constantly rushing cyclone of gas, rainbow hued like a volatile oil slick.

Rusty appeared suddenly by his side. "What's that?"

Doc was somewhat dazed. "Why, I think it's a bomb—a dragon death bomb waiting to be dropped on some far corner of the Earth."

"Well, it looks like we got here just in time."

Now the rest of the war party gathered around. Sandra wrapped her soft, warm arms around Doc and kissed him resoundingly. "They're gone. They're running away. Like ants after their eggs."

"Yes, I should imagine they are." Doc still had a faraway look in his eyes; his thoughts were somewhere else. "Well, I—I guess we had better get on with the mission. I've done just about all I can do. It's in your hands now."

"Aren't you coming with us?" Scott said.

"I could do nothing but slow you down. This has taken so much out of me. And I'm quite confident in your abilities. I think it would be best if I were to stay here and—stand guard over the weapons."

"Good idea," Sandra said.

The smell of burning plastic filled the air, and with it was the horrible mephitic stench of scorched flesh. The loud hissing sound that was carried with it was not all due to the consuming flames: many dragons, young and old alike, were being destroyed in the rampant conflagration.

Sandra stared hard into Doc's eyes. Her own brown eyes flashed with the scintillation of polished jewels. "Doc, I—I'd like to say thanks. For everything. And I'd like to apologize for, well, for the way I—"

Doc pulled her close for a hug. His eyes were squeezed tightly shut. "Think nothing of it, my dear. You've certainly done your part. And well, I might add. You all have."

Doc held back tears. He was overawed by the gripping sense of fellowship this venture had brought him. As she stepped back, he swept back her partially singed hair. His eyes shifted to the tiny pendant that hung from her delicate lobe. He was caught by its luster. Then he felt in him a queasiness that sapped the strength from his already weakened legs. "My dear, where did you get that?"

Sandra pulled away slightly, and laughed. "Doc, this is no time to admire my jewelry."

But she was trapped in his suddenly iron grip. "Where did you get it?"

Sandra beheld his astonished gaze. "Look, if it means that much to you, my mother gave it to me."

Doc seemed to wilt where he stood. "Ah, I suspected as much." His teeth gnashed together like a squirrel grinding nuts. "My child, all of you, warriors and killers of dragons, you've done a fine job. No matter what happens now, no one can ever take that away from you. But the most important part of our task yet remains. For humanity's sake the time transporter must be destroyed, and the prisoners must be rescued.

Now flee. Flee all of you. And may honor and righteousness guide your way."

He ushered them to the giant doorway.

In the orange glow of flames the four warriors, who had fought together through so much, hugged and shook hands. The street had been deserted ever since the dual explosions. Only the dead and dying remained.

Then Sandra turned to Scott and Rusty. "Take care of yourselves. I love both of you." She nodded to Death Wind, and together they left the armory and ran up the slanted street. Scott and Rusty took off in the opposite direction, downhill.

Doc wistfully watched them go, for he loved them all. But years of training and hardship had taught him that duty comes before joy. There was still important work to be done.

Back inside, he studied the death machine lying in its cradle. Softly, almost lovingly, he ran his hand over the alien mechanism, sensing through his fingers the awesome power it contained.

A wry grin touched his weathered lips. "Oh, boys, if you only knew," he said, thinking aloud. "This time I've got an idea of my own—and it scares me to the very depths of my soul."

CHAPTER 28

Scott and Rusty sneaked up on the intersection. The street was thick with dragons, streaming by only a few feet away from where the two crouched in the shadow of the wall. Yet, none so much as glanced in their direction. They all had only one thought in mind: the hatchery.

Rusty drooped under the weight of the explosives pack. "How are we going to get through that?"

Scott shoved the beamer back into the holster. These were unarmed slaves, and not dangerous. "Over this wall?" He jumped up and took a look. Below him was a courtyard, but visible in the distance were flames leaping a hundred feet into the air as the fire, which had started to die down after the first furious blast from the twin missiles, found more fuel. The dry plant growth in which the eggs were covered during the night kept feeding the blaze, while the air rushing in to fill the void fanned it out of control.

He dropped back down. "It's all clear." Automatically clasping his fingers together, he held his hands down low so Rusty could put his foot into them. Then he boosted his friend up and Rusty clambered up onto the ledge. Scott easily swung himself over, jumped down, then helped Rusty to the patio floor.

For a moment they had been in almost full view of the dragon throng, yet none had taken the slightest notice of them. The slaves were too dull, too stupid, too mechanical to know better. They were programmed for simple functions, and beyond the scope of their training they were helpless.

They worked their way through the darkened enclosure, around scattered furniture. At the other end the twenty-foot wall of a house provided the only means of egress. The tall, oblong doorways were like monstrous mouths waiting for victims. Scott stepped inside, beamer in hand. The room was deserted. With Rusty right behind him, he bounded up a set of poured plastic stairs.

The second floor was full of doorways, one of which led to a common porch that was a parapet connecting the entire block, like a private sidewalk ten feet above the crowded street. From this height Scott could easily see the cave opening which was the entrance to the time transporter. It glowed with an eerie blue light that coruscated slightly and spilled out into a plaza that was surrounded by the same seven-foot-high walls that lined all the streets. From only several hundred yards away the mountain looked like a giant gumdrop, granite colored, set in orange plastic as if it were a caramel candy.

"They don't even know we're here." Scott led the way along the parapet completely unopposed, while below scores of dragons rushed in exodus toward the hatchery, attracted like moths to a flame. Interspersed among the numerous naked slaves were vested technicians and several richly caparisoned leaders with flowing capes. None bothered to look up.

When they got to within a hundred yards of the cave entrance the block of plastic buildings curved around and veered off. This close to the plaza there was very little traffic. The dragons Scott saw now were mostly soldiers milling around haphazardly like any military outfit. They did not appear to be an attacking force; rather, they were a rear guard with little to do.

Scott lowered himself to an alley, then turned to help Rusty. "I can't make it down with this pack."

"All right, then hand it down." Scott reached up and took the explosives at arm's length. When Rusty alighted beside him he placed it on his back.

Scott took careful stock of the situation. They were in an alleyway that opened directly into the main thoroughfare, pitching down into the plaza and straight into the glowing entrance. The half dozen dragons lounging around, weapons holstered, did not appear to present any tactical problem. But an uncounted number might be waiting for them just inside the cave opening.

"Let's take them on the run."

Rusty took a firm grip on the straps. "Okay, but I can't run too fast with this weight on my back."

Scott pulled out the beamer. "Just do your best. I'll cover you."

Rusty took a deep breath, and nodded. Scott stepped out into the moonlight. For several seconds no one took notice of them.

Then, a wary soldier swung its long neck in their direction, registered surprise with a hiss, and started to draw its gun. Before it was halfway out of its holster Scott's laser stabbed into the tawny breast with a surge of power that stunned the wielder: the capacitor must have been supercharged, for the dragon was literally cooked on the spot as the beam went straight through and exploded in the bushes covering the mountain.

"The jig is up!" As quickly as he could, Scott beamed down three more guards before their reptilian tripartite brains had time to handle the concept of foul play. Daggers of light transfixed them with the same violent intensity that had slain the first: they were burned to a crisp.

Blasting right and left, Scott ran into the midst of the no longer unsuspecting dragons. Enemy laser beams poured out of niches and doorways. "It's a trap!" But it was too late to back out now. They were committed.

"I'm right behind you." Rusty lost his footing for a moment over a sudden dip in the street, but regained his balance by skipping along awkwardly without slowing down.

The soldiers chose him for a target, shooting from all corners of the plaza. Half a dozen laser beams lashed out over the shuffling redhead. One dragon was cut down by a bolt of lightning shot by another. Blobs of molten plastic flew in all directions as the walls were picked apart.

Rusty raced into the cave unscathed, while Scott was still outside shooting cover fire. Then the blond ran in after him. They had run the gauntlet successfully.

But in the weird light that pulsated with an electrical charge that made his hair stand on end, Scott suddenly felt his heart sink. Barring their way to the time transporter was a stout, floor to ceiling, case-hardened steel gate.

Doc inspected the bomb carriage and discovered that it had roller bearing-type wheels. Six axles distributed the load evenly. A long handle either extended straight forward for pulling, or folded over the top for storage. It had two mechanical calipers that were brakes as well as a steering mechanism: squeezing the left caliper caused the chassis to swerve that way, and vice versa. There was no motor, for with unlimited slave power there was no need.

Even though the bomb must have weighed hundreds of

pounds, it moved easily on its lubricated and closely machined wheels. Leaning back with all his might he was able to move it himself. And once started, it took equally as great an effort to stop it.

Straining, pushing, pulling, and twisting the handle, Doc managed to extricate the cumbersome device from where it was wedged between shelving and miscellaneous equipment. He crashed it back and forth until it was free.

By that time he was exhausted; his bad leg ached where it was forced to bend against unused muscles. Still, he worked the carriage out from the back of the armory. He had to get that bomb out of there.

The future—and presence—of humanity depended on it.

Sandra and Death Wind stalked up the street like two thieves. There was nothing in their way for the first block except dead dragon bodies stretched out helter-skelter. The odor of burnt flesh permeated the air, not only from the still blazing nursery but from the roasted soldiers as well. To Sandra's nostrils it was the scent of victory.

When they reached the first intersection they slunk into an alcove filled with street-cleaning tools. From among the long plastic handles they watched the panic-stricken horde of dragons sweeping along the wide avenue. Not all were slaves, for many caped individuals were tagged by their covering as belonging to the high echelon. But all shared the mindless terror that drove them relentlessly onward, unaware of their surroundings.

After several minutes it became apparent to Sandra that there was no end to the stampede. "Come on, let's cut a path through this mob."

"We cannot shoot. There are no soldiers."

Sandra was not bound by any sense of fair play. She was prepared to immolate every dragon that came between her and her mother. Without any qualms she stepped out into full view of the passing parade and cleared a swath through the street, beaming down slaves with unmerciful abandon. Dragons hissed hideously, perishing sequentially as the separate brains fought to coordinate their inputs. Some of them were literally half dead.

"Come on, shoot the bastards." Sandra could not understand Death Wind's immobilization, or Nomadic ethics. All she knew was that this was the enemy, that they were on the rout, and that this was her chance for revenge. "Kill them!"

Sandra pulled the trigger mindlessly, blasting left and right. Then, as if a traffic signal had decreed it, all dragon movement came to a standstill. The two long-haired youths casually scuttled across the street weaving through the parboiled bodies. Glazed reptilian eyes did not even follow their hasty track, but merely waited a suitable period of time before resuming their instinctive pilgrimage. The dead and dying were completely ignored.

Death Wind had not yet fired a shot. "Prison this way." He cut through a maze of alleys and cross streets that avoided further confrontation. Sandra shot off a bolt at every stray dragon, but the savage would not slow down simply to fight. He seemed determined to get to the captives with the minimum amount of squabble and at the maximum speed.

Before long, Sandra was grateful that he had. Bright flashes warned her of discharging beamers ahead, while screams of pain and cries of anguish cast evil foreboding.

The prisoners were being massacred!

Rusty stared at the insurmountable obstacle in front of them. "Now what?"

"Start beaming the hinges." Scott aimed at the massive metal joints on which the doors pivoted. Rusty averted his eyes. With the supercharged battery pack the beamer cut through steel like a steak knife through hot butter. After a dozen blasts both doors sagged. Scott ran forward and kicked the locking mechanism with a high thrust of his foot. The gates swung open and tore off the hinges, and crashed in an upright position against the rock walls. Scott put the heel of his hand against his forehead. "Oh, no. It wasn't even locked."

Then they hurried through the rest of the short tunnel and into the immense inner chamber that housed the time transporter. Two hundred feet across and a hundred feet high, every available space on the arched walls was covered with power packs identical to the ones that charged the beamers. Protruding out of each one was a single, ten-foot-long needle that resembled closely the disruptor beam nozzles that buoyed up the flyers. Crammed side by side, the inside of the hollowed-out cavern bristled like an inverted porcupine skin.

In the middle of the room was an intensely blue spherical

shield at which the needles were aimed. The shield was coruscating with the leakage of static charge that continuously pulsed from the focusing nodes. Along the circumference of the floor were the huge whining generators that were even now winding up the capacitors to a full charge.

So potent was the energy in the cave that each individual needle tip glowed with a purple luminescence that filled the air with an eerie, and tangible, shimmering light. Every hair on Scott's body stood up from the electrical inductance, and his skin crawled as if covered with slimy worms.

Rusty stood with mouth agape, studying the raw potential, the advanced technology, the scientific curiosity they were about to destroy. Then he was jerked aside as Scott yanked the pack off his back and flung it to the floor.

"We don't have time to admire it." He started taking out the cylinders from the dismantled warhead. With an armful of explosives he dashed away and started depositing them at strategic locations: between pairs of generators. His will to live was stronger than his sense of marvel.

Hurriedly Rusty unrolled the spool of detonation cord and started walking it out, leaving a long loop at each canister. The idea was to wire all the charges together so they would go off with one gigantic bang.

There was a commotion at the entranceway. "Uh oh, here they come." Scott raced back and fired half a dozen bolts of lightning up the tunnel, then took another armful of canisters. His job was done easily, so while Rusty made the connections he kept the dragons at bay. They were trying to sneak in along the rough-hewn wall, hiding in jagged, rocky corrugations. Scott ran back and forth inside the opening so he could direct his beamer at both sides. He picked them off one by one as they became either too bold or too careless.

"We've got them good. They're afraid to shoot." Any laser beams that went past him were sure to hit some of the delicate and complicated time transporting equipment.

Halfway around the curved cavern Rusty attached blasting caps to the explosive canisters. He pushed them against the wall when they were made up so the resultant blast would use the walls and floor as a springboard to hurl the destructiveness upward and outward, and destroy the capacitor banks as well as the generators.

"Hey, watch out."

Rusty was concentrating on his work when a dragon technician stepped out of a work cubicle in front of him and swung a heavy tool at his head. Scott was too far away to shoot accurately, and he started running, aghast, as he saw his friend swing around. He did not have time to duck before the metal object made contact with his red hair.

The wagon with the plague bomb was taxing Doc's strength.

He had ruined half the armory working the carriage through the plastic shelving. He would struggle to get it moving only to have it crash into a wall or stanchion before he could get it to turn, for its forward momentum kept it going where it was aimed. Then he would have to back it off and push it forward again.

By now he was panting heavily, and rubbing his injured leg where the bone had not healed properly. In addition, his chest pain had returned, although not as severely. He had completely forgotten that he was supposed to guard the armory against infiltration. It suddenly seemed as if the most important thing in the world was to get this bomb out of there.

Finally he could see the light. Just around the corner of the doorway the dying embers of the conflagration wrought strange, flickering shadows. Doc wiped sweat off his forehead, and rubbed his damp palm across his mouth. Positioning himself in front of the wagon he gave a mighty tug and started it rolling. Now there was room to maneuver, so he used the alternate brakes to steer.

He cast a glance over his shoulder. One of the shadows coalesced into an eight-foot-tall form, squat near the base and sinuous near the top. Silhouetted against smoke and flame the dragon lifted its paw and pointed it at the man. The golden gun gleamed brightly.

Behind it two more tall forms lurked. And behind them were more—many more. There seemed no way out.

Four dragon guards walked along a parapet that surrounded the stockade. A caped leader was there, too, hissing orders to his troops. The soldiers fired their beamers downward, into a crowded throng of humanity—one of whom was Sandra's mother.

There was no compassion in the girl's heart as she lashed out

with the stolen weapon. She zapped the two closest dragons
before they were aware of her presence down in the dark street.
By the time the other two turned around one of them had its
head blown off. The first two had not yet crumpled from their
posts.

Death Wind ran ahead while Sandra dispatched the last
dragon soldier. He tried to get into position to shoot the leader,
but two more dragons stepped out of a guard shack and opened
fire. Dodging quickly, he got out of one beamer's path, while
another crackled by his ear. He fired twice, his aim as straight
as his arrows. Both soldiers fell, but the leader slunk away.

"Darn." Sandra sent a beam of light after the beast. She
melted plastic, but nothing more.

"Let us hurry. It will bring more."

Sandra nodded. Through the barred gate she could see
people picking themselves up from the ground. She concentrated her fire on the thick jambs and blew away the mounts for
the steel hinges. The entire structure crashed to the ground.

Inside the stockade a mass of people, perhaps fifty in all,
were reacting to the attack. Most of those that wore complete
lizard-skin outfits huddled against the far wall. Those dressed
in loincloths and breast skins stood poised to leap erratically in
order to evade beamer fire. They had been in a constant state
of movement during the whole operation in a bold attempt to
outwit the slow-moving dragons and their slower response
systems. There was mumbled surprise when they saw the two
desperate youths limned in the garish glow of the moon.

"*Sandra! Is that you?*"

A trim but ragged woman with long, dark hair and fair
features ran out from the crowd. She was taller than Sandra,
and more mature, but the resemblance was immediately
apparent.

"Mother!" Sandra let the gun dangle by its power cord and
ran toward the woman's open arms. They came together in the
middle of the stockade, mother and child, hugging and kissing
and weeping openly.

Now the prisoners began to realize that the crashing of the
gate was an act of liberation, not an invasion of dragon
soldiers. More people climbed out of cubicles into the courtyard, milling with those already there, until the crowd swelled
to several hundred. Excitement ran high, the din of voices

crescendoed. To those who had been incarcerated for so long, it was impossible to believe that they had been rescued.

One man cheered as he wrapped his arms around Sandra and her mother. It was Ned, ragged and much the worse for wear, but alive. The three made a happy spectacle.

"Sandra, how did you find—I mean—how did you— Sandra, what are you doing here?"

"I came to get my mother."

Only a few feet away another man strode forward. He was tall, gaunt, and dark-skinned—his bearing was unbroken by the harshness of captivity. Long, black hair covered his shoulders, a breechcloth hid his hips and muscular thighs. Deep-set eyes peered out from behind a face that was firm and stolid, but in which swelled unfathomable depths of emotion.

"Son."

"Father." Death Wind stood at arm's length, and spoke in a monotone that belied his feelings. But to a Nomad, that one word exchange expressed volumes.

Death Wind's father placed two strong hands on his son's broad shoulders. Death Wind returned the gesture. It was the Nomad family greeting.

A woman only slightly shorter, and dressed in lizard-skin breechcloth and halter top, came to stand next to Death Wind's father. With a quick glance Death Wind acknowledged her presence. Releasing his father's embrace, he stepped to one side and kissed the woman on the cheek, where tear tracks were already glistening. She returned his kiss.

"Son."

"Mother."

Many Nomads crowded close behind the chief and his wife, watching the event in controlled admiration. Beyond were other Nomads, from other tribes, as well as oddly dressed strangers who must have been itinerants much as Sandra's mother.

Death Wind faced his father once more. In a voice loud enough for all to hear, he said, "Talk later. Fight now. Follow me."

Without further word or expression he turned on his heels and trotted out of the open stockade gate. Behind him every able-bodied Nomad, whether man or woman or child, took up the trot. And behind them, slower to respond, came the rest. They all understood that the fight was not yet over.

Indeed, it had just begun.

CHAPTER 29

It was pure instinct that made Rusty duck, but it was training and experience that permitted him to roll to the side and draw the forty-five from his belt. The blow on the head stunned him, but was lessened by his movement away from it. When he came up onto one knee the weapon was already in his hand. In the next instant, before the metal tool descended, he burped the last three slugs into the monster's grisly face.

The two antagonists froze in this position: Rusty with arm outstretched holding the now useless gun, the dragon dead with the signal not yet received in its alien brain. Then they both collapsed, Rusty into unconsciousness and the dragon into death.

When he came to, Scott was hovering over him. "Are you all right?"

His scalp was bleeding where a chunk of skin was torn off. He groaned and shook his head. "I—I guess so." Without thinking he brushed his hand through his hair, winced with pain. He made an enigmatic laugh that came out like a huff. "That was a close shave."

"More like a haircut." Scott glanced at the entrance. "Can you make the rest of the connections by yourself? I've got a whole roomful of dragons just dying to get in here."

"If I can't I'll call for help. I'm just a little dizzy, that's all." Rusty followed Scott's gaze. He had to look right through the center of the materialization ring, and the swirling, coruscating image accentuated his dizziness.

"Okay. I haven't got time to chat." Without waiting for further acknowledgment Scott ran around the perimeter of the room, staying as far away as he could from the cyclonic central sphere. The eerie purple glow was gaining in strength. It flickered like a strobe, highlighting his motions like sequences cut from poorly adapted stop-action photography. And at the node half-formed images, like wraiths, soughed into and out of focus.

217

Rusty quickly worked his way back to the entranceway. A dragon entered the time warp room but before it had time to swing its head around on its snakelike neck Scott fried it. An ugly gash was seared through the potbelly, spilling organs and intestines. Before the beast hit the floor Scott took up a new station and sent blasts along the corridor as fast as his power pack would recycle. Some of the soldiers had taken refuge in the corrugations and stayed there for protection. Scott's shots ricocheted all around, but did not hit any more. At least he was holding them at bay.

Overhead, power packs hummed and the long needle points whined and danced with fire. The capacitor bank was nearing full charge. It suddenly occurred to Rusty that if they did not hurry they might find a party of dragons materializing right in their midst.

"Would you hurry up and blow that thing? This stalemate isn't going to last forever." Scott fired two more blasts up the tunnel. Molten chips of granite exploded into the air, but no dragons were hit. The weapon that was their greatest offense now proved their downfall, for they had no shield against it.

There was an impasse between reptile and human.

Rusty crabbed across the floor, trailing the detonation cord behind him. He dragged the battery out of the pack and started wiring the last connection.

"I can't hold them off much longer." Scott fired one shot at each side of the tunnel just to let the dragons know he had not fallen asleep. "They're bound to think of something."

Rusty worked wordlessly, sorting out the wires with attached alligator clips. His head throbbed, dulling his concentration.

There came a crashing sound from the outside entrance of the cave. Dragons erupted from the walls where they had been hiding. Something that looked like a huge battering ram sped past the downed gates with unstoppable momentum.

"I need a few more seconds."

With grim determination Scott stepped out into the open, beamer in hand. He had lost so much already, so long ago in that other world in which he had once lived, that it was easy for him to make one last sacrifice.

Even had he wanted to Doc could not have stopped the bomb-laden carriage. Once he had the mass moving the tremendous kinetic energy was not so easily lost.

He ducked under the outstretched arm of the nearest dragon and trundled past. There was a pain-filled hiss as the front wheels rolled over extended reptilian digits, crushing claws and bones. The next two dragons were raising their weapons to fire as Doc slipped between them, shoving for all he was worth on one good leg and one slightly misshapen one. By the time they fired he was no longer there, and the crossed laser beams gouged plastic and hit one soldier in the leg.

Once on the slanted street the carriage began to get away from him. He hobbled alongside trying in vain to keep hold of the handle that controlled the brakes. But they were not holding. Metal was grinding against metal as the roller bearings heated up and shrieked mechanically.

Laser beams flicked overhead. Human shouts chorused in the background. But Doc was in no position to make explanations. As he barreled through the dragon army he heard Death Wind's whoop and Sandra's cry as they led the newly drafted troops into the armory.

He had both brake handles squeezed tightly and was still not able to keep up with the wagon. He grabbed the metal collar on the bomb as he ran alongside. This did not help slow it down; instead, it swept him along faster than he could run. He clung desperately to the rampaging vehicle. It was no longer under his control.

Before he knew it he was approaching an intersection where thinning dragon hordes were still rushing toward the blast area. With resignation he swung his left leg, the bad one, over the top of the bomb as if he were mounting a saddle. He clung precariously to the carriage for several seconds before he was able to climb onto a more stable position. Then he was riding the racing bomb like a wild cowboy on a bucking bronco: lying down hugging it with both legs while he kept a firm grip on the reins, in this case the steering handle.

He held this pose for only a second. Then, as he entered the crossroad he released the squealing right brake; the continued pressure on the other caliper caused the carriage to slew around to the left. Skidding sideways, the wagon upended as the wheels on one side left the ground. As they did so they also lost their braking power, and the wagon straightened out until it fell back down with a crash and the brakes took control again. The wagon banged up and down in this manner while Doc negotiated the turn and miraculously threaded a path through nonplussed dragons, crashing into more than one and bowling them over like tenpins.

He was knocked from his perch when the wagon first slammed down, so that he rode the side of the bomb like an Indian warrior riding his pony into battle. His long white hair and beard streamed back in the wind, and he grinned maniacally at the adventure. He felt like the young, reckless scout he had once been.

The wagon barely made the turn without flipping over. It made such a wide arc that his back scraped the opposite wall and his shirt was torn to shreds. The screaming brakes were a warning that he was on the warpath, but startled, slow-reacting and dull-witted reptiles could not get out of his way in time. Then he clambered back on top.

He gripped the steering handle and swerved drunkenly through the mob, trying to avoid the worst collisions. Glancing blows knocked dragons to the ground and sent some reeling into others. The street was soon turned into a madcap replay of the Keystone Cops.

He grazed the left retaining wall for only an instant, but that was enough time for one of the two retaining straps that held the bomb in place to wear through. The flayed strap dangled uselessly, flapping in the breeze. The cylindrical bomb was still nestled firmly in the grooved floor.

By this time Doc could hardly see where he was going, for there were tears in his eyes as the air bit savagely into them. His hair billowed out like a lion's mane. With the brakes still screeching like a banshee the bomb carriage was like some mythical monster swooping through the city.

The wagon hit a dip in the roadway with such speed that it traveled ten feet in the air before its roller bearings touched the ground. The resultant jolt not only broke Doc's grip on the collar, but it knocked the bomb sideways in the carriage. The rear strap took up the strain, but threatened to snap. The bomb was half out of the groove now, sticking off at an angle. Doc's leg slipped to the ground with a painful jar. A few seconds contact with the smooth plastic surface at this speed was enough to rip several layers off his skin.

He lost his grip on the steering handle and the front of the bomb veered too close to the wall. It hit with a jarring crash.

*   *   *

At first Scott could not tell what was happening. The flickering purple light behind him cast an eerie glow of light up the tunnel. By the awful sound of things the dragons were engaging some new kind of weapon, for he could hear it winding up like a charging capacitor.

All he knew for certain was that some large object was about to run him down. He leveled the beamer. Licking his lips, he cast a glance at Rusty.

The redhead looked up just then. "I'm almost ready."

But there was no more time. The battering ram was there. The only thing left for Scott to do was to try to blast it apart, or stop it with his body.

The bomb carriage veered sickeningly to the right and rose high up on one side to the point of overbalance. With strength he did not know he had, Doc pulled himself back up onto the bomb, which was now pointed at an oblique angle to the forward motion of the wagon. The carriage came down onto all its wheels with a crash. The bomb would have slid off had not Doc retained his grip on the metal collar.

Instead, it reseated itself into the curved groove, the one retaining strap preventing it from rocking out of the cradle on the other side. It happened so quickly that Doc rolled over the other side of the bomb, as if he were an acrobatic stuntman performing tricks. He almost had to laugh at himself.

Ahead he could see the brightly lit maw that was the entrance to the cave. The plaza in front of it was filled with soldiers and technicians, milling and hissing hysterically. They did not even notice his approach, despite the still shrieking brakes.

Doc carefully aimed the wagon to avoid congregations of dragons. So fast was he moving that the soldiers did not have time to draw their weapons as he zoomed past. Then he was in the clear, for there was a long corridor empty of dragons, as if they were afraid to stand where the purple light spread like a beacon.

Then he was in the tunnel, rushing forward with jetlike speed. The time warp node was dead ahead, in the middle of the cave. With his peripheral vision he noticed dragons hiding in the corrugations along the side of the tunnel. But in front of him there was only one barrier.

"Get out of the way," he shouted when he recognized Scott standing in his path.

Scott was too stupefied to move at first, until his eyes focused on the white head, the long-flowing beard. "Doc?" At the last second he jumped aside as the wagon thundered past.

"Blow it up," Doc shouted as he rode by. "Blow it up now."

Then Doc, the plague bomb, and the lumbering carriage sped into the high arched cave. The purple radiance was noontime bright, and the focusing nodes glowed and sparkled with potential merging on full capacity. The time warp was wound up to full excitement. Electricity arced and crackled; the smell of ozone was thick in the air.

The last hundred feet was covered in a matter of seconds. Then Doc rolled off the bomb and was swallowed up by the miasma of pulsating purple haze emitted from the warp screen.

There was no time to jump for cover. Rusty made the last connection, touched the battery terminal with a bare wire. The entire cave seemed to detonate at once. Hundreds of power packs were discharged at the same moment the explosive canisters were detonated.

Scott crashed into Rusty and hurled him into an alcove by the entrance. At the same time the dragons in the corridor, hearing the violent discharge, evacuated their hiding places and ran as fast as their lizard legs would carry them. It proved to be their undoing.

The discharging warp field was accentuated by the destruction of the generators, power packs, and focusing nodes. Every piece of equipment in the transporter room was ripped from its foundations, flung outward, then spliced through the wreckage of equipment flying inward from the opposite wall. Part of this debris was blasted violently into the time warp. But the dragon bomb, if it exploded, was already sixty million years in the past.

The cave was at once a moving, chaotic pit of hurtling metal and plastic shards. Showers of sparks, electrically as well as frictionally generated, scintillated among tons of passing parts. Sophisticated electronic components were converted to shrapnel and spun around the circular walls like water in a maelstrom.

The burst of heat melted plastic and made metal glow. The

hot, expanding gases could not be confined in the cave, and were forced out the entrance tunnel like a blast from a cannon. The dragons that were caught in the barrel were wiped out in an instant, their dismembered bodies vaporized and spread out across the city like so much stew. The funneled discharge leveled buildings and disintegrated plastic ramparts, leaving in its wake smoking, orange globules.

The mountain shrugged under the tremendous impact, and expanded for a moment like a balloon. Then it deflated as uprooted trees were shed like falling hair. Thousands of tons of dirt slid down the gumdrop-shaped exterior leaving a naked granite mountain behind, and burying all that lay at its base.

In the tunnel, in an alcove, two huddled, blackened bodies sought to extricate themselves from the dust and debris. They had stopped breathing while the heat wave passed. Their clothes were virtually burned off their backs. They had scores of cuts and bruises. But they were alive.

Somehow, when Scott had grabbed him, Rusty had held onto the pack. Now he rummaged through it for a couple of torches, and a flint and stone with which to light them. In the darkness Scott poured oil over the bundled sticks. Rusty struck a spark, and gloom was dispelled. Then they climbed over the heaps of rubble into the center of the cave.

All was quiet.

There was a tinkle of glass. Shadows moved in the torch-light. A confusion of wire and electrical parts and blobs of fused plastic, like some weird mechanical monster, rose up out of the ash, shedding shards and components like leaves off a tree in autumn.

"You could lend an old man a hand," said a soft, familiar voice.

"Doc!" Two voices rang out simultaneously.

Scott and Rusty dashed forward and in a flash pulled him clear of the trash. They cheered, hugged, slapped, and jumped up and down—and never noticed that his snowy hair had turned black.

"What happened to the bomb?" Rusty said.

Doc raised bushy eyebrows that were covered with soot. "It was sucked into the vortex of time and sent back to its makers. Peace be with them."

With their arms around Doc's weary shoulders, they half carried the tired old man out of the cave, through the entrance tunnel, over the mound of dirt filling the plaza, and into the cool nighttime air where the stars shone overhead and the moon glowed like a beacon of hope.

A cheer arose as the three stood in the open, torches held high. Several hundred yards away, with beamers flashing in exultation, hundreds of people, the freemen of the world, honored those who had released them from bondage.

Then came another sound, high-pitched and ominous. The vibration in the air filled everyone with dread, for there were none who did not recognize it—or fear it.

"Oh, no." Doc looked with despair up the hill toward the armory.

Way up in the coal-black sky, but descending purposefully on shimmering disruptor beams, the last of the dragon warships was returning like a maddened hornet to its molested nest. Already it touched the tops of the tallest buildings, melting them down like icicles under a blowtorch. The hundred-foot-wide swath meant destruction for the city, and all who stood in its path.

In victory, there is death.

CHAPTER 30

People ran for their lives: along the streets, over walls, into buildings. They scattered as widely as they could. Beamers fired at the flyer like wolves nipping at the heels of their prey, inflicting damage. But it came on relentlessly, suicidally.

The stockade was incinerated in a flash, and the flyer moved quickly down the street after the pockets of humanity. Walls and ramparts melted into garish puddles. Multi-story structures sagged into squat masses, or twisted over on their sides in molten blobs. Orange plastic ran in rivulets.

Screaming people ran toward the sanctity of the cave. Sandra spared a second to glance over her shoulder at the awful spectacle. The flyer was dangerously close, but it seemed as if they might make it—until someone fell headlong and could not get up.

It was her mother! Sandra stopped and dashed back to help her up. She was dazed, and only half conscious. When Sandra tried to pull her to her feet she was like a dead weight. The purple radiance loomed practically overhead, blotting out the sky.

Suddenly Death Wind was at her side. With one easy motion he threw off the power pack, lifted the slender woman onto his shoulders, and trotted off with his burden. Sandra lagged along with him while everyone else made for safety.

The flyer hammered on mercilessly, its deep-throated humming filling the air with a presentiment of death. The glowing disruptor beams stabbed at their heels; Sandra's legs felt the warmth, then the heat, then the burning.

Then there was a helping hand beside her. Death Wind's father grabbed hold of the woman's legs and took some of the weight off his son's shoulders. With the shared load they surged ahead, moving faster—but not fast enough. The pounding in Sandra's ears told her that the flyer was drawing inexorably closer, that no power could make them move any quicker, that they would never reach the cave where Doc, Scott, and Rusty were beckoning.

They reached the loose dirt and debris from the hillside. Sandra slipped, fell, tried to get up, and could not. She crawled on her knees, watching Death Wind and his father carry her mother onward. She did not cry out for help. She rolled over and brought her own beamer to bear. She would not die without a fight.

A meteor descended from the star-studded heavens with incredible speed, pushed by a needle of bright yellow flame. Sandra could hardly comprehend what was happening when it contacted the flyer with a dull thud, followed immediately by a loud boom and a billow of bright gas.

At first the flyer absorbed the shock, dipping slightly with the weight of the impact. Then half the disruptor beams winked out, and it canted to an acute angle propelled by only part of its power nozzles. The still working light beams unstabilized the flyer, driving it around in a circle. It seesawed crazily, retracing its route, then lost altitude until its leading edge crashed into a watchtower. The fiery beams acted as a lever, flipping the flyer upside down and flattening walls. Then it blew up violently as the pent-up power in its capacitor banks was released all at once. The pyrotechnic display sent flaming metal parts thousands of feet into the air, and lighted what was left of the dragon city with solar brilliance.

The last missile, fired automatically when the flyer came into sensing range, vanquished the last dragon defense.

Doc sank heavily to the ground as Scott and Rusty ran forward past Death Wind to Sandra. Scott cradled her head in his arms. "Sandra, are you all right?"

She was slow to respond. She shook her head from side to side, blinking her eyes. "Three strikes and you're out. The next time a flyer comes after me it's sure to get me. I hate having to thank you guys again for saving my life."

Scott laughed. "There won't be a next time. They're all gone. It's just a sweeping operation now. We'll just kill off the ones that are left."

Sandra slid her arms out of the straps of the power pack. When she sat up it stayed on the ground. "Most of the soldiers are dead. And we left the slaves alone."

"Then you leave it to me. I'll kill every last one of them."

"Scott, you don't have to. They're only slaves, and they're unarmed."

"They're dragons," Scott snarled. "They're the enemy, remember? And we came here to kill them. All of them. If you're too squeamish, then get out of the way. Here, Rusty, take his beamer."

Scott pushed Sandra aside and lifted the power pack to put on his friend's back. Rusty hesitated. "You know, maybe she's right."

"She's not right, she's just selfish. Now that she's got her mother she doesn't care about our fight." He gave Sandra an angry look. "Always thinking of yourself, aren't you? You don't care about anyone but you. All right, if you don't want to fight, I can't make you. But don't try to stop me." Looking up at Rusty, Scott gestured with the power pack. "Are you with me?"

Rusty glanced at Sandra, then back at Scott. He demurred for a moment, then nodded wordlessly. He donned the pack and palmed the golden gun.

Then Death Wind approached, with his father by his side. "Let us go. We have work to finish."

"Not you, too. You wouldn't—" Sandra bit off whatever she had to say because Death Wind was no longer there. He was gone along with the rest of the Nomads, women and children included, and all the people who had been captured by the dragons in their sweep across the continent. "It doesn't matter, now. We've won." But there was no one there to hear her.

Then her mother was by her side, and Sandra buried her face in her breast and cried. She did not know why.

"Hello, Helen." Doc was lighted by the glow of the still burning flyer. He smiled, and tenderly reached out with one blackened hand.

"Hi, Dad." Helen's lips twitched and formed a tender smile. She placed a palm lovingly against Doc's face, then kissed him on the lips. "Just like old times, isn't it?"

Now it was Doc's turn to smile. "It seems as if I'm always getting into trouble."

"You'll never change." Helen shook her head with chagrin. Sandra watched the exchange of words completely baffled. Then her mother looked down at her. "Sandra, I'd like you to meet your grandfather."

"I'm happy to make your acquaintance, my child."

Sandra's jaw hung slack. She looked from mother to grandfather to mother, and repeated the process until the slow realization crept into her brain. "But how can you—that is, I didn't know—I mean, why didn't you say—"

"Until recently I only suspected myself. The resemblance was striking, to be sure. And you had your mother's courage, individuality, vanity, and lack of respect."

"Dad!"

Doc ignored Helen's pout. "But I was not really sure until I saw—" Here he swept back her long, dark hair, now mussed and singed, and pinched the shining pendants hanging from her lobes. "—your earrings."

"Dad gave them to me when I was a child. I passed them on to you because it was part of the family heritage. And he was no longer around—he had a world to conquer and there was no way of stopping him."

"It was not easy for me to leave, you know?"

Helen pursed her lips. "Yes, I know that now. But I couldn't understand it then. I needed you."

"But, Doc—er—Grandfather—er, Dad— Heck, what do I call you now?"

Doc laughed out loud. "That's for you to decide."

"But, what's going to happen now? What are they doing?" Sandra made a sweeping gesture over the city. Beneath Sandra's blood-splattered shirt lay a troubled heart. She had had enough of killing, of death, of destruction, of fear and anger.

Doc's smile faded. "They are putting an end to dragon rule."

Twin pearls of water rolled down Sandra's quivering cheeks, washing away the dirt. Her own ruthlessness faded. She was only a girl who did not understand the cruelties of life.

"But why must the slaves, and the babies, be killed. Death Wind says the enemy are the leaders, and the soldiers. It seems so—brutal."

"Remember, my dear, that the dragons killed four human beings without so much as a warning—or an afterthought."

"And you don't know what it was like being a prisoner. We were beaten, starved, kept thirsty, waiting for the day when we would be dragged off and used for their inhuman experiments.

None ever returned from the torture chamber. At least, not in one piece."

Sandra's heart was in turmoil. "But these are just slaves, mindless animals. They aren't responsible, and they can't fight back. It just doesn't seem right."

Doc held her chin in her hand. "Not because it is right, but because it is necessary. There is a time for strength, and a time for righteousness. Now is the time for strength. Let us hope we do not lose our sense of righteousness."

The orange flames from the downed flyer were dying out. But beyond, a brighter ball of fire was rising. The eastern sky was tinged with color as the deep blue of the night slowly faded. The stars were gone, and the moon was a pale ghost dipping westward.

Doc took the weight off his bad leg and leaned against Helen. She put one arm around her father, the other around her daughter. "You haven't changed at all, have you, Dad?"

Doc suppressed a smile. "I've tried not to. I did get lost along the way, but these young people found me and nudged me back onto the right path. And in my own way I nudged them along as well."

Sandra wiped the tears from her eyes. "Grandpa!"

"Yes, my dear?"

"Nothing. I just like the sound of it. I think I'll call you Grandpa."

Helen and Doc looked at each other, and laughed. "Well, you've always called me exactly what you wanted in the past. And I suppose I still have no control over you. Yes, Grandpa has a nice ring to it. I accept it."

Still entwined, the reunited family strode across the dirt-filled plaza to enjoy the first free dawn of humanity's new beginning.

It was a weary group of warriors who straggled into the slag heap that had once been a broad courtyard. Death Wind led Scott and Rusty to where Doc set up a temporary command post, and reported on operations. "Guards all set. Dragons no escape."

"Guards! What guards?" Sandra wanted to know.

Scott shrugged off his beamer, then helped Rusty with his. He scowled with contempt. "They wouldn't let us kill them all—only the ones who wouldn't give up. The rest were rounded up and herded into makeshift prisons. I think it's a big mistake."

"My boy, mercy is the one quality that differentiates raw intelligence from civilized learning. It is that social grace—our humaneness—that separates humanity from the dragons. To their dishonor, it is what their culture lacked."

"You knew it would turn out this way, didn't you?" Sandra said.

White teeth showed on Doc's newly scrubbed face. "I know the Nomad way, and had faith in them."

Rusty shrugged. "I guess I'm not sorry we let them live. In a way, it shows we're better than they are."

Death Wind doffed his own beamer and stood next to Sandra. He drew her closer to him. She bent her head against his brawny, naked chest. Helen looked at the couple perplexedly.

"Or more stupid." Scott shook his empty canteen. "Come on, Rusty. Let's go get some water. I need a drink."

They left through one melted opening in the courtyard just as two Nomads entered through another on the other side. "Death Wind!"

Death Wind saw his father approaching. He was puzzled, because he had not yet told him what name he had conferred upon himself after completion of his trial. He was even more puzzled when his father shook Doc's hand in the Nomad greeting and exchanged the ritualistic "Men stick together. It is code."

"From what your boy told me I never thought I'd see you again, Bold One. Nor you, Slender Petal."

"Dragon destroy village, kill many people, capture others. We live, but no escape." Turning proudly to his son, he smiled and placed a strong bronzed hand on his shoulder. "Son rescue."

Death Wind was now the proudest person alive, for he had earned more than the Nomad title of warrior; he had earned his father's respect as well. But there were still things he did not understand.

Addressing his father, he pointed to Doc. "You know?"

Bold One nodded. "Know for many moons. Killer of dragon, helper of old, healer of sick. We fight together, side by side. He is great man, brave scout. We call him—Death Wind!"

Death Wind, the Nomad, recoiled in horror. Suddenly things became all too apparent: Doc's knowledge of the world, his knowledge of Nomad ways, even his hauntingly familiar face. Vaguely, Death Wind saw images in his mind of when he was a child playing with toy arrows. He remembered the strong, oddly white-skinned man who had lived, and fought, with his tribe during their migrations.

Doc laughed heartily. "Yes, it's only one of the many names I picked up during a rather long and hazardous career. I borrowed it myself from a western writer named Zane Grey. Now I fear I'm getting too old to keep up the image. I think the name would do better on a younger man, someone bold and brave, some killer of many dragons—someone like yourself." Pausing dramatically, Doc added with glee, "Therefore, I hereby bestow upon you the name of Death Wind. May you carry it faithfully for a long and useful life."

Death Wind grasped arms with Doc. "Men stick together. It is code."

No sooner had they completed the chant when there was another shout of "Death Wind." Rusty raced back into the compound swinging his canteen. His carrot top looked lopsided now that he had combed the hair away from his scalp wound. Scott walked sullenly behind him.

Death Wind cringed, for he saw the quizzical expression on his father's face. Bold One had no way of knowing that Death Wind had already chosen that name for himself.

Rusty stopped in front of the Nomad. "Death Wind, uh, I was wondering if that offer was still open. You know, when you said we could come and live with you. I don't know what's going to happen from here on out, but I'd still like to be, well, part of the family."

Bold One looked seriously at his son. The simple nod he received carried with it reams of Nomad understanding. He stepped up to Rusty and put his hands on his shoulders. "Son." Then he held out his hands for Scott. The blond came forward reluctantly. "Son." Then Bold One stepped back and waved his hands in a way that included all who were present. "Family."

Rusty beamed, but Scott was not so easily put off. "What about the dragons? What do we do with them now?"

"Those that have survived will be allowed to live out the rest of their days," Doc said. "Perhaps we can even get some work out of them."

"Do you think that's smart?"

"Dragons have intelligence, but man has wisdom. We will do what is just, as well as what is wise."

"And those in the past?"

"Time is like an endless river: it has no past or future, only flow. The dragons made their own destiny, now we must make ours."

Doc shielded his eyes from the hot, bright sun. He grinned apishly. "And right now, my destiny lies with breakfast. What say we scrounge around and try to scare up some food. I'm starved." He leaned on Helen and took the weight off his bad leg. "And by the way, someone's going to have to carve a new cane for me. I can't depend on my daughter's support forever."

"On the contrary, I don't think you can live without me. And anyway, I don't intend to give you the chance. You need me." She fluffed up his long white hair. "And when was the last time you washed behind your ears?"

Amid the laughter of all, Doc stared at the sky as if to plead with a higher authority. "It seems as if I've freed everyone except myself."

There was a great deal of work to do. The pieces of the world were lying there to be picked up. In order to pick them up properly it was important for men to stick together.

It is code.